THE MOTHER'S PROMISE

THE MOTHER'S
PROMISE

SALLY
HEPWORTH

ST. MARTIN'S PRESS ☒ NEW YORK

THE MOTHER'S PROMISE. Copyright © 2017 by Sally Hepworth. All rights reserved.
Printed in the United States of America. For information, address
St. Martin's Press, 175 Fifth Avenue, New York, N.Y. 10010.

www.stmartins.com

Designed by Anna Gorovoy

The Library of Congress Cataloging-in-Publication Data is available upon request.

ISBN 978-1-250-07775-2 (hardcover)
ISBN 978-1-4668-8992-7 (e-book)

Our books may be purchased in bulk for promotional, educational,
or business use. Please contact your local bookseller or the Macmillan
Corporate and Premium Sales Department at 1-800-221-7945, extension 5442,
or by e-mail at MacmillanSpecialMarkets@macmillan.com.

First Edition: February 2017

10 9 8 7 6 5 4 3 2 1

FOR CHRISTIAN

ACKNOWLEDGMENTS

I'd like to thank my brilliant editor, Jennifer Enderlin, whose keen insight and thoughtful advice make me look so much more impressive than I am. And to the rest of my dream team at St. Martin's—particularly Caitlin Dareff, Olga Grlic, Brant Janeway and Lisa Senz . . . and, of course, the best publicist in the world, Katie Bassel—thank you for all that you do. To my publishers around the world, particularly my beloved Australian team at PanMacmillan—Haylee Nash and Alex Lloyd—thank you for everything.

To my agent, Rob Weisbach, who takes care of everything else so I can focus on my favorite thing—writing. If it weren't for you, I'd still be writing entertaining e-mails to my friends and daydreaming about being an author.

To those who helped me with this book, especially Maree White, for your medical expertise (I suspect the text messages about chemo, tumor markers, and salpingo-oophorectomies must have run into the thousands), this book would not have been possible without you. Also, to Sasha Milinkovic, who shared with me the human element of cancer—the fear, the fancy cookies, the red pee—the stuff you cannot find in books.

To my critique partners—Jane Cockram, Anna George, Meredith Jaeger—for lots of things, but mostly for being my crew.

Writing is a solitary profession and I'd truly be in the madhouse without you guys.

To my friends (and my friends' mothers!), who get so preposterously excited about my books—and buy more copies than they can carry—I wish everyone had cheerleaders like you.

To my children, who make writing incredibly difficult, and to my husband, who makes it so much easier—thank you for being the lead characters of my life. You guys are the happy ending every person deserves.

Finally, to my readers, not only for buying my books, but for coming to my events, visiting my Facebook page, and e-mailing me to let me know how much you love my writing—it is because of your support that I can do my dream job. This, and every book, is for you.

ONE

With what price we pay for the glory of motherhood.

—ISADORA DUNCAN

1

When the doctor gave Alice Stanhope the news, she was thinking about Zoe. Was she all right? Was today a bad day? What was she doing? In fact, Alice was so swept up in thoughts of Zoe that when the doctor cleared his throat she startled.

"Sorry," she said. "I zoned out for a second."

Dr. Brookes glanced at the nurse on Alice's right, who sat with her hand close to, but not quite touching, Alice's. The nurse's role in this hadn't been entirely clear until this moment, when she scooted a little closer on her chair. Clearly she was here to translate the medical speak. "Alice, Dr. Brookes was just saying that, unfortunately, your test results . . . they're not what we hoped for. Given the ultrasound, and now these test results, I'm afraid . . ."

On the wall clock, Alice noticed the time: 10:14 A.M. Zoe would be in third period. Science. Or would she? Some days, if she wasn't feeling up to it, she skipped a class or two in the middle of the day. Alice always covered for her. In fact, if it weren't for this appointment, she might have suggested Zoe have a day at home today. Instead she'd watched as Zoe packed up her books and bravely headed out the door. In a way, the brave days were the worst. The strained smile, the *I'm fine, Mom*, was somehow more painful to take than the *I ache, Mom, I can't face the day*.

"Alice?"

Alice looked at the nurse, whose name she'd forgotten, and apologized again. She tried to focus, but Zoe lurked in the shadows of her thoughts—so much that the nurse started to *look* a little like Zoe. The nurse was older, of course—thirtyish, maybe—but she was pretty, with the same chestnut hair and pink lips Zoe had, the same heart-shaped face. She even had Zoe's pallor, off-white with purplish shadows under her eyes.

"Would you like to go over it again?" the nurse suggested.

Alice nodded and tried to concentrate as the nurse talked about a "mass," a CA 125 score, a *something-or-other*-ectomy. She knew this nurse—Kate, according to her name badge—and Dr. Brookes didn't think she was taking it seriously enough, but Alice simply couldn't seem to conjure up the required feelings of fear and dread. She'd been through it too many times. The irregular Pap smear, the unusual breast lump, the rash no one could seem to diagnose. She seemed to have a knack for attracting illnesses and ailments that required just enough investigation to be financially and emotionally draining, but—and she knew she ought to be grateful for this—always stopped short of the main event. Now it was happening again. She was prepared to go through the motions—as a single mother, she was committed to looking after her health—but what she really wanted was to get it over with, so she could get to work.

"Alice," Kate was saying, "I'm concerned that you're here alone. Is there someone I can call for you? There was no emergency contact listed on your paperwork. Perhaps you have a family member or a friend . . . ?"

"No."

"You don't have anyone?"

"No," she said. "It's just my daughter and me."

The doctor and nurse exchanged a look.

Alice knew what they were thinking. *How could she not have anyone? Where are her family and friends?* They probably couldn't wait to leave so they could talk about her. Alice couldn't wait to leave too.

"How old is your daughter?" Kate asked finally.

"Zoe just turned fifteen."

"And . . . Zoe's father . . . ?"

". . . isn't in the picture."

Alice braced for a reaction. Whenever she imparted this particular piece of information, women tended to wince and then offer a sympathetic noise as if she'd told them she'd broken a toe. But the nurse didn't react at all. It raised her slightly in Alice's opinion.

"What about your parents?" she asked. "Siblings?"

"My parents have both passed away. My brother would be less than useless as an emergency contact."

"Are you sure," she started. "Because—"

"He's an alcoholic. A *practicing* alcoholic. Not that he needs the practice . . ."

Not so much as a smile from either of them. Dr. Brookes sat forward. "Mrs. Stanhope—"

"Ms. Stanhope," Alice corrected. "Or Alice."

"Alice. We need to schedule you for surgery as soon as possible."

"Okay." Alice reached into her tote and pulled out her day planner. She flicked it to today's date. "Is it possible to do a Friday, because I don't work Fridays. Except the first Friday in the month, when I drive Mrs. Buxton to her Scrabble meeting—"

"Mrs. Buxton?" Kate said, suddenly animated. Alice realized the nurse had mistaken her for a potential support person.

"Oh no," Alice explained. "She's eighty-three. I look after *her*, not the other way around. It's my job. I mean, I'm not a nurse or anything. I keep elderly people company, cook and clean a bit. Drive them around. Atherton Home Helpers, that's my business." Alice was rambling; she needed to get it together. "So . . . the operation . . . is it a day procedure?"

There was a short silence.

"No, Alice, I'm afraid it's not," Dr. Brookes said. His eyes were incredulous. "A salpingo-oophorectomy is major surgery where we take out the ovaries and fallopian tubes. You'll have to stay in the hospital for at least a few nights. Maybe up to a week, depending on what we find."

Something hardened in the back of Alice's throat. "A . . . week?"

"Yes."

"Oh." She stopped, swallowed. Tried again. "Well, uh, when can you do it?"

"As soon as possible. Monday, if I can arrange it."

Alice felt a strange jolt, a lurch, into awareness. Kate's hand finally touched hers, and maybe it was the shock, or maybe their earlier moment of camaraderie, but Alice allowed it.

"Maybe your daughter should be here," Kate said. "If she is going to be your primary support she probably needs to—"

"No," Alice said, pulling her hands back into her lap.

"This will be hard for her," Dr. Brookes said thoughtfully, "and we will be mindful of that. But at fifteen, she might be able to handle more than you—"

"No," Alice repeated. "Zoe doesn't need to be involved in this. She can't handle this. She isn't like a normal teenager."

Dr. Brookes raised his eyebrows, but Alice didn't bother explaining further. Doctors always turned it around on her, making it seem like the whole thing was her fault—or, worse, Zoe's.

"Zoe won't be my support person," Alice said, with finality. "She doesn't need to know about any of this."

Dr. Brookes sighed. "Alice, I don't think you fully understand—"

"Maybe there's someone else, Alice?" Kate interrupted. "A friend? Even an acquaintance? Someone to drive you home from surgery, to be at these kinds of appointments?"

Alice shook her head. Dr. Brookes and Kate conferred with their eyes.

"We can get a social worker to contact you," Kate said, finally. "They'll be able to attend appointments with you, they might be able to organize meals, or even get access to special funding to help with out-of-pocket costs." To Kate's credit, she wasn't reeling off a speech; she appeared genuinely engaged in what she was saying. "The thing is, Alice, you *are* going to need someone. We need to do more tests, but the current information we have indicates that your condition is very serious. You have a mass in your ovaries, your CA 125 levels are up in the thousands, and you have a buildup of fluid in the abdomen, indicating the cancer may have already spread. Even in the best-case scenario, if everything goes well in the surgery you will most likely have to have chemotherapy. We will do everything we can, but I promise you . . . you *are* going to need someone."

If she'd felt a jolt earlier, this was a cannon, blowing a giant hole right through her. "Cancer." Had they used that word earlier? She didn't remember it.

Apparently appeased by her expression—finally the reaction they'd been waiting for—the doctor began to explain it all again, a third or maybe fourth time. Once again, Alice zoned out. Because . . . she couldn't have cancer. She was barely forty, she ate well, exercised occasionally. More importantly, she *couldn't* have cancer. She had Zoe.

Dr. Brookes finished his spiel and asked her if she had any questions. Alice opened her mouth, but no sound came out. She thought again about what Kate had said. *You* are *going to need someone.* Alice wanted to tell her she was wrong. Because if what she was saying was true, Alice wasn't going to need someone. Zoe was.

2

As cancer-care coordinator, Kate Littleton delivered bad news for a living. In five years at the job she'd given hundreds of people what was, arguably, the worst news of their lives, and in five years it hadn't got any easier. Today's appointment was no exception. When the doctor explained to Alice Stanhope that she had cancer, it was almost as though she didn't hear. A severe case of denial, most likely, which was why they asked patients to bring a support person to appointments—so they could hear what the patient could not.

There wasn't anyone, Alice had said. Was that possible? In five years at Stanford Health Care, Kate had never heard this. Most patients were surrounded by people, in chemotherapy, in post-op; usually Kate's problem was getting them all to leave so the patient could rest. The ideal scenario, in Kate's experience, was for patients to have one primary support person. There was something about pairs—the yin and the yang of it. When one fell apart, the other was strong; when one zoned out, the other would listen. Yet Alice Stanhope didn't have a single person she felt she could nominate to walk beside her in what was going to be the hardest journey of her life. Which meant that Kate would have to do her job a little better than usual.

Kate knew there was one thing that a patient needed more than a doctor, more than a nurse, even more than medicine, and that was a mother. Someone to reassure them, to fluff their pillows, to give them that look of certainty that said they were in good hands. Someone to *fight* for them. At the age of nine, after an emergency appendectomy, Kate had learned this firsthand. Her father, widowed when Kate was just a toddler, had visited her every night, but it was Ann, Kate's nurse with the short brown hair and thick ankles, who'd cuddled her before she fell asleep. It was Ann who shooed the younger nurses out of her room and wheeled in the old TV and VCR along with kids' movies she'd rented at Blockbuster on her way to her shift. It was Ann who'd told her that under no circumstances was she to eat her vegetables. For those two weeks, Kate had had a mother. Now Kate strived to be that mother for her patients.

"Lunch?"

Kate looked up from her desk. Dr. Brookes—Chris—stood in her doorway. He was so tall his head almost brushed the top of the doorframe. His top button was undone and his skin had a bluish tinge.

"Lunch?" Kate glanced at her watch. "It's not even eleven A.M."

"When you are called into surgery at three A.M., lunchtime is whenever you have a break," he said. "Oh, I managed to get Alice Stanhope's surgery scheduled for Monday."

"Perfect." Kate reached for a pen. "What time?"

"First up. Eight A.M."

Kate wrote the details on her desk calendar.

Alice Stanhope: Bilateral Salpingo-Oophorectomy.

The one thing Kate couldn't get used to was that you couldn't *see* the cancer. Alice, in particular, looked well. Blondish and slim with short tousled hair, she was the picture of Meg Ryan, back in her heyday. The image of health. It was always a shock to learn that someone like that had cancer.

Chris leaned against the doorframe. "What do you think was up with Alice's daughter? What did she say . . . that she isn't like a normal teenager?"

"I wondered that myself," Kate said. "Who knows? Some kind of special needs, maybe?' "

"Geez, I hope not," he said, and they both drifted into silence for a moment. Eventually Chris shook his head. "Well, we'll just have to take extra-good care of her mother, won't we?"

Sometimes Kate loved Chris Brookes.

"All right," he said, "I guess I'll get one of those plastic salads from the cafeteria. Those salads are probably causing the cancer that we treat here, you know. We're probably keeping ourselves in business."

When he had drifted off down the corridor, Kate listened to her voice mail. She had two messages: the first from an anxious middle-aged woman wanting information about her newly diagnosed breast cancer, the second from David, who had seen cheap fares to Cancún and thought it was high time for a second honeymoon. "Or, what do they call them nowadays," he'd added, "a babymoon?"

Kate's eyes drifted back to her desk calendar, specifically to the Post-it on the bottom of tomorrow's date. Twelve weeks. She'd written it eleven weeks and two days earlier when she'd seen the two pink lines appear on the pregnancy test she'd promised her fertility doctor she wouldn't take. Twice before she'd written this note on a Post-it—but those had ended up in the trash at seven and nine weeks respectively. This time, she'd made it to twelve weeks. Almost.

It was the final piece of her puzzle, growing inside her, ready to make them whole. All Kate needed to do was hold on to it.

3

n third-period science, Zoe was trying to follow the rules. Not the class rules, her own. And her own rules were far more extensive.

- Never place both feet on the ground while sitting.
- Never touch the sides of the chair.
- Never be the first or last person to take their seat.
- It's okay to look around the classroom, but never out the window.
- Don't let anything weird pop into your head.
- If forced to answer a question never start your response with "Um" or "I think."

Two seats to her left, Cameron Freeman was folding up scraps of paper and attempting to throw them at the back of Billy Dyer's head (yeah, real cool, Cameron, picking on a kid because he's deaf), but the paper was falling well short of its target. Zoe wanted to tell Cameron to cut it out, but Zoe didn't do things like that. It wasn't that she cared about what Cameron Freeman thought about her—she didn't—it was merely the fact that if she stood up to him people would notice she was alive, and that was something Zoe tried to avoid at all costs.

"Okay, class," Mr. Bahr said. "Everyone find a partner."

Zoe's stomach plunged. There were few things more heinous than having to find a partner in class. The looking around, the making eye contact, the inevitable rejection. All around her people paired up with the ease of magnet and metal. Even now Zoe couldn't help but marvel. How did they do it? Were they really as carefree as they looked? Usually, when the class was asked to partner up, Zoe lunged for Emily, her one and only friend. When Emily wasn't in her class—like third-period science—she simply kept her eyes down and tried to be invisible. Eventually the teacher would pair her up with whoever was left, usually Billy or Jessie Lee Simons, the emo with the turquoise hair and the piercings. But today, as she pondered her defect, her inability to be normal, she found herself staring straight ahead, and that's when she noticed Harry Lynch, bent around in his chair with one elbow draped on the front of her desk.

"What?" she whispered, when he didn't look away.

"You just said my name."

Was he crazy? Why on earth would she say his name? "No I didn't."

"You did. First *and last*." Harry spoke matter-of-factly rather than with ridicule. "Why else would I be looking at you?"

Zoe felt her cheeks pool with hot, shameful color. It was a good question, which made it all the more humiliating. Someone like Harry would never look at Zoe spontaneously. Harry wasn't good-looking exactly, but he managed to hide it well by being big and looking more or less like all the other guys who played football. Maybe she had said his name out loud? She did do weird things like that sometimes. Once, in gym class, she'd accidentally started singing out loud (she needed to sing internally to get through the horror of exercising and wearing gym shorts in public). Maybe she was actually as crazy as she thought she was?

Harry opened his mouth to say something else, but before he could, Amber Jeffries was practically sitting in his lap. "Partner, Harry?"

She gave him the kind of slow sexy smile that was both ador-able and sickeningly desperate. Harry's gaze flickered to Amber's. "Sure."

As he turned back to face the front, Zoe's heart started to beat again. Another bullet dodged. Just about another five hundred billion to go.

Until tomorrow.

Once, Zoe's mom had asked her to describe what it felt like, being her. For a heartbeat, she'd considered telling her the truth.

It's like being anchored to damp sand, she'd imagined saying. Your head is toward the ocean, your ears are wet, and you're waiting for the next wave. You want to turn and look, to see what's coming, but you can't move. So you just lie there and wonder. Are the waves big today? Will they come, tease me a bit, then recede away? Or will they come at speed, dumping on me again and again, filling my nose and mouth with water until my lungs are burning and ready to explode? The awful part is, you don't know. So you wait, helplessly, expecting the worst.

Zoe had pictured what her mom's face would look like if she were actually to say these words. And then she'd said, "It kind of feels like being out of breath. You know, a little light-headed, a little fluttery. But it only stays for a few minutes and then it fades away."

It was bad enough that one of them knew the truth.

4

As she hurried along the hospital corridor, Sonja caught her reflection in the window and winced. She'd overdone the Botox. She *knew* she'd overdone the Botox. She wasn't sure why she'd started doing it in the first place, but once she'd started, it had become surprisingly addictive. First her forehead, then the deep lines that bracketed her mouth. Before she knew it she had become utterly expressionless. Now, no matter how she tried, she couldn't show how she felt. Which, come to think of it, wasn't the worst thing in the world.

By the time she found Kate's door, she was a little breathless. "It's me," she said, knocking.

"Come in!" Kate smiled. It was the kind of smile that warmed you through. She gave off an almost serene aura of goodness, Sonja thought. Or perhaps it was simply youth? Kate was in her mid-thirties, at a guess. A hundred and fifty years younger than her.

"I hear you have a case for me?" Sonja said.

As a hospital social worker, Sonja had "cases" that varied widely. One day she'd be dealing with a child who'd been admitted with injuries consistent with abuse, the next with a family who'd lost their primary breadwinner in an accident. When she was dealing with a cancer patient, her role was usually more

administrative—putting the person in touch with community services, providing assistance filling out forms and dealing with
insurance companies. But no two days were the same. Once, it
was what Sonja had loved about the job. Lately, the uncertainty
of what lay ahead felt unsettling to her.

"I do," Kate said. "Come in, sit down."

Sonja did, eyeing the picture on Kate's desk—of Kate and a man
who must have been her husband, judging by their body language.
In the picture Kate was sitting in his lap and they both laughed
into the camera, heads tilted up, eyes squinting. It was the kind
of photo that came with the frame—beautiful people with a perfect life. People who had a lot of mutually satisfying sex.

"I have a single mother scheduled for a salpingo-oophorectomy
on Monday," Kate started. "Alice Stanhope is her name. She has
a teenage daughter and no support people."

Sonja looked away from the photo. "How old is Alice?"

"Forty."

"Forty?" Sonja felt her eyebrows rise. Most forty-year-olds had
spouses, siblings, and friends coming out of their eyeballs. Tennis clubs and social groups providing meals on rotation every
night of the week. It was rare to find a person so young without
a network to rely on.

"Yes, I'm not sure exactly what's going on," Kate said, reading
her mind. "She said she doesn't have any family other than her
daughter."

Kate pushed a file over to Sonja. Sonja opened it and scanned
the top page. "How old is her daughter?"

"Fifteen."

"And Alice's financial situation?"

"I'm not sure. I thought you could discuss this with her. She
seemed very concerned about her daughter, so she might need
some support there too."

"Is she expecting my call?" Sonja asked. She glanced into the
file to make sure all the information was there.

"Yes, but it's hard to say how receptive she'll be."

Sonja nodded. Unfortunately it was often the case that the people who needed the most help were the least likely to take it.

"I'll call her today," she said, fully intending to stand up. And yet she remained in her chair. Some days, when she sat, she wondered if she'd ever get up again.

"How are you settling in to the area?" Kate asked, mistaking her inability to stand as a desire to chat. "You live in Atherton, right? So do I."

Sonja nodded. "I'm missing San Francisco a bit," she admitted. The sudden move had been George's idea—a segue into retirement, he'd said. Sonja went along with it, but six months later she wasn't entirely sure what they were doing there. Atherton was a desirable place to live, certainly—in fact, it had been ranked the number one most affluent zip code in the United States by *Forbes* a few years ago. A twenty-minute drive from Silicon Valley, it was home to Facebook's Sheryl Sandberg, Hewlett Packard's Meg Whitman, and Google's Eric Schmidt. (Sonja had found this out when she'd Googled Atherton.) Most homes, Sonja's included, were fenced and gated and on a minimum lot size of an acre. On the street people smiled and kept walking, minding their own business. It unnerved Sonja a little, even if it was, strangely, perfect for her. "But Atherton's very nice. Small, but nice."

Kate nodded politely.

Sonja glanced again at the photo on Kate's desk. *Is your marriage as good as it looks?* she had a sudden urge to ask. *Are you happy all of the time? Or do you have days when things are good and other days when you think about swerving into oncoming traffic?* But she couldn't ask any of these things, of course. So instead she smiled and said, "Well, I guess I'll call Alice today."

5

"ancer."

An hour after leaving her appointment, Alice was still in the hospital parking lot. Like a crazy lady, she said the word aloud, listened to the way it sounded. "Cancer." "*Cancer.*" It was strange. She must have said the word a hundred times before but today it felt different on her tongue. Rounder, and in a way, ridiculous—like the words "leprechaun" or "scapegoat." But then the whole thing was ridiculous, wasn't it?

Two weeks ago she'd gone to the doctor with some discomfort in her shoulder. She'd had one of her increasingly rare sessions at the gym (brought on by a newly paunchy stomach she'd she blamed on too much eggnog at Christmas) and had, she thought, overdone it with the overhead weights. But when the pain continued for nearly a week, in spite of Advil, Alice finally made a visit to her family doctor.

"Shoulder tip discomfort?" Dr. Hadley asked when Alice finished explaining.

"Well . . . I guess it's the tip, yes."

"Does it get better or worse when you move your arm or head?"

Alice tried moving. "No," she said. "It's pretty much the same all the time."

"And you're otherwise well?"

"Yes."

"You couldn't be pregnant?"

"Does that still require sex?"

Alice chuckled at her own joke. It was hard to believe that once, sex had once been her drug, something that had never been far from her mind. Now sex was like a childhood friend that she remembered vaguely, a friend she had no intention of reconnecting with.

Dr. Hadley, bless her heart, let the comment go. "You're menstruating regularly?"

Alice thought about that. She wasn't clockwork regular, but more or less. And there hadn't been any change in that regard.

Except.

"Well it's probably not relevant but . . . my flow has been a little heavier than usual lately, I guess. And a few months ago, I did have a . . . gush."

She'd been playing bridge with Marie Holland, a ninety-year-old client, when she'd felt it. They had nearly finished with the game, so Alice had decided to plow ahead. But she'd had to keep her back to the wall when she'd excused herself a few minutes later. There'd been enough blood to soak her underwear and her trousers and leave a faint stain on the armchair. She'd sponged it clean and covered it with a cushion and attributed it to changing menstrual cycles as she'd got older. Then she'd made a mental note to mention it the next time she went to the doctor. Which she was doing. Although she failed to see what any of this had to do with her shoulder.

"Okay," Dr. Hadley said. "I'd like to palpate your abdomen if that's all right with you. Make sure everything feels normal."

"Sure," Alice asked. "But you know I'm here for my shoulder, right?"

"I do." Dr. Hadley grinned as she guided Alice toward the table. "What I'm trying to ascertain is whether the discomfort you're feeling in your shoulder is what we call referred pain."

Alice lay down on the table. "Referred pain?"

Dr. Hadley began to touch her belly. "It's a pain perceived at a location other than the stimulus. An example is when a person is having a heart attack and they feel pain in the neck or the jaw, rather than the chest."

Dr. Hadley's fingertips, Alice noticed, had slowed in one particular area. She glanced at Alice's face as she pressed down on it. "That sore?"

"A little uncomfortable," she admitted. "Why?"

Dr. Hadley continued examining her stomach in silence, leaving Alice to wait. It wasn't like Dr. Hadley to leave a question hanging like that.

"Why?" Alice repeated. "Do you feel something?"

"I'm going to refer you for an ultrasound. Your abdomen feels distended and I think it's best to be safe."

"What do you think it is?" she asked.

"It could be a cyst, or possibly even gallstones. Or"—she smiled—"it could be a sore shoulder. An ultrasound will tell us more."

Two weeks later Alice was in the hospital parking lot. With ovarian cancer. The same cancer that killed her mother.

She put the car into gear. She was, she decided, going to work. It wasn't as ridiculous as it sounded. She and Mrs. Featherstone were going grocery shopping in Menlo Park this morning, then perhaps to the nail salon. Alice could handle a little grocery shopping, even today. If there was anyone used to going about her business with an unspoken tragedy in her pocket, it was Alice.

On the way to Mrs. Featherstone's house, things looked the same, evidence that nothing had changed. Mrs. Featherstone lived close to Alice, in the part of town just north of the train station that Alice and Zoe lovingly called "the slums of Atherton." Despite its name, this part of town was lovely, just modest in comparison with the rest of the area. Alice preferred it to Atherton's

West, with its opulent homes and lack of sidewalks (which always made Alice feel unwelcome, like she was trespassing when she walked down the street). Today people were out walking their dogs or taking a stroll, enjoying the warm weather. Alice passed a couple that must have been in their mid-twenties, strolling with their arms resting lightly above each other's bottom. They both wore T-shirts and cutoffs and large sunglasses and their lives seemed to be brimming with possibility, almost as though they'd been planted there to remind Alice how life once was. It was working. The sight of them brought up images—actual, visual snapshots—of Alice at a similar age, only with shorter shorts and bigger glasses. Right before everything changed. It was amazing how easily it all came back to her, almost sixteen years later. Alice should have known that, today of all days, it was only a matter of time before her thoughts turned to Zoe's father. Still, it always astonished her—her capacity for hate.

Alice arrived at Mrs. Featherstone's fifteen minutes early, and parked around the corner. Then she pulled her phone from her purse.

"I know it's tempting," Nurse Kate had said before she left, "but whatever you do, do *not* go onto Google."

As she thumbed the words "ovarian cancer" into her iPhone Alice wondered how many people followed that advice. Alice wasn't exactly a rebel, and yet she'd known, even in the moment, that it was advice she wouldn't take. Could anyone? Knowing there was a world of information at her fingertips? She did know a thing or two about ovarian cancer, of course—her mother had died of it—but there hadn't been Google back then. She'd relied on what the doctor told her—or rather, what *her mother* told her the doctor told her. Now she had a veritable glut of information at her fingertips.

She hit Search, and a Wikipedia link popped up. *What is ovarian cancer?* Alice hovered over it for a second or two, and then she tapped it.

Ovarian cancer is a cancer that begins in an ovary.

Helpful, Alice thought. She read on.

Symptoms may include bloating, pelvic pain, and abdominal swelling, among others.

Alice scanned the symptoms. Bloating, okay, but she was, after all, a woman. Pelvic pain, no. Abdominal swelling, well, wasn't that the same as bloating? So the symptoms were . . . bloating? If that was the case, every woman she knew had ovarian cancer too, at least once every twenty-eight days.

There, she thought. *It had all been a terrible mistake.*

Alice scanned the links. Forums. Early warning signs. It was called the "whispering illness," apparently, which had, to Alice, an almost glamorous ring to it. But having watched her mother go through it, she knew there was nothing glamorous about ovarian cancer.

Alice returned to Google and added the word "cure" to her search.

The screen filled again. She tapped a few links, recognizing some of the terms as ones that had been mentioned at her appointment. Salpingo-oophorectomy—that was the operation she was scheduled for on Monday. She tapped an article.

Salpingo-oophorectomy is the surgical removal of both the fallopian tube (salpingectomy) and ovary (oophorectomy). A unilateral salpingo-oophorectomy is generally performed on patients in the case where an ovary is unable to be preserved, such as: cases of ruptured ectopic pregnancy where hemostasis is unable to be achieved without removal of the tube and ovary; a tuboovarian abscess that does not respond to antibiotics; adnexal torsion where the ovary and tube are necrotic; or when no viable healthy ovarian tissue is able to be

preserved if a benign ovarian mass is present. A bilateral
salpingo-oophorectomy is usually one of three classifications:
elective at time of hysterectomy in the case of benign
conditions, prophylactic in women when there is an increased
risk of ovarian cancer, or due to malignancy.

Alice read over the description again. She didn't think the
doctor had suggested a unilateral salpingo-oophorectomy, so she
supposed hers must be a bilateral one. She wondered if she should
read something into that. Did it mean it was bad if they had to
take out both ovaries? Then again, why not whip them both out?
She didn't need her ovaries anymore, so why have them just sitting there, gathering cancer? Taking them both out was a good
thing, she decided. It would sort it all right out, and then it would
be over.

Good.

She put down her phone, and gave herself a little shake. *Get
it together, Alice—it's time for work.* At Mrs. Featherstone's front
door, she pressed the doorbell and then let herself in using her
key. She was barely inside when a figure appeared in the wide
hallway.

"Alice!"

Alice supposed she should be pleased that Mrs. Featherstone's
daughter, Mary, was happy to see her, but instead she felt an immediate sense of dread. Mary had been the one to hire Alice, saying that she couldn't *possibly* take care of her mother, not when
she had a family of her own (two grown married children and a
retired husband) to take care of. Alice had expected that, in light
of this, Mary wouldn't be around very often. No such luck.

In the open-plan kitchen/living room, Mrs. Featherstone was
seated on her usual chair. Alice sent her a wink, which she promptly
returned. Beside her, Mary sank into the sofa. Alice slipped behind the kitchen counter and pulled a notepad from her purse.

"Well, it's official," Mary announced. "I hate him."

Mrs. Featherstone raised her eyebrows at Alice—an apology.

A lot of their exchanges were this way: silent. It was difficult to believe that someone as discerning with words as Mrs. Featherstone had birthed a talker like Mary. (Once, Mrs. Featherstone had said to Alice, "I love my children, but I do wonder, as a mother, if my job will ever be done.")

Alice opened the fridge and bent to survey its contents. There were a tomato and a carrot that had seen better days—but they might be okay in a Bolognese sauce. "Waste not, want not" was Mrs. Featherstone's motto. Alice added ground beef to her list, and an onion.

"I'm talking about Michael of course," Mary continued.

As if she needed to clarify. Mary had complained consistently about her son-in-law, Michael, for the entire three years Alice had worked for Mrs. Featherstone. He didn't sound so bad to Alice. There were no allegations of affairs or violence; he was just particular about personal boundaries. Which, with Mary as a mother-in-law, seemed to Alice a wise thing.

She checked the use-by date of the milk and yogurt.

"After everything I've done for them, he turns around and tells me to give Audrey some space! He says she needs to get used to being alone with the baby. Can you believe it? I'm the grandma! Every girl needs her mother around when she has her first baby."

Alice wondered if she had a point here. She would have loved to have had her mother around when Zoe was a baby, but she died while Alice was pregnant. Seven months from diagnosis to death.

"Audrey had said nothing of the sort, obviously. That's how I know he's interfering. She would have told me if she wanted time alone."

"Would she though, Mary?" Mrs. Featherstone asked.

"Of course she would. She's my daughter. Mothers and daughters don't have secrets. They have a soul connection. Right, Alice?"

Alice stood, a limp lettuce in her hand.

"Anyway, I told him he had no right to tell me what to do with my own daughter—no right at all—not after the way I've supported them," Mary continued before Alice could speak. "Emotionally not to mention financially. I actually have a good mind to cut them off. See how they'd do then! Audrey, she'd be lost without me. She couldn't function . . ."

The lettuce rolled off Alice's hand, onto the floor, landing with a thud.

"Alice?" she heard Mrs. Featherstone say. "Alice? Are you all right, dear?"

Mothers and daughters don't have secrets. . . .

She'd be lost without me. . . .

She couldn't function. . . .

Alice wanted to respond but she couldn't make her mouth comply. She took a breath and tried again, but all at once it hit her—a profound sense of horror. She caught her reflection in the window. Her arms were wrapped around her middle and she rocked like a woman going mad.

6

Ten minutes before lunchtime Zoe put up her hand. The class had broken into groups to discuss an assignment, so there was a general hum of noise in the room, which made it slightly more bearable. Still, with her hand in the air, she felt under a spotlight, onstage. Like a thousand bugs were crawling on her.

"Yes, Zoe?" Mr. Crew said when he finally noticed her. It had taken at least a minute, which wasn't even close to a record. She made it easy for people to not know that she existed.

"Can I use the restroom?" she said in a small voice.

Mr. Crew tapped his ear as though he were trying to shake something loose. "I'm getting deafer every year. What did you say?"

"The restroom," Zoe repeated, mortified. "I need to go."

It was the catch-22 she dealt with every day. She could use the bathroom at lunchtime with a bunch of people right outside the door (torture), or put up her hand and ask to go during class (also torture). Some days she'd do neither and instead wait until she got home. But today she really needed to pee.

"There's ten minutes until lunchtime, Zoe," he said, glancing at his watch. "Can't you wait?"

A few kids glanced up from their desks. Zoe shrank down in her seat. "Uh, no," she whispered. "I can't."

He rolled his eyes. "Fine. Go ahead."

She could feel everyone's eyes on her back as she walked out. She could also hear their thoughts. *Why is she so weird? Why does she blush so much? Why does she always need to pee?* For the zillionth time Zoe yearned to be invisible.

She used the stall at the end, the one with the sink inside so she didn't have to look in the mirror as she washed her hands. She'd taken to avoiding mirrors ever since she'd reached puberty and her breasts had failed to get the memo. Mercifully, she hadn't fallen victim to the cruel acne that resided on every second teenager's chin and nose, but she *had* been cursed with an abnormally large forehead, something she'd hoped was all in her mind until last week, when she'd dropped five bucks in the cafeteria and someone had called after her, "Yo, forehead, you dropped your cash!" When she'd asked Emily, "Do I have a giant forehead?," Emily had frowned and said, "I mean . . . you do have a bit of a Rihanna thing going on. But it's cuuute!" Emily once called a pimple "cuuute," so Zoe wasn't reassured.

Zoe walked ridiculously slowly back to class. The bell would go any minute and she could live without the spectacle of walking in again. At these kinds of times she yearned for a Klonopin. Just one sweet tablet to make everything—if not okay, better. But the problem with anxiety was that you worried about everything, including taking medication. What if the pills made her do strange things, what if she became addicted? The debate had culminated in a full-blown panic attack two weeks after the Klonopin had been prescribed, as she stood in the bathroom, bottle in hand, debating whether to take it. (Since then the bottle had remained in her bathroom cabinet, for emergencies.) Therapy had ended in a similar way—hello? One-on-one conversation; it had made Zoe so anxious she'd forced her mom to let her discontinue it over a year ago.

And so she steeled herself.

Lunchtime was, hands down, the worst part of Zoe's day every day, but today was made crueler by the fact that Emily was meeting her in the cafeteria rather than at the stairs where they normally met. Zoe felt absurdly self-conscious as she slunk through the hallway. Was she walking too slouchily? Too straight? Was her fly undone? Her T-shirt tucked into her undies? Were people looking at her giant forehead? It was bad enough walking in with Emily, but going alone was a kind of torture.

When the bell went, she made for the line, snatched up a tray—something to hold on to—then slunk toward the cashier, trying to blend in. The trio of girls in front of her loaded up their trays with oily white food—Tater Tots, mac 'n' cheese, fries. They were caught up in a conversation about reality TV, a conversation so easy and natural it made Zoe want to cry. All around her, people chatted easily while Zoe pretended to be totally gripped by the disgusting food behind the steamed-up glass. She shot a longing look at the lunch ladies, wishing she could be one of them: busy at her station, not required to sit, be sociable, make small talk. When she reached the end of the line, she swiped up some onion rings (she wouldn't eat them, but she could push them around her plate for fifty minutes to give herself something to do) and proceeded to the cashier.

Having paid, Zoe did a discreet assessment of the room. She and Emily didn't have, like, a regular spot; they "freestyled"—a term Emily had coined to mean that they moved around. Zoe would have preferred to have a regular table, a place she knew she could always head toward, but if Emily wanted to freestyle, they freestyled.

Zoe and Emily weren't geeks exactly; they were more like nobodies—didn't register on anyone's dial at all. This was fine by Zoe, but Emily was determined to improve their social standing at any cost. She'd taken to brazenly talking to the coolest guys as if they were good friends. ("Hey, Fred, great game last night, man! Next stop, Super Bowl?") Her optimism was sweet, if majorly embarrassing. (Like the day she stopped Amber in the parking lot and asked for a ride home. Amber hadn't even tried to contain her amusement and roared with laughter as she drove away. Em's cheeks had pinkened a little but she got it together and waved as Amber screeched out of the parking lot.) Zoe knew Emily longed to be part of the cool crowd, but rather than get down about being on the outer circle, she stayed focused on having a plan— the next person they could befriend, the next party they could attend. Luckily for Zoe, Emily's plans never quite worked out.

Zoe had sat next to Emily in homeroom on the first day of school and Emily had latched on to her (weirdly, it wasn't the other way around) saying she thought she had "this mysterious vibe going on" and she "so *wished* she could be mysterious." Zoe doubted that, but she welcomed the friendship. Emily had invited herself to Zoe's house that first day, and Zoe was floored to find that the prospect didn't make her freak out. Her mom nearly choked on her wine when Emily bounced in, all bubbly and happy. Zoe's previous "friends" had been made up of freaks and creepers (like Carla, the morbidly obese kid who, during a sleepover one night, had crept into their kitchen and eaten the entire contents of their fridge, including the condiments, and then stole away into the night and never talked to Zoe again). Then along came Emily, this fairly normal, nice girl, who thought Zoe was awesome. And around Emily—as long as they were alone— Zoe *was* awesome. There was no good explanation for it; Emily was simply one of her safe people. She'd come up with the term "safe people" in one of her few therapy sessions, and it seemed to fit. But there weren't many safe people. There was her mother. Emily. Her grandpa before he died. Some of the old people her mom looked after (there was something so wonderfully nonthreatening about the elderly). And once upon a time, a few of her misfit friends, who, once they'd realized what was wrong with her, had moved on to greener pastures of friendship. Like Emily was bound to do eventually.

Zoe walked slowly, searching for somewhere to sit. There were a few tables that had spaces, but none had room for two. There were some empty tables at the back of the room, but they were a bad idea—anyone could come and sit there and she'd be stuck with them for the entire hour. Harry Lynch, she noticed, sat alone at a corner table, rather than in his usual spot with the other football players—but when you were as cool as he was, you could do that. A sandwich was in his hand, suspended halfway between his plate and his mouth. He observed it for a moment then returned it to his plate.

Zoe hurried on.

Finally, she sat at an empty table, crossed her legs, and pushed her onion rings around her plate. Zoe didn't have an eating disorder exactly; she simply didn't eat in front of people. The way she figured, there was just so much potential for it to go bad. She became consumed by the way she chewed, the way her mouth opened and closed, whether she'd left a shiny oil residue on her lips. Not to mention the unholy minefield of something sticking in her teeth. They were normal worries, but where a normal person would carry a mirror or wet wipes in their purse, Zoe stopped eating in public.

"Sorry!" Emily said, clattering her tray against the table. "Whew."

"Where'd you go?" Zoe asked, then immediately chastised herself. She didn't want to be that possessive friend who wanted a full report every time her friend went to the bathroom. Mostly because Emily had told her she'd once had a friend like that and it had really annoyed her.

"I have news," Emily announced, dragging the word "news" out and making it two syllables, and delivering it in an opera-style voice. It was cute and endearing, just like Emily. It made Zoe long to be cute and endearing.

"What is it?"

Emily pierced her with her blue gaze. "Um, just the most amazeable thing that could possibly happen. You're not going to eat these, right?" She gestured to Zoe's onion rings.

Zoe bumped them toward her. "Tell me."

"I have a date with . . . wait for it . . . Cameron Freeman!"

"Cameron Freeman?" Zoe exclaimed, hoping it came across as excited disbelief rather than the truth, which was that she thought Cameron was a jerk.

Emily nodded, her red curls bouncing. She hated those curls, but Zoe would have loved them. Her own hair, black and straight, was as bland as she was. "And it's all because of you."

"It is?"

"Uh-huh. The reason it all happened is because Seth wants to date you."

Zoe paused for a beat. "He does?"

"Yes!" Emily squealed.

Seth was in several of Zoe's classes but they'd never exchanged so much as a word. Then again, Zoe didn't exchange words with many people. But now that she thought about it, he had sat next to her on a couple of occasions, and perhaps even smiled once or twice.

Zoe's face fell.

"Oh come on," Emily said. "Seth is adorkable."

Seth *was* adorkable. Small and prepubescent-looking, much like Zoe herself. He and Cameron were cousins and this was most likely the only reason they came as a pair. Without a cool cousin, Seth would have been relegated to a regular nobody, just like Zoe and Emily. He probably would have been perfect for her. If she went on dates.

"You should have seen Seth just now, he was having a full-on joygasm!" Emily adopted a wide-eyed expression. "'Do you think she'd really go out with me? You don't think she's out of my league?'" She crunched on an onion ring cheerfully.

Zoe tried to imagine the scenario that Emily had just described. Emily and Seth standing around, talking about *her*.

"I told him you'd go, but only if I came along—I played up the shy thing. Then I said it would be majorly awks with just the three of us, and then . . . ta da . . . Cameron said he'd come too. Which was what I'd been angling for all along."

Zoe felt the blood drain from her face. "You told him I'd go?"

"Oh no, don't do that." Emily's eyes narrowed.

"Do what?"

"Go all cray-cray. This is *good*. Seth is cute."

Zoe tried to breathe, to act normal. But Emily was looking at her too closely. Zoe focused on uncrossing and recrossing her legs, being careful to keep one off the floor at all times.

"It's not forevs, Zo, it's just a date. I even suggested a movie so you don't have to talk."

With this last statement, Emily's demeanor had changed a little—only slightly, but Zoe was attuned to these kinds of things. Her voice held an edge. A warning. *Do this.* Panic started to flood Zoe. This was it. She'd been handed an ultimatum—this date or her friendship. Except, in her case, it wasn't an ultimatum. An ultimatum indicated choice.

"I know you hate people and generally being social," Emily continued. "I get it. Hey, I even dig it. You're weird-chic. But *come on!* This is one night. If you're my friend, you'll do this for me." Emily was pleading. Zoe had never heard Emily plead. "You know I'd do it for you."

Zoe did know that. Emily had more than proven herself. Sat with her, just the two of them, because that's what Zoe preferred. Spent Saturday nights watching movies. Let her borrow (and then keep) the black skirt that always made Zoe feel slightly less horrible, even though it looked amazing on Emily.

"Zo, it will be fine, okay, I promise." Emily had softened now. "I'll be right there with you. And Seth is so crazy about you he won't even care if you don't speak. Think of it as a date with me. You don't freak out when we go to the movies, right?"

"No."

Emily smiled at her with a sense of finality that said, *There, that's settled then.* And Zoe fought the tears that welled in her eyes. And, as usual, she had an immediate, sharp longing for her mother. She wondered what it said about her that, at fifteen, when things didn't go according to plan, the first thing she wanted was her mommy.

7

Alice lay on the couch, dry-eyed and numb. Her brain ticked over the same three things in rotation—cancer, Zoe, her breakdown in front of Mrs. Featherstone and Mary. Amazingly, Mrs. Featherstone had been the one to take control, instructing Mary to find tissues and insisting that Alice head straight home.

Now Alice crossed her ankles on the coffee table, narrowly missing Kenny. Damn cat was always underfoot. Kenny had always unnerved Alice, the way he slunk around, smirking as though he knew her most guarded secret and was going to tell. Zoe said it was the cat's "wisdom" that made him look like that. One thing to be said for the cat was that it was one of very few living things that Zoe felt comfortable with, and indeed, relaxed around. And for that, Kenny had Alice's begrudging respect.

Next to her feet was a stack of bills, including those from her medical appointments, out-of-pocket expenses that she had to find the money for. As she flipped through them, Alice considered how her diagnosis would affect her financially. Her business was steady—in fact she had so much work that she'd recently hired two part-timers—but it wasn't enormously profitable. She always managed to get the bills paid but there was no safety net, no additional pool of money they had to dip into, other than her salary. She allowed herself to fantasize, just for a moment, about having two salaries to rely on. Two parents. The kind of life where an illness meant an opportunity to rest, to sleep, to be cared for by loving relatives. She could concentrate on getting better and leave all the daily stresses of her life to others. She was ashamed to admit that she found that scenario somewhat appealing. As though cancer were a health spa, an opportunity for some "me" time. In that scenario, money wasn't the concern of the sick person. She wondered if this was how it would have been had she married. Indulgently, she let herself sit with that thought for a moment. But only a moment. If she thought too hard, she'd remember why she hadn't.

The phone rang. It was Kate, the nurse from the hospital.

"How are you doing," she asked gently, "after this morning?"

"I'm fine," Alice said. "I've taken the afternoon off work."

"I think that's wise. It's a lot to take in."

"So, what do I need to know?" Alice asked once the niceties were out of the way.

"You shouldn't eat anything after midnight the night before the operation. On the day you're to wear no makeup, no lotion, no antiperspirant, no jewelry, no piercings or acrylic nails—"

"Nothing to tempt the doctors away from their wives," Alice said. "Got it."

There was a short silence and for a horrible moment, Alice thought she'd have to explain that she was joking. Then, finally, came the stilted laugh.

All at once Alice had a sharp longing for her father. If he'd been here, she knew, he'd have been chuckling. She thought of that strange, sad day she'd returned to her family home after her mother had died. Alice had been twenty-five. Alice's brother, Paul, of course, had turned to his best friend Jack Daniel's to help him through the ordeal, so it was up to Alice to support her father through his grief. He was sitting on the green velvet couch, watching a black-and-white family movie, when she got there. As

Alice peered into the room, she saw him crying openly, while an image of her mother, visibly pregnant and smoking a cigarette (because you did in those days), talked to the camera. Alice tried to duck away without being seen, but her father glanced up suddenly, slyly wiping away a tear.

"I was looking for my dirty movies," he said finally with a shrug. "This was all I could find."

Humor, Alice always thought, was tragedy's best friend. Her dad had agreed. A few years back, minutes before his own death, he'd startled a nurse in the hospital who, noticing that his chest had stilled, had leaned over him to listen to his breathing. He waited until she was nice and close before whispering "Boo!" into her ear. Alice was still chuckling a few minutes later when he slowly slipped from this world.

Kate continued with the list. Alice tuned out until the part where she said, "If you have a living will, bring it on the day of surgery."

A *living will*, Alice thought. Try as she might, she couldn't think of anything funny about that.

"Sonja, one of our hospital social workers, will be in touch with you about providing support these next few weeks. And Alice? I'm here if you have any questions. My cell is on the card I gave you, and you can call twenty-four hours."

Alice hung up, remembering only the barest details of what she'd been told, but feeling certain that everything would be in the e-mail Kate promised to send. She was comfortingly earnest, Alice thought. Whether it was staged or not, Alice did believe that Nurse Kate would, indeed, be there if she had any questions.

She tossed the phone onto the couch beside her and immediately it began to ring again. Alice silenced it. She didn't want to talk any more. She planned to spend the rest of the afternoon— or at least until Zoe got home—wallowing in self-pity. But the time went quickly and before she knew it, keys were jiggling in the door.

"Mom?"

Alice uncrossed her legs and lay back, trying to look relaxed. "In here, Mouse."

It had always been such a perfect name for Zoe. She was so small and easy to miss, and inclined to scurry away when someone noticed her. A few seconds went by; then Zoe's dainty little face appeared in the doorway. "Why are you lying down?" she said.

Alice sat up. The girl didn't miss a trick. "What? Can't a woman rest?"

Zoe's eyes narrowed. "How was your doctor's appointment today?"

Alice searched for some truth she could tell her daughter— a truth that wasn't terrifying. "Nothing to worry about," she said eventually. "Though I do have to have a small surgery on Monday."

Zoe's face paled a few shades. Since she was a child she'd been plagued with terror that something would happen to Alice, and even now, whenever Alice seemed threatened with some ailment—be it a dentist appointment or tonsillitis—Zoe was paying attention.

"What's the surgery for?"

"Gallstones." Alice hadn't planned to lie; it just slipped out. Immediately she felt the weight of it.

Zoe dragged in a breath. "But . . . aren't gallstones, like, painful?"

"They can be when they flare up," Alice said, hoping she sounded authoritative. "That's why they want to take them out— before they cause me any more problems. I'll have to stay in the hospital for a few days."

"A few days?" The rest of the color drained from Zoe's face. "So I'll stay here by myself?"

Zoe hated being home by herself, even during the day. It was one of the ironies of social anxiety disorder. Zoe didn't like being by herself; in fact, she wanted nothing more than to be with people and in places surrounded by chatter and noise. Problem was, when she was in that kind of situation, she became so caught up in what everyone thought about her, she either had a panic attack or had to leave.

Unfortunately, staying at a friend's place wasn't an option. Apart from an attempt at a sleepover when she was ten (which didn't end well), she'd never slept anywhere but in her own home in her entire life.

"Maybe you could ask Emily to stay with you?" Alice suggested.

Zoe's cheeks flushed.

"Mouse?" Alice pressed. "What is it? Did you and Em have a fight?"

"Worse," Zoe said. "She wants me to go on a double date."

Alice's heart plummeted.

"I mean . . . I can't go, obviously," Zoe continued. "But if I don't, Emily can't go either. It's an all-in kind of thing. I don't know what to do."

Zoe was fighting back tears and Alice felt a little like crying herself. *Not Emily!* she wanted to shout to the universe. *Not today. What else are you going to take from us today?* The arrival of Emily had been a godsend. Since their friendship had started, Zoe had, well, not exactly transformed, but improved. She'd started sitting in the cafeteria during the lunch hour instead of by herself outside on the lawn, and at home she spent hours holed up in her room with Emily, hunched over their cell phones, like normal teens. Occasionally Alice had even heard Zoe use the lingo, like "douche" or "cray-cray" or "I literally can't" (though immediately she would blush, giving away the fact that it hadn't come naturally). On the weekends, Zoe and Emily sprawled all over the sofa watching movies while scrolling through Instagram or Facebook or whatever was hip these days. Once Zoe caught her watching them and called her "creepy," which only made Alice happier. She was the annoying mom! It was all she'd ever wanted to be. It was unthinkable that it could all be taken away from them because of (the lack of) a double date.

"What's the worst that could happen?" Alice asked.

For years they'd played this game when Zoe was afraid to do something. Alice would ask her to come up with the worst thing that could possibly happen; then they'd compare it to something much worse. ("I could fall over and land on my face," Zoe might say, to which Alice would respond, "Which isn't bad at all compared to . . ." "Drowning in elephant poop," Zoe would finish.) At worst it made them laugh. At best it gave her the courage to do whatever it was she was afraid of.

"I could be humiliated and lose my best friend," Zoe replied.

"Which would be terrible," Alice agreed. "But not bad at all, compared to . . ."

". . . something happening to you." Zoe stepped forward and gave her a sudden, impromptu hug. Talk of gallstones had obviously affected her. Alice tried to swallow, but her throat had suddenly swollen shut.

Zoe pulled away.

"What if I come with you?" Alice joked. "I can wear a disguise and sit in the row behind."

"Mom!"

"Or I could hang out in the foyer?" Alice grinned.

"No."

"Or maybe," Alice said, her smile slipping away, "you can actually do this?"

Alice nodded at Zoe with what she hoped looked like full confidence. She knew that, at best, Zoe would be back within the hour. At worst she wouldn't make it out the door.

"Without you, you mean?" Zoe asked.

A lump rose in Alice's throat. Could Zoe do it without her? Zoe looked at her expectantly and finally Alice smiled and nodded. *Yes, you can do it without me,* her smile said. But she couldn't bring herself to say the words.

8

At 6 P.M., Kate looked in the mirror, assessing. Her hair, recently cut to shoulder length, fell in carefully constructed haphazard waves. She wore patterned silk pants, a black top, and ankle boots. An oversize beaded necklace to add some festivity. It was, after all, a special occasion. She was rounder, she decided, around the jaw. She'd gained a little weight—two pounds to be exact. Not much, but enough to make it real.

Lately, it seemed, Kate's number had been two. There was the husband, who was on his second marriage, with two teenage children of his own. Two years of trying for a baby followed by two years of fertility treatments. Two pregnancies, followed by two miscarriages. But this was the third time. Kate hoped that, as the saying went, the third time was the charm.

She turned to the side and pulled her top down so it was taut over her stomach. "What do you think?" she said to David as he entered the bedroom. He glanced over at her for only a second before heading toward the bedside table.

"You look enormous," he said without missing a beat. "It's definitely twins."

She rolled her eyes. "It's not twins."

"Honey," he said, "every woman wishes she could look like you when she's pregnant. When Hilary was pregnant with Jake, she looked like she'd swallowed a watermelon. And that was just in the first trimester!"

This was David's favorite story about his ex-wife; he sometimes teased her about it when she came to pick up the kids.

"More like four watermelons," Hilary would agree wearily. "What those kids did to my pelvic floor!"

David and Hilary had this sickeningly well-adjusted relationship for the sake of sixteen-year-old Jake and fourteen-year-old Scarlett, who divided their time equally between their parents. Perhaps the most sickening part was that even Kate liked Hilary. When Kate had become pregnant the first time, Hilary—and her new husband, Danny—had sent flowers. The second time she'd pumped Kate's hands warmly and wished her the best of luck. They hadn't told her this time. Twice bitten and all that.

As David reached for his iPhone on the bedside table, Kate spun around. "What are you doing?"

"I'm going to have a game of Pokémon Go with the kids. *What?*"

Kate was glaring at him. "You're not playing now! Dad's coming to dinner, remember?" She looked at her watch. "Any minute."

Right on cue the doorbell rang.

Grumbling, David returned the iPhone to the bedside table. Kate glanced in the mirror. She looked calm and together, the opposite of how she felt. Strange as it was, she always felt uncomfortable— nervous even—around her father. Almost as uncomfortable as he seemed around her.

By the time they had walked downstairs, Jake and her father were having an awkward handshake, and Scarlett was attempting to answer a question about her "studies." Kate's dad had no idea how to talk to teenagers, and he had a habit of deferring to interview-type questions about college that kids always hated. Jake and Scarlett were polite and they endured them, but Kate knew they found her father hard work.

"Hi, Dad," Kate said. She raised her arms to give her father a hug, but at the same time he dipped to kiss her cheek. Finally they both stepped back and he thrust a bunch of flowers at her. "Oh, these are nice," she said, taking them. "Thank you."

"You're welcome." Her father nodded brusquely at the floor.

"Nice to see you, William," David said. His friendly voice seemed to warm the air around them. He shook her father's hand and this time the connection worked out. "Come on, let's get you a beer."

Kate trailed behind them to the back room. Every time she saw her father, like a fool she hoped it would be different. Even now as an adult, long after the proverbial ship had sailed, she hoped for some kind of connection with her only living parent. And every time she was left bereft when it didn't eventuate. Whenever people heard that she'd been raised by a single father, they always said the same thing: "You must be close." And Kate always responded, "We are," because what else could she say? He was a perfectly nice man. He wasn't abusive or neglectful. How could she admit that she rarely had anything to say to him? That he seemed to have even less to say to her.

According to her grandma—his own mother—her father had always been aloof, even as a baby. "Didn't suckle well," her gran was fond of saying, and also, "William never talked much." That was perhaps the hardest part. When her dad was uncomfortable, he went quiet. When Kate was uncomfortable, she talked. It baffled her, how different they were.

"You're like your mother," her gran had always told her. Kate had no idea if this was true (her mother had been hit by a car while cycling to work when Kate was only two) but Kate liked the idea that they were similar, even if it made her absence a little harder. Tonight, especially, Kate longed to have her mother present—the night she was going to announce that a grandchild was on its way.

"Where should I sit?" her dad asked when they reached the dining room.

"Wherever you like," Kate said. She was used to his habit of immediately sitting at the dining table when he arrived—even though part of her always wondered if it meant he was eager to get the evening over with. She fetched two beers and a platter of dips from the kitchen, where the kids were already hiding out, side by side, staring at their phones. Scarlett looked up guiltily but Kate just smiled at her. When she returned to the dining table, David and her dad were sitting side by side. Her father kept his eyes down, running his fingers over the table's surface as though admiring something new, even though he'd sat at this very table a dozen times.

"So . . . how was your day?" Kate asked, sitting down at the head. "Did you do anything special?"

"Read the papers." Her dad took a cracker and dipped it. "Drove Arthur to pick up his truck from the shop."

"And how *is* Arthur?" Kate persisted. Arthur, her father's oldest friend and another Stanford professor of artificial intelligence, was perhaps the only person on the planet who had less to talk about than her father (other than artificial intelligence, of course). Still, you never knew. Perhaps Arthur was more interesting than she thought.

Her father frowned. "He's . . . Arthur."

"Yes," she said. "Yes, I guess he is."

They drifted into silence once again. Kate was racking her brain for another topic of conversation when her dad turned his back on her and launched into conversation with David. And that, she supposed, was the end of that.

When her dad visited, he often spent the entire evening talking *at* David about something dull and intellectual, which wasn't a problem exactly, apart from the fact that generally David had no idea what he was talking about. David had gone directly to work from high school and then started an office-cleaning business that had, over the last thirty years, grown from him and a mop to a national organization—one of the top twenty in the U.S. "You don't need brains to be a success" was one of David's favorite sayings, which always made her father bristle. "Just common sense and hard work." Sometimes Kate wondered if her dad had any-

thing to talk about other than his career. If he *cared* about anything else.

She hoped he might care about one thing.

"Well," Kate said, when conversation came to a natural pause.
"We invited you here tonight for a reason. We have some news."

The kids had joined them at the table a few minutes earlier.
There must have been something in her voice, because Jake, who'd
been digging into the eggplant dip, froze. Scarlett looked up too,
a note of interest registering on her face.

"As you all know, we've been trying for a while to have a baby.
We've had a few false starts along the way, but we're excited to
say"—she shot a look at David—"that I'm pregnant."

It was a strange thing announcing a pregnancy after two miscarriages. Kate could actually *feel* the excitement swell in the
room and then immediately recede, as if everyone was afraid
to feel it. Although it made her sad, Kate understood. She hadn't
allowed herself to be excited until now. Everyone just needed a
minute to catch up.

Scarlett was the first to respond. She came over to Kate and
hugged her with such painstaking gentleness that it brought tears
to Kate's eyes. "I'm keeping everything crossed," she said into
Kate's ear.

Beside them, Jake hugged David. As he moved to give Kate a
peck on the cheek, she noticed a cautious smile on his face.

Kate shot a furtive glance at her father. He was yet to react, but
that was his way, always measured.

"Pregnant?" he said finally. "Again?"

Kate nodded, conscientiously ignoring the *again* part. Her
stomach reached new levels of activity—clamping, stretching,
churning. Waiting. "Twelve weeks tomorrow."

He weighed that up for a moment, frowning. "Tomorrow? But . . .
aren't you supposed to wait until twelve weeks to announce?"

The silence in the room carried for a beat. Kate was about to
laugh nervously, to make a joke, to do *something*, but David beat
her to it.

"The expectant mother can tell her family any time she likes, William," David said, the cheeriness of his voice notably absent. "And the correct response, I believe, is 'Congratulations.'"

David's mouth set in a thin line. Scarlett's and Jake's eyes flew back and forth between David and her dad. The low, dragging feeling in Kate's belly became heavier.

"Yes," her father said quickly. "I'm sorry. Congratulations."

"I'll get dinner," Kate said, standing.

An hour later Kate squirted a long line of liquid soap into the sink and watched the water turn to bubbles. Dinner hadn't lasted long. The atmosphere had been tense and eventually her father had excused himself, before even dessert had been served. Kate felt the tears come to her eyes but she chased them away with a steely thought. *Who cares?* she told herself. *What did it matter?*

Anyway, what had she expected? That her awkward old dad would suddenly become Pa Ingalls upon hearing he was going to become a grandfather? No, she hadn't expected that. Hoped, but not expected.

"What are you doing, Kate?" David said, appearing behind her. He entered the kitchen slowly, as though with each step he might chance upon a rogue grenade.

"What does it look like?" she said tonelessly. "The dishes."

"I already stacked the dishwasher."

"I know." She kept her eyes on the dishes. "Thank you. I just wanted to give them a quick wash before they go through the cycle. Otherwise they never come out clean."

David looked perplexed. "You're *washing* the dishes before putting them in the dishwasher? With soap and everything? That's nuts, even for you."

Kate exhaled, exhausted. "So let me be nuts."

On the word "nuts" her voice broke. She felt David move in close behind her and she wanted to fall against him—feel the warmth of his chest against her back. But she remained straight-backed—scrubbing an already clean dish with new vigor.

"Kate—"

"I'm fine."

She picked up a new dish and wiped the pastry crumbs from one side. She'd spent hours making the beef and burgundy pie which her father had barely touched, because he'd once commented how much he enjoyed the beef and burgundy pie he had at the club on Fridays after golf. Why did she try so hard with him? Why didn't she, like David suggested, order a pizza when her father came to dinner and call it a night?

"Why don't you head up to bed?" David said.

"I have to finish this."

"I'll finish it," he said. "I will," he insisted at her skeptical look. "I'll wash the dishes and then put them in the dishwasher. And when they're finished, I'll drive them down to the car wash and give them a run-through there, make sure they're really shipshape."

Kate felt a small smile pull at her lips.

"You know what, to hell with it," he continued. "Let's just throw out these dishes and buy new, clean ones. What kind of peasants are we, anyway, eating off these filthy old things?"

She smiled, properly now, and let herself rest against him. He was warm and, as always, a tremendous comfort.

"Don't let him get to you, Katie," he said into her hair. "I won't have anyone upsetting the mother of my baby."

He reached her belly, gave it a little rub.

"All right," she said. "I won't. Just let me finish up here and I'll come to bed."

David kissed her forehead again, then headed upstairs while Kate finished the dishes. But just as Kate had convinced herself that it didn't matter what her dad thought, she went to the bathroom and noticed the streak in her underwear. Red-brown.

9

n a small circle of people, Sonja was pretending to follow a conversation with an impressively chatty thirty-something woman when she felt George's lips against her temple and the coolness of a glass against her fingertips. His sudden presence made her jump.

"Oh." She accepted the champagne and took a sip. "Thank you."

"You're welcome."

George stood next to her and smiled at the small group. They all smiled back with considerably more enthusiasm. George wore a gray suit and had a name badge pinned to his right pocket, bearing the logo of the organization that was putting on this event and his name above the words KEYNOTE SPEAKER.

"I've just been chewing your wife's ear off about you," said the chatty woman. "I'm Laurel, a social worker for the county of San Francisco." Laurel wore a tight black skirt suit and stiletto heels. "One of our directives this year is to address the mental illness problem in homeless teens, so I'm really looking forward to your speech."

Laurel was young enough to be George's daughter, but her body language—legs slightly parted, leaning inward—made it clear that she thought of him as anything but fatherly.

"Sonja's a social worker too," George said, reading the situation accurately. After ten minutes of small talk, Sonja knew about Laurel's rescue dog (Roger), her root canal gone wrong, and the family rift created over her grandmother's inheritance, yet Laurel hadn't even bothered to ask Sonja what she did for a living.

"You don't say?" Laurel said. She eyed Sonja's black shift dress, her pearls, her gold bangle. Her hair, pale blond and bobbed. *You don't look like a social worker,* Laurel wanted to say (Sonja could tell). *And you don't look like you belong with George.*

It was true that Sonja, by an outsider's standards, was doing well for herself. George was a good-looking man, even at sixty. He was intelligent and charismatic and impressive. Oddly enough, someone like Laurel might be a better fit for him. Young and pretty, not to mention so clearly *up for it.* Then again, Sonja had been *up for it* once too. Before she understood what *up for it* meant with George.

Sonja had met George at one of these sessions. Back then, her clothes were less expensive but her waist was narrower and the lines on her face were not yet Botoxed. At forty-two she'd considered herself attractive. But twelve years could make a difference. It had been a small workshop, held at a hospital in San Francisco. George had been speaking about depression in the caretakers of the terminally ill, and Sonja had been in the front row. He'd glanced in her direction more often than seemed necessary, enough to make her cheeks hot, and make her unable to look at him. After the presentation he didn't even try to play it cool—he just bowled up to her and said, "You dropped this."

"What?" she said.

"My business card," he said smoothly, tucking it into the palm of her hand. "Call me."

And then he stole away into the crowd to speak to her superiors.

Sonja had thought it bold that he expected *her* to call. But she was so hypnotized by him, she put it out of her mind. Women like Sonja didn't date men like George. They dated men who drove

cabs or sold used cars or didn't work at all. Men who chatted up other women in bars and spent the grocery money on a horse that "just can't lose." In comparison, George was a prize. Who cared that he wanted her to call? Perhaps he was a feminist?

"Are you nervous?" Laurel asked George now.

George smiled into his drink because it was a tough one to answer. To not be nervous is to be arrogant. But to admit nerves is to care too deeply about ego. The best response was to simply dodge the question entirely. Or let his wife answer it. And Sonja answered right on cue: "George is more comfortable behind a lectern than he is in his own living room!"

Laurel and George laughed and, ridiculous as it was, Sonja felt pleased that she had got it right. In this world—George's world—she never really knew. The rules were just different. For one thing, people never said what they meant. They told people their hideous outfit was lovely, and they laughed at things that weren't funny. And they always pretended things were great, because admitting your life was less than perfect brought shame upon you—even if the shame rightfully belonged to someone else—for having the audacity to actually talk about it. It was the curse, Sonja thought, of the middle class.

In the world Sonja grew up in, people came right out and said things, usually loudly.

"My husband's a shit."

"Can't go the movies. I'm broke."

"The kids are driving me nuts."

"Frank was completely wasted last night. Woke up the entire street. I was ready to call the cops on him!"

It always felt peculiar to Sonja, the way everyone pretended. And yet, unwittingly, she had joined them. Now Sonja was the expert in pretending.

A man appeared at George's shoulder and whispered something. George nodded. "Excuse me, everyone," he said. "Looks like I'm required to give a speech."

Everyone laughed and started to drink up their drinks and

shuffle toward the double doors. George's hand grazed Sonja's bottom and, on instinct, she jerked away. He raised his eyebrows at her—*Are you all right?*—and she nodded that she was. Pretending, yet again.

"Good luck," she whispered, and then took her seat in the front row. George strode confidently toward the podium. He was going to dazzle everyone tonight. He was going to dazzle *her*. He'd be pumped—he always was after a speaking engagement. And that was what terrified her.

10

A "missed miscarriage," that was what they called it. A *missed miscarriage*. The phrase swirled in Kate's mind as she lay on the gurney in Emergency, too numb to talk or move, even to cry. Her baby had died nearly two weeks earlier—they could tell from the size—but her body had held on to it, almost as if her mind had forbidden her cervix to open. But as it turned out, the mind could only do so much. Finally her cervix couldn't hold on any more and all remaining traces of her baby had flushed out.

The funny thing about being pregnant, Kate thought, was that you were never ever alone. There was no other time in your life like it. Sure, if you had a toddler, you might feel like you were never alone, but there were always little pockets of time. When you went to check the mailbox. When you nipped to the store for milk. When your husband gave the little one a bath. But when you were pregnant, wherever you were your baby was too. Even if you were by yourself, they were with you.

Until they weren't.

Emergency had been bustling when she'd arrived. Kate hadn't known the doctor, and for that she *was* grateful. Some might have felt comforted by a familiar face, but Kate wasn't one of them.

Familiar faces were great for good news, but for bad she'd always found comfort in the unassuming stranger.

Having been through this twice before, Kate knew the drill. And yet, like a fool, she'd allowed herself to hope. There hadn't been *that* much blood, the cramps hadn't been *that* bad. As the doctor did his thing with the ultrasound she squinted at the screen waiting for a tiny heartbeat to come into view. But of course there was no heartbeat. David, she noticed, didn't look. Inexplicably, it enraged her. Perhaps it was because it made her feel foolish, looking when it was so painfully obvious nothing would be there?

The doctor said they could stay as long as they wanted. They always said that. Kate herself had said it to patients, though she was always surprised when they did stay. Wouldn't they rather be home? Now, suddenly, Kate understood. Cancer or miscarriage, as soon as they walked out the door it was the end of a chapter of their life.

"Katie," David said. Kate rolled to face him, but he had nothing else to say. It might have been the light, but his face seemed an odd gray color. She observed the contours of his face as though they were individual, separate entities rather than part of a whole man.

"What's wrong with me?" she whispered.

David smile was anguished. He didn't try to respond. Probably because she knew the answer.

Unexplained infertility.

She'd assumed, at first, that the issue was David's—a fair assumption, given that when they'd met David was being treated for testicular cancer. With Hilary on his arm, supporting him through treatment, Kate had been taken aback by the way he looked at her during appointments. He had seemed like such a family man—a handsome family man. It was Hilary who explained the situation, one day, while David was having his chemo.

"Oh we're not together," she'd said, chortling as though the very idea was preposterous.

David had burst out laughing too. "Us? Good God, no."

"So you are . . . "

"Exes," Hilary said cheerfully. "We were young," she said by way of explanation. "And desperate. We came from a small town."

David struggled with chemo. Kate did a home visit when Hilary called to say how ill he was, and she found he was mildly dehydrated, mildly delirious. She wanted to admit him for IV fluids, but he promised to drink a whole liter of water if she'd just hold his hand while he slept for a while. It wasn't the first time she'd held a patient's hand while they slept, but it had a new intimacy in the patient's bedroom. His bed was enormous—bigger even than king-size—and his sheets were masculine and expensive. She remembered a fleeting, inappropriate thought about what it would be like to sleep in this bed, curled around this man. Even during chemo he was a ball of pure muscle, from his broad chest, which was just visible above the sheet, to his calves—one of which had flung free of the blankets. As she looked at him, she felt both horrified and thrilled by what he was stirring up in her. After an hour, she'd wriggled her hand free.

"I'm sorry," he said as she was halfway across the room.

"No, I am," she said. "I'm afraid I have to go."

"I manipulated you. Making you hold hands with a dying old man."

"You're not dying," she said automatically. And it was true. David's prognosis was good. Unfortunately it didn't make the chemo process any less ghastly.

He looked sheepish. "You were meant to say I'm not old."

She smiled. David looked terrible, but there was an unmistakable twinkle in his eye. "You're not *that* old," she allowed.

She went to leave, then paused at the door. "Anyway, I'm sure a man like you doesn't need cancer to get a girl to hold his hand."

"I don't," he admitted. "But cancer has to be good for something."

She didn't agree to go on a date with him until after his treatment was finished. Apart from the ethical issues, she assured

David that he didn't have the strength to be starting a new relationship and battling cancer at the same time. He reluctantly waited, but later admitted to her that it was that kernel of hope that helped him endure the chemo.

Three years later, when despite their best efforts a baby hadn't been conceived, it made sense that he should be the one to be tested. He'd had a testicle removed, but the test showed that the other one was performing well. Above average even. And so it followed that the problem must be hers.

She had ultrasounds. Laparoscopies. Dye injected into her fallopian tubes and followed on a screen. Test after test came back normal. Which left them with . . .

Unexplained infertility. The treatment prescribed: IVF.

Kate knew that David wasn't thrilled by the prospect. But once they got through the first couple of squeamish appointments, it actually brought them closer. Every night, at the same time, he'd inject her with drugs (including one night at a country wedding when the pair of them had to shimmy into a portable toilet to get it done). It wasn't a wonderful time by any stretch, but it was a close time in their relationship. As though they shared a secret.

When they got the call, they drove to the clinic to *harvest* Kate's eggs. Even the word "harvest" hadn't been enough to rain on Kate's parade.

"Harvest my eggs!" she'd exclaimed on the road.

"Yeah, baby!" David sang. "Harvest my wife."

David's contribution had to be made eighteen hours later. Like everything to do with IVF, it was time-sensitive, but he wanted to do it at home rather than in a magazine-filled cubicle at the clinic. Kate liked the idea. Their baby could still be conceived as an act of love, an act of passion. She lit a candle, put on some music, and made sure it would memorable. But despite their best efforts, only one embryo was fertilized. An embryo that wasn't to be.

The second time, when it was time for David's contribution, they didn't bother with a candle. Again, only one embryo was created. And failed to thrive.

The third time, Kate was distracted. It wasn't happening for David, and time was of the essence.

"David, can you just . . ." She glanced at the clock. "I mean, why don't we try—"

"Jesus, Kate," he'd said, pushing her off him. "Just . . . can you just let me do this? I'll be out in a minute."

In the living room, Kate waited on the edge of the sofa. Then they drove to the clinic in silence.

With hindsight, she should have known this baby would be doomed. Conceived by a frozen egg and a reluctant sperm. What hope had this poor baby ever had?

Now, she squeezed his hand. "It will work next time," she said with a breeziness that she recognized sounded plain wrong in this setting. David didn't reply. He looked spent. Normally she only noticed his age in terms of how distinguished it made him, but today he looked old.

"Right?" she pressed.

He closed his eyes, pinched the bridge of his nose. "Let's not worry about that just now, okay, babe? Let's just take care of you."

"But it will work. Next time. Won't it?"

She heard the crazy in her voice. But you were allowed to be crazy in the face of tragedy, weren't you? People made allowances for it.

David stood. "Can you walk or do you want me to get you a wheelchair?"

"David."

He dropped his gaze. "Let's not talk about it now," he said, and Kate felt her heart splinter.

"Katie." He ran his fingers through her hair. "I don't want to see you like this. That's why I think . . ."

"Stop," she said into his chest. "Don't say it. I can't handle you saying it."

"Okay," he said quietly, kissing her forehead. "I won't. Shhh. I won't say it."

But as Kate sobbed into her husband's chest she realized he already had.

11

You know that dream people always talked about—the one about going to school naked? Zoe had never had it. Ironic, right? The sad truth was, Zoe's subconscious never needed to go that far. In Zoe's anxiety dreams she walked the hallway fully dressed. People stood around, at their lockers or in groups, glancing at her—checking out her giant forehead or last season's sneakers and laughing. This dream always had her jerking awake, drenched in sweat, her heart thundering. And the worst thing about it was, her anxiety dream was also her reality.

It was 8:00 P.M. on Saturday, and Zoe was outside the movie theater in Redwood City, which was nothing short of a miracle. People walked by, glancing at her and then quickly away. Under their brief gaze, Zoe felt bigger than she actually was. Freakishly big, like a kite puppet on a freeway, bobbing and waving in the wind. What was she doing here? Like a fool she'd told herself she'd be able to do this.

I lie to myself all the time. But I never believe me. The words came at her suddenly. They were from *The Outsiders*. They were studying the novel this year in English and Zoe had never found so much truth between two covers.

Emily had offered to give her a ride but Zoe had made an excuse about needing to finish her math project, and Emily was too caught up in the prospect of a date with Cameron to notice how unlikely that actually was. Only an hour ago Zoe still didn't know if she was going to do this. Even if it wasn't for the *date* thing, movie theaters terrified her, almost as much as the school cafeteria. The airlessness, the artificial light, the people (mostly the people).

Through the glass doors, Zoe could see that the foyer was full. There must have been a kids' movie about to start, because the place was full of moms with kids ranging from ages three to ten, and the floor was sticky and dotted with popcorn. A kid had dropped his drink and an employee had erected a CAUTION: WET FLOOR sign while he mopped it up. This created a bowl-like opening in the wall of people, and through it, from behind the pole where she stood, Zoe could see Emily, Cameron, and Seth.

Emily was wearing a dark blue T-shirt dress that was tight around her chest and stopped at her upper thigh. It must have been new as Zoe hadn't seen it before. She'd straightened her hair and she was laughing at something Cameron had said a little too enthusiastically. Seth appeared to be half listening, smiling a little, but he kept glancing around, looking for her.

Zoe wasn't sure if it was the anticipation or the strong smell of popcorn, but she was feeling woozy. Perhaps it was just the closed-in-ness of the movies? She imagined having a panic attack right here, in front of all these people—the shame of it. Someone might give her a paper bag to breathe into. Someone else might call an ambulance. Afterward she'd overhear people say, "What was *wrong* with that girl?"

Even as she took her first shallow breath, Zoe could see the ridiculousness of her thoughts. She was panicking over the idea of panicking! She silently recited some affirmations—*I am calm, collected, and in control. I am calm, collected, and in control*—and then she peeked around the pole again. Emily said something and then Seth and Cameron went and stood in the ticket line. Then she got her phone out and was texting. A heartbeat later, Zoe's phone beeped.

Where r u? U'd better b coming.

Suddenly Zoe saw an "out." She could text a response—she was sick! Something had come up! Texting was a godsend for someone like Zoe. With written words, she could say exactly what she wanted without being crippled by fear about what the other person was thinking. It was like braille for a blind person, signing for a deaf person. A way for her to communicate where she was impaired. She lifted her phone and started to reply, but her thumbs were jelly. She wiped her hands on her jeans. They were sweaty, useless. Heat crept up Zoe's neck, and her heart started its horrible, rapid thrum. She tugged at the neck of her T-shirt.

I am in a safe place, she told her panic. *This will pass.* She asked herself, *What is the worst that can happen if you go? Seth and Cameron might think you're an idiot, but then again, they probably already do. But what is the worst thing that can happen if you don't go? Emily won't be your friend anymore.* Zoe closed her eyes for a second. Then, she stepped out from behind the pole and pushed through the glass doors.

The kids' movie must have started because the foyer had cleared. It helped a little. Emily was concentrating on her phone but, as if feeling Zoe's presence, she looked up.

"Zo!" Emily exclaimed. "I just texted you!" Her concentration had already melted into relief. "I was worried you were going to be a no-show."

"Nope." Zoe smiled weakly. "I'm here."

"Great, the boys are getting the tickets. Seth is reeeeeeally excited!"

"Cool," she mouthed, but no sound came out.

"Do you want anything from the concession stand? Popcorn? Gummy bears?"

Zoe tried to speak but her mouth was dry. She shook her head.

"Okay, well—let's go." Emily looped her arm around Zoe's and started to walk. "I don't want to be stuck in the front row, not with Cameron sitting beside me! We might need a little privacy if you know what I . . ."

The room began to soften at the edges. What would she say when she greeted Seth? What would she do if, afterward, he wanted to hang out, just the two of them? What if—and even in her stressed-out state she realized the irony of this—he *didn't* want to hang out afterward, just the two of them? There would be relief in that, but there would be shame too. Like everything in Zoe's life, she was damned if she did, and damned if she didn't.

"What?" Emily said, turning around.

Zoe blinked. Had she spoken aloud again? Jesus, what was wrong with her? "Nothing," she muttered, and Emily turned around again happily.

How were all these people all breathing normally? Zoe wondered as Emily dragged her along. She couldn't seem to get a lungful of air. It felt so real, even though Zoe knew it was all in her mind. There was air all around her. Why couldn't she feel it in her lungs?

Suddenly she planted her feet. "I . . . can't do this."

Emily glanced back over her shoulder. "What?"

"I'm s . . . sorry, Em. I can't."

Emily stopped, not understanding. "You can't go to the movie?"

Zoe shook her head, taking a deep rasping breath. She pressed her hand to her pounding chest.

Emily stared at her for a moment. And for the briefest flash, Zoe saw something in her eyes. It was as if, after all these months of friendship, something had clicked into place and she got it. Zoe was not just shy. There was something wrong with her.

But just as quickly, the look was gone. "How will I explain this to the boys?" She lifted her hand and let it slap against her side. "Jesus! What is wrong with you?"

Zoe was shaking now. It was as though her lungs were a vacuum bag and someone was sucking out the air. Behind Emily, Cameron and Seth approached holding sodas and popcorn.

"There they are," Emily said. She thought for a minute, then sighed. "I'll be with you the whole time, okay? I'll even sit between you and Seth. . . ." Her expression was pleading. "You don't even have to speak to him. But please don't leave."

Seth stepped forward. "Hi, Zoe," he said, holding out a soda. "Em said you liked Pepsi."

Zoe looked at the drink then back at Seth. Did no one *see her*? She couldn't breathe! She felt Seth's eyes, and Cameron's, wondering what was up. And she felt Emily, willing her to stop making a scene and let her get on with her date. She wanted, more than anything, to go on the date. But it was far too late for that.

"I'm sorry," she said, a final time, and then she sprinted out the glass doors, into the night air.

12

Alice sat on the floor in front of the television with her portable filing system on her lap, sliding the paid bills in one by one. Zoe had finally decided to go to the movies. Alice had given her a high five and a giant grin as she walked out the door, but once Zoe was gone she felt positively ill with nerves. Going to the movies with guys was a big deal for her daughter. Alice didn't have high hopes.

She shoved the last bill into its pocket, wondering why she kept the blasted things. Her file was close to bursting. She glanced into it, looking for things she could toss, and pulled out a folded piece of newspaper in the W section—work. It was the article the local newspaper had done on Atherton Home Helpers last year. Alice scanned it.

When Helping Others Becomes a Career

Alice Stanhope was working as a receptionist in a psychology practice when she got news that her great-grandmother was going to be transferred to a nursing home.

"I knew she wouldn't want to go into a nursing home," Alice said. "Joan was a homebody. She found the idea of having strangers around her very distressing."

While many 25-year-olds would have been too absorbed in their own lives to worry about their relatives, Alice moved from her native San Francisco to Atherton, where she lived and cared for her great-grandmother in her own home.

"It made sense for all of us. I was pregnant with my first child and about to start caring full time for my child. I thought, why can't I care for them both?"

After her great-grandmother's death 2 years later, Alice found herself at a crossroads. She'd been out of the workforce for 2 years and, as a single mother, she needed to get back to work.

"It occurred to me that Joan wasn't the only elderly person who needed help. I'm not a nurse, but I can do grocery shopping, housework and drive people to and from appointments. Some people just like the company."

At first, part of the appeal for clients was that Alice, a single mother, brought her young daughter to work with her. "Zoe used to come to work with me when she was little, and clients loved that. She's 14 now, so she has other places to be."

Alice now offers in-home help to over 20 elderly residents of the Atherton area.

At the bottom of the article were the company Web site and a photograph of Alice sitting beside Ida Keaney, who'd died last year.

Alice had been thrilled to receive the coverage. It had prompted the spike in business that required her to hire a part-timer, and then another. But she'd been annoyed with herself for using Zoe's name. She should have expected it. Of course a community newspaper would be looking for the human element—the elderly woman, the single mother, the child. But Alice had always been protective of Zoe in public—making her use a pseudonym on Facebook and Instagram. Zoe thought she was being over-the-top, and she probably was, but the idea that someone (one person in particular) could cyberstalk her daughter terrified her.

She stuffed the newspaper article back into the bursting file, annoyed at herself for thinking about him. Again. But the sad truth was, she thought about him more than she cared to admit. But how could she not? She had a living, breathing reminder of him that she looked at every day. And that reminder was the reason that she could never regret that night. That reminder was why it was the very best thing that ever happened to her.

13

When Zoe was ten, she was invited to a sleepover. The fact that she'd been invited was beyond exciting, even if she knew she wouldn't go. And she'd known she wouldn't go from the moment she saw the pink envelope. Parties were something other kids did, normal kids. Like Jordan, the diabetic kid in her class, she knew her limitations.

But the birthday girl, Jane, was insistent. *All the girls in the class are coming*, she said. *It won't be the same without you.* It was nice. One common misunderstanding about Zoe was that she *wanted* to be a recluse. On the contrary, she longed be part of things. She just longed to be part of things without being plagued by debilitating fear.

Her mom said it was up to her, but Zoe saw the fear in her mom's eyes. That was what finally made up her mind. If Zoe started trying to be normal, maybe her mom could be normal too. Have friends, go out—have her own life.

She arrived at Jane's house with dread in her heart and a sleeping bag under her arm. While the girls set up on the living room floor, unrolling their sleeping bags and opening packets of candy, her mom gathered with the other moms in the kitchen. Zoe heard a pop of champagne and a giggle. Her mom would love this.

Meanwhile, the girls all stretched out in the living room,

deciding on a movie to watch. Zoe saw the effortless way the other girls interacted—giggling, talking. She wanted to be like them. She wanted to *be* them. But every time she tried—to laugh at a shared joke, or squeal when Jane's brother squirted his water pistol at them—it felt forced, fake, not like the others. And then she hated herself for being different.

After about an hour, the moms started to leave.

"If you need anything, I'll be here in a flash," Zoe's mom said into her ear. "I promise."

Zoe nodded, working hard to keep the tears at bay. It would be okay, she told herself. What was the worst that could happen?

After the video ended, they played a game of truth or dare.

"Zoe," Jane said when it was her turn. "Truth or dare?"

Immediately Zoe was blushing. "Uh . . . truth, I guess."

Of this, at least, Zoe was certain. She wanted no part in stealing Jane's brother's baseball cards, or knocking on the neighbor's door and running away. And, being Zoe, she hadn't done enough stuff to have any secrets.

"Have you ever wet the bed?"

"No," she said immediately. It was the truth. Sleep was one of those blissful places where she was relieved of the burdens she carried during the waking hours. She was far more likely to wet her pants when she was awake and stressed. Still, her blush deepened.

"Are you sure?" Jane said.

Zoe nodded. It was horrible. She knew she looked guilty but this knowledge just made her face hotter. Now everyone was staring at her, little smirks on their faces. She wanted to cry.

"How do we know you're not lying?" one of the other girls said.

"I . . . I don't know." She tried hard to sound indifferent. "You just have to believe me."

"I want proof," Jane said.

Zoe felt the heat rash start to creep up her neck. She didn't know what to do. Sophie had been the last one to pick truth, and when Sophie answered that no, she didn't want to kiss Wayne

Langford, she hadn't had to prove it, even though no one, including Zoe, had believed her.

"Whose turn it is next?" Zoe said desperately.

Eventually the game moved on to the next person, but Zoe was still stuck. What was wrong with her? If she had just laughed, like Sophie did, or teased someone else, everyone would have left her alone. Why did she have to be such a freak?

After a while something else started to prey on her mind. What did that mean, they wanted proof? What was going to happen, after she fell asleep? Was someone going to do the old trick of putting her hand into a glass of water?

Her lungs began to constrict, her veins began to prickle.

"I need to go to the bathroom," she said, standing up.

"Why, are you going to pee yourself?" Jane laughed and a couple of others joined in.

Zoe wondered if that was exactly what she was going to do. The room was dark and she felt for the light switch on the wall. What had she been thinking, coming here? She wanted her mom, her apartment, her own bed—where she could sleep peacefully. *I am in a safe place*, she told herself. *I am calm, collected, and in control.*

But she felt a swell in her bladder, and panic gripped her. She pinned her knees together.

"Oh my God!" Jane said, turning her attention from whomever it was she was grilling. "Zoe *is* going to pee her pants."

By the time the others looked, it was already streaming down Zoe's legs. The girls flew to their feet, and then backed away, as if it might knock them down—a tsunami of pee instead of a small puddle at her feet. Zoe couldn't bear to raise her head, so she just ran out of the room.

If you need anything, I'll be here in a flash, her mom had said. But Zoe couldn't find a phone. She picked her way along the corridor toward the front door—looking for a hallstand, somewhere a telephone would be. Down the hall she could hear the television—Jane's parents watching TV. She tried to breathe, but her throat felt blocked. Her chest was close to bursting. Her heart hammered. She leaned against the wall for support. Her lungs felt flat and tight, a plastic bag void of air.

This was *it*; she was going to die. She had visions of the girls finding her here, flat on the floor, white-cold. Their terrified faces being the last ones Zoe saw before she blacked out of this world. She wanted her mom.

Just then the sensor light on the front porch flicked on. In the window Zoe saw her mother's face. She was hallucinating.

"Zoe," her mother instructed. "Open the door."

Zoe did. She wondered how her mom could possibly have known that she needed her at that exact moment. Was that something mothers just knew?

"Are you all right?" her mother asked.

Zoe shook her head, gasping.

"Okay, just breathe," her mother said. "Slowly, not too deep. Come outside and breathe in some fresh air."

Still light-headed, Zoe allowed her mother to guide her into the cool night air. "Mom," she gasped. "My chest. I'm . . . going . . . to die."

"It's just a panic attack, you're not going to die." Her mother's voice was a cool stream on a hot day. She looked Zoe over, her eyes stopping at her soaked pajama pants but only for a second. "We've been through this before, it will all be over in a minute if you just relax."

Zoe let her mom hold her and she weakened in her arms. When it was over, her mother put her into the car while she ran inside to get her things and explain what had happened to Jane's mother. While she waited, Zoe noticed a blanket on the driver's seat and a book and her mother's reading glasses.

"How did you get here so fast?" she asked when her mother returned to the car.

For an instant, she looked guilty. "I just . . . wanted to be nearby. You know, in case you needed me."

"Thank you," Zoe said. But as they drove home, Zoe thought a more appropriate response would have been "Sorry."

"Why so loud?" Dulcie cried when Zoe reached her apartment. "When I was a girl we *walked* up the stairs."

Dulcie was sitting in a folding chair on the landing—she did that sometimes. As for the stairs, they were carpeted, so Zoe had literally been soundless as she'd run upstairs.

Dulcie lived in the apartment across the hall from them and was approximately a hundred and fifty years old. Around five years ago Zoe's mom had offered to do Dulcie's grocery shopping. Since she looked after old people for a living, she'd thought why not help out a sweet elderly neighbor? Problem was, Dulcie wasn't sweet. She'd stopped thanking her mom for buying groceries several years ago and instead started treating her like the delivery person, making her stand there as she checked the groceries against her list to make sure that she'd got everything she asked for (and then usually shortchanging her mom). Once, Zoe had watched a TV comedian talk about the two types of elderly people. The fat ones who adored children, gave them sweets, and told them they were lovely. And the thin ones who complained about "young people being the problem with society these days."

Dulcie was thin.

"Sorry, Dulcie," Zoe said turning toward her own door.

"What if I'd been trying to sleep?" Dulcie cried. "You would have woken me up!"

Zoe apologized again, even though it was eight thirty on a Saturday night, and scrambled for her keys with useless, uncooperative hands. She just wanted to get out of this hallway into her apartment. Away from Dulcie and away from *people*. Finally she found her key and slid it into the door.

"Young people these days," Dulcie muttered.

Inside, the lights were off, and it took Zoe a second or two to locate her mother on the couch, watching TV. A comforter was slung over her hips and a pizza box sat on the floor beside her.

She looked up, instantly panicked. "Mouse?"

Zoe had managed to hold back the tears all the way home, but at the sight of her mother she broke into a full-blown ugly cry.

"What happened? Oh, no. Come here."

Her mom opened the comforter and Zoe crawled in. She laid her head on her mom's chest, drenching her.

"I tried, Mom," she said when her sobs had slowed enough for her to talk. "I went to the mall. I even talked to Em. But then the boys came up and I . . . I started to panic. I ran away in front of everyone. I ran!"

Zoe could see her mother's face in the window reflection. She shook her head, resolute. "At least you tried. You should be proud of yourself."

Zoe knew she'd say something like this, and yet today it made her angry. "Proud of myself? I'm a freak, Mom. A fucking freak."

Once again she liquefied into tears.

"I know it seems hard to believe now," her mom said, "but this is not the end of the world."

Zoe felt her face mangle in pain. "I lost my best friend. My *only* friend. For a high school student, that's the end of the world."

"You don't know you've lost her, hon. I'm sure Em will understand."

Her mom's voice was still calm, still soothing. But when Zoe snuck a look at her mom's face in the reflection she saw a mangled mirror image of her own.

14

Alice knocked on Paul's door fifteen or twenty times before finally letting herself in with her key. She'd driven an hour to get here; she wasn't leaving without seeing him. Something heavy was behind the door and she had to put her whole shoulder into it to edge it open. A wet rolled-up towel, as it turned out. She didn't want to know why that was there. The last time Alice had let herself in to her brother's apartment, he'd been in bed with a woman. Sleeping, thankfully. Passed out, actually. That time it had taken several hard slaps before Paul came to, but today he was awake, plodding wearily into the living room.

"Alice!"

He grinned. It was something, she supposed, that he was pleased to see her even if it did raise the odds that he was still drunk.

"I knocked," she said.

He nodded, sheepish. "I heard."

She looked around. She hadn't remembered the place looking this bad. It had never looked good—a decrepit apartment with a shared kitchen and bathroom. The carpet, which had once been cream, was now gray and littered with beanbag fill. The curtains had just three hooks still attached; the rest had been affixed with electrical tape so they were permanently closed save for one corner where a triangle of light beamed in. The glass coffee table was covered in ashtrays and coffee mugs and half-empty bottles of wine and Jack Daniel's and Coke. There was a faint smell of vomit and whiskey.

Paul glanced at her empty hands and failed to conceal his disappointment. Usually Alice brought food. She knew better than to bring cash. He had enough to survive. Alice collected his disability payments and had set up an account for him, releasing funds in small amounts every few days so he couldn't kill himself on a booze-filled bender. Still he did, invariably, spend the majority on booze, so he was always happy when she arrived with groceries.

Well, not today.

"So," he said. "What brings you by?"

She sighed. "Take a seat, would you?"

Alice swept a bag of chips and a coffee mug off the chair and sat herself. Paul did the same, a serious expression registering on his face.

"Is it Zoe?" he asked.

"No, thank God. It's me." She decided there was no point in sugarcoating it, especially for Paul. "I have cancer."

Paul blinked, presumably in shock, but it only served to make him look like more of a stoner. She braced herself for him to say something like "Fuck, man." She ached, in that moment, to have a brother who actually had his shit together. A brother she could have this conversation with over sushi during his lunch break, a brother who would grab his suit jacket, call his secretary and tell her to cancel his meetings for the rest of the day so he could spend the afternoon driving around to specialists he knew, to get a second opinion. At the very least, a brother who could say, "Well don't worry a bit about the financial side, I've got you covered. And Zoe will have a home with us forever. She'll never want for anything."

Instead, Alice had Paul.

"Shit, Al," he said, shaking his head. "That's . . . that's shit."

"Yeah," she agreed.

"What kind of cancer?"

"Ovarian."

"Same as Mom."

"Yep."

"Fuck."

He was so out of his depth. It was like Alice was having a conversation with a teenager rather than a forty-three-year-old man.

"So . . . how bad is it?" he asked.

"I have an operation scheduled tomorrow," she said. "They're going to take out my ovaries and fallopian tubes."

He waited a few seconds, at least, before reaching for the bottle of Jack Daniel's on the table. "Do you mind if I . . . ?"

"Actually I do." Alice took the bottle. "If you could just wait until I leave, I'd appreciate it."

He nodded, as though he'd expected it. "Well . . . what can I do?"

It wasn't so much the question as the way he said it. Emphasis on the "I." What can *I* do? As if she had asked him how to single-handedly solve the world's hunger problem. It pissed her off. "What can *you* do?"

"I mean . . . ," he stammered, "I don't have any money, and I . . . you wouldn't want to leave Zoe with me, surely?"

Alice couldn't believe she was having this conversation. That *this* was her only support person. Alice held her hands to her mouth and nose, trying to hold in the crazy. "Do you know what I want you to do? I want you to *grow the fuck up*."

Paul winced. "I'm sorry."

"Don't be sorry."

"What do you want me to be?"

She laughed—a light airy sound, tinged with rage. "I want you to be a man."

He stared at his hands.

"I realize you don't have any money," Alice said, when she'd calmed slightly. "And no, I wouldn't want to leave Zoe with you. But here's the situation. We don't have any parents. I don't have a husband. I don't have any family . . . except you. And in the next little while I'm going to need some help."

"What kind of help?" he asked warily.

"As I said, I'm going into the hospital tomorrow. It would be great if I had someone to stay in the apartment with Zoe while I'm gone. After I get out, I might need someone to drive me to and from appointments, in a sober state. I might need someone to be my family."

Alice didn't know at what point she'd started crying. It hadn't reflected in her voice. Paul sat back in his ripped vinyl chair, bone-white, and on the verge of tears himself. Then he started crying too.

"Paul—"

He reached for the bottle in her hand and this time she let him take it. And just like that, Alice realized there wasn't a chance in the world that he was going to be able to be the person she needed. That she was, pure and simple, in this thing alone.

15

Alice arrived at the hospital at 7 A.M.—half an hour before her scheduled arrival time. She'd awoken early with a strange sense of calm. Yes, she was short on family support, but she'd been short on that for years and she'd always done okay. And today was the day they were going to take the cancer out of her! It was all going to be all right.

A social worker named Sonja had joined her in the waiting room a few minutes earlier. Alice had, of course, insisted that she didn't require a social worker, but apparently she didn't have a choice. Sonja was one of those curiously ageless people who could have been forty as easily as sixty. She was attractive without being beautiful, tall and impeccably dressed, right down to a string of pearls, but she was a nervous type, rattling off a list of services that Alice was entitled to while patting her repeatedly with a cold hand.

"There are, of course, certain financial grants that we can apply for, depending on your income level," she was saying. "Charitable organizations et cetera."

Alice hadn't been listening, but at this, her ears pricked up. They hadn't discussed finances in her appointment with the doctor, or if they had, she hadn't been listening. She had health insurance, but it never covered everything.

"I understand you have a daughter," Sonja said, once her spiel was complete.

"Yes, Zoe."

"And where is Zoe now?"

Alice might have been imagining it, but it felt like Sonja's eyes had become vaguely beady.

"She's at home. Hopefully getting ready for school."

"Hopefully?"

"She *is*." Alice made a mental note not to joke with Sonja. "She *is* getting ready for school."

"Is she at home unsupervised often?"

The only other people in the waiting room were a middle-aged couple. The man—paunchy and balding—had his hand on the woman's thigh. They glanced around the room, pretending they weren't listening.

"She's fifteen, so it's hardly neglect," Alice snapped.

"I wasn't suggesting—"

"—but, as it happens, no, she's not home unsupervised often. Major abdominal surgery is something of a rarity in our household."

Sonja opened her mouth again, but before she could speak, a nurse crouched in front of Alice.

"Alice Stanhope?"

"Yes?"

"It's nice to meet you," she said. "My name is Kerry and I'll be looking after you prior to your operation."

Alice frowned. "But . . . where's Kate?"

"She's not on today, hon."

"Well, where is she?"

"Couldn't tell you, I'm afraid," she said, shrugging. "Can I take your bag? Come this way."

Kerry had thick auburn ringlets and a wide gap between her front teeth. She seemed perfectly nice. And yet Alice felt irrationally put out. She felt comfortable with Kate. There was just something about her—Alice couldn't put her finger on it—that made her feel cared for. Being greeted by another nurse, Alice felt like she was starting all over again.

"All . . . right," she muttered.

Alice found her feet and trundled off after Kerry. Sonja, unfortunately, followed. When they got to her room, Sonja sat in the corner scribbling into a notebook while Kerry dispatched a gown and confirmed that Alice had followed her pre-op instructions. While she was finalizing her paperwork, Dr. Brookes came in.

He was nicer than Alice remembered—introduced himself as Chris. Maybe he'd been nice last time and she just hadn't noticed? Or maybe her mind was playing tricks on her now, needing to believe that someone in the operating room cared about her. His hair, Alice observed, was still wet from the shower, which made her picture him in the shower—not an entirely unwelcome thought—and then think about his morning routine thus far. Had he flicked through the newspaper while eating a bowl of cornflakes? Made love to his wife? Fed the dog? Had he done all the regular things one did before heading off to work in the morning, unmoved by the fact that he'd be scooping organs out of his patient in just a few hours?

Dr. Brookes introduced Alice to another doctor, an anesthesiologist who trotted out some jokes that Alice somehow knew he used on every patient. As such, they failed to make her laugh. He explained to her what drugs he was going to use, his post-op pain-management regime. He did all the things he could to make her feel at ease. Then they waved good-bye to Sonja (who hastily put down her notes and wished her luck) and the three of them—Kerry, Dr. Brookes, and the anesthesiologist—rolled her down the hallway to the operating room, where at least another four people were setting up for surgery. For the first time since arriving, Alice felt in grave danger of falling apart.

She lay there for a while, watching as people buzzed about her, wheeling carts, carrying trays. The anesthesiologist put a needle in her hand and attached a tube. Alice thought back to the balding man in the waiting room, patting his wife's thigh. No one was waiting for her. When more people arrived in the operating room, Alice marveled. How many people did it take to scoop out some organs? She must have said it out loud, because Dr. Brookes laughed and said, "Yes, I'm sure it does seem like a lot of people are in here. But everyone has an important role, I assure you."

A few minutes later, the anesthesiologist told her to count backward from twenty. Soon, he said, she would feel sleepy. Alice thought of the waiting room again, of the fact that there was no one waiting for her.

"Alice? Can you count?"

"Twenty, nineteen, eighteen . . . ," she started.

Once upon a time she would have had a roomful of people waiting for her. Her mother, her father. Maybe even her brother. Not anymore. How sad would it be if she died on this table and no one was waiting? What would happen to Zoe? Who would give her the news?

"Alice?"

"Seventeen, sixteen, fifteen . . . ," she continued.

Alice had a sudden urge to rip the tube out of her arm and run away. What was she doing, lying on this table, leaving her daughter alone to fend for herself? What if the worst *did* happen? She had an almost overpowering yearning for Zoe. But she also felt drowsy. She couldn't be bothered counting anymore, so she ignored the anesthesiologist when he called to her. She felt something brush her eyelashes.

"Okay," the anesthesiologist said. "She's out."

No, she wanted to say, *I'm not. I'm not out! You have to let me go and see my daughter.*

But then, a moment later, she was out.

16

Zoe had a secret. That, in itself, was pretty hard to believe. She wasn't the kind of teenager who kept everything from her parents—of course she didn't, she didn't *have* anything to keep from her mom. Except this. She did it when she was alone in her bedroom when the house was empty and quiet. To unwind, but more important, to chase away the voices of self-loathing. To help her get up in the morning.

She watched speeches.

She had her favorites. Obama's inauguration speech, Steve Jobs's Stanford commencement address, pretty much any TED Talk. It didn't really matter what the speech was about, so long as there were gasps when there were meant to be gasps, and claps when there were meant to be claps. So long as people were enthralled. So long as they were moved to tears or laughter or both. So long as they were on the edge of their seats.

When Zoe found a speech she liked, she watched it on her laptop until she'd memorized every word and gesture, every pause and hand movement. Then she delivered them. The funny thing was, when she spoke to her wall, her voice held power. Her heart didn't race. Her hands didn't tremble. She felt the absence of her fear as strongly as if it were a presence. A balloon of air, a feeling of fullness, pushing out the blackness that she always felt. In her bedroom, the silence was people on tenterhooks for her next word, the looks were of admiration. And she wanted, for once, to be noticed.

As far as vices went, it could have been worse. And yet, in a way, it was a form of self-harm. Like the kid in the wheelchair who dreamed of being an Olympic high jumper, the mute who dreamed of being an opera singer—she was dreaming about something that would never be possible for her. Which meant the best she could hope for was delivering speeches to a wall.

On Monday morning, Zoe's walk to school was long. It was always long—almost forty minutes' walk—but she preferred it to the world of potential horror that existed inside the bus. The side of the road in Atherton was never busy because most people drove. The people Zoe did pass—bringing their garbage out, or returning from walking the dog—were friendly enough, but despite talk of Atherton's strong sense of community, no one chatted over the fences. They couldn't; the fences were too high. It made Zoe wonder how many people were actually like her—wanting to be surrounded by people, but needing to shut them out.

At six that morning Zoe had felt her mom's lips brush her cheek before she'd headed off to the hospital. Zoe had kept her eyes closed, wanting to linger in that not-quite-awake bliss where the terror of the day hadn't crashed in on her yet, but now she wondered when she had done that. Her mom was probably lying on an operating table somewhere right now and Zoe hadn't even bothered to wake up and say good-bye? What did that say about her?

Keyhole surgery, a Web site had said when she'd Googled the gallstones operation over breakfast. Very safe. Patients should be able to return to normal activities after a week. It seemed reassuring, Zoe thought, until she scrolled down to "Risks." Infection of an incision. Internal bleeding. Bile leaking into the abdominal cavity. The liver being cut. Death.

Death.

As she thought about it, her mind brought up an image, a B-grade-film-type image, of her being called into Mrs. Hunt's office that morning and told the news. "We're very sorry, Zoe, but your mom, she didn't make it."

And Zoe hadn't even bothered to say good-bye.

She could feel herself spiraling then, picturing it all in minute detail. The casket and eulogies, the outfit she'd wear to the funeral, herself crying on a pew that was empty apart from herself. She wouldn't have to go to school for a few days, or even a few weeks. Emily would forgive her—because what friend held a grudge against someone whose mother had just died?—and she'd spend a few weeks holed up in her apartment, eating frozen meals that had been left on her doorstep by one of her mom's clients. It played out almost like a fantasy, a horrible fantasy, and yet it soothed her somehow. Which went to show that she was a truly horrible person who didn't deserve her mom, or anything else.

At the gate a senior guy bumped into her (heavily) and, after taking a quick glance, exclaimed, "Watch it, would you?"

She jumped back, horrified. If there had been a hole to jump into, Zoe would have jumped. And she would have stayed in that hole all day, safe from people's eyes. Safe, even, from her best friend's eyes.

Zoe hadn't heard anything from Emily since the movies, despite sending several texts. She'd thought about calling, but the phone was terrifying to Zoe at the best of times—the pauses, the silences, the inability to read facial cues—and this time there were just too many uncertainties. *What if she doesn't answer? What if she screams at me? What if she is screening the call and laughing?* In the end Zoe had just put her phone in a drawer and hadn't looked at it until this morning. There was still nothing from Em.

Zoe had known Emily would be mad, but the silence was not like her. It worried her. What had happened with Cameron? Had he been a jerk to her? Or had it all worked out and she'd spent the whole weekend in loved-up bliss, too busy to check her messages? Whatever it was, Zoe was fairly sure it wasn't good news.

When she arrived at her locker, she twisted in the code and shuffled books around unnecessarily until she noticed Emily. There were a few people around—Jessie Lee crouched at her lower locker next to Emily's, looking typically weird in big bullet-style earrings and a red T-shirt with giant slashes over a black bustier and black lace-up boots. Lucy Barker was also there, talking to no one in particular about her haircut, which she hated. But this was probably the best opportunity Zoe would get. She steeled herself and came up behind Emily.

"Em?"

Emily kept her back to her. "Maybe your bangs *are* a little short," she said to Lucy, who was now looking in the mirror on her locker door. "But otherwise I'd say your hair is totally on trend."

Zoe glanced at Lucy's hair. Lucy was one of those people who on first glance looked really pretty, but on closer inspection she had a strangely equine look about her that had meant the majority of the student body, Emily included, called her Seabiscuit behind her back. Her hair, now cut into a short, shaggy style, only made her look horsier.

Zoe waited, but Emily didn't turn around. Had she heard? Lucy looked away from the mirror and right at Zoe, making it clear that *she* had heard.

"Em?" Zoe tried to look casual, but her facial muscles were too tense. "Can I talk to you? In private?"

"Emily?" Jessie Lee said, from her locker. "Zoe is talking to you."

The silence that followed was as long and uncomfortable as any Zoe had ever experienced. Emily stiffened but she didn't turn or acknowledge Zoe. She didn't even acknowledge Jessie Lee.

"I wouldn't worry about it," she said to Lucy finally. "Hair grows! I mean, there's just two weeks between a good haircut and a bad haircut, right?"

A second later the bell rang and Emily shut her locker. "Okay," she said, "time for math."

And she was gone. Zoe stood there for a moment, shame and horror ballooning inside her. All around, people headed off to class in twos or threes, chewing gum and laughing and being normal. Zoe longed to run to the bathroom and hide out for the rest of the day, or even just crawl inside her locker and shut the door. Instead, she went to class.

During math, Emily didn't once look in her direction. Seth and Cameron sat in the back row snickering, and though Zoe kept her eyes forward, she was sure they were laughing at her. Harry Lynch, once again, sat in the seat right in front of Zoe, and Zoe spent most of the time staring at his giant football-playing shoulders—actually, now that she looked at them, they weren't as giant as she remembered—but even that came to an end when he got up in the middle of class and walked out. Harry did that every now and again. They'd be in the middle of class when, bang, he'd just get up and leave. The teachers rarely asked where he was going, and if they did, his answer was always "Fishin'." It was weird.

Science was next, then history, and Emily wasn't in those classes.

And then it was lunchtime.

Zoe moved quickly through the cafeteria, grabbing a tray and joining the line. Alone. When the cashier spat her out the other end with a carton of potato wedges, she headed toward Emily in the back corner. She couldn't give her the silent treatment forever, Zoe told herself. And if they could just speak privately, Zoe could explain everything.

Zoe walked purposefully toward her, but just a few paces away she pulled up sharp. Emily was sitting with Lucy Barker.

"Hey!" came a voice behind her, a guy with dreadlocks. "Are you just gonna stand there? Move along!"

Zoe jumped out of the way, and straight into someone else's way. Finally she pulled up a seat at the nearest table and sat, trying to disappear. She crossed her legs so only one foot was on the ground. When she looked up, she noticed Harry, in the far corner of the table, hunched over what looked like another home-made sandwich. Did he always bring his lunch from home?

"Oh." Her chair screeched as she stood again. "Sorry."

You couldn't just go and sit with anyone in high school. That wasn't how it worked. Some people would be polite about it—just give you major side-eye and exchange glances until you went away. Other people would be more vocal about it. Zoe didn't know which type Harry was, and she wasn't willing to take the risk.

"Zoe?"

Zoe blinked. Emily was standing at the end of the table. "Em, hey," she said pathetically.

"You could at least have had the decency to come and say you're sorry. And a text message isn't the same." Her voice was mortifyingly loud.

"I'm sorry."

"What is wrong with you anyway?" Emily stared at her for a long minute. "Why can't you just be normal?"

"Normal is overrated," Harry muttered.

Zoe and Emily both turned to look at him, but he kept his head down as if he hadn't spoken. Maybe he hadn't?

Emily looked back at Zoe. "Do you know what else is over-rated? People who can't inconvenience themselves for one night to help out a friend. People who are so selfish they can't see how their actions affect others. People who call themselves your best friend, when really their best friend is *themselves*." Horrifyingly, Emily's voice was climbing. Three or four people at the next table spun in their chairs and listened unashamedly. "People who spend so much time thinking about what other people think of them that it escapes them that no one thinks about them at all, because no one has a clue that they exist!"

At the next table there was a gasp, and a snicker. Someone said, "Bitch fight."

The air in the room started to vanish. *I can't breathe*, Zoe thought. Spots of purple and red appeared in front of her eyes, and her heart—it felt like it might burst. *I am in a safe place*, she told herself. *I'm in control.*

But she wasn't. And Emily was still talking.

"Hey," someone said. "Zoe? Are you all right?"

Breathe, Zoe told herself. *You know what this is. Just breathe and you'll be all right.*

"Zoe!"

"I have to go," she said, and stood so fast her seat flew backward. She ran across the cafeteria, swerving to avoid someone and slamming instead into the wall.

As if she weren't humiliated enough.

17

As Sonja fed her prepaid ticket into the machine and the boom gate opened, she was thinking about Alice Stanhope. More specifically, she was thinking about Alice's daughter. Supporting the patient's family fell under Sonja's job description as hospital social worker as well, and Alice had seemed, well, cavalier to say the least, when Sonja had asked about her daughter staying home by herself. This concerned Sonja. Teenage brains weren't yet fully formed, at least that's what George always said. He should know. When he'd been in private practice he'd seen adolescents almost exclusively. In the state of California, there was no law that stipulated the age at which you could leave a child home alone, it came down to whether the child was considered "fit." And so Sonja determined it would be prudent to do a home visit, to determine how "fit" Alice's daughter was.

As she drove out of the hospital parking lot, Sonja's phone began to ring. She tried to answer it, but it was harder than it sounded. George, who was far more technologically inclined than she, had paired it up to her car's blue-tooth something or other, which in theory, made it "hands-free," but in practice just made it unusable. She jabbed uselessly at the phone, which sat in its holster, taunting her.

"Answer," she said, feeling foolish. She remembered George saying something about voice activation. But surely saying "answer" couldn't connect a call?

"Sonja?" George's voice filled the car.

"George?"

"Guess what?" he said.

"What?" Although the air conditioner was blasting, Sonja's hands were suddenly sweaty on the wheel. She wondered if it was strange that her husband could make her feel that way.

"I've got an appointment with the student counselor at Westleigh," he said. "She sounded very keen for my input on their young-people-in-crisis program."

"Fantastic," Sonja said, even though, in truth, she didn't really understand his desperation to volunteer in the community. He wasn't a student trying to get experience; he was a renowned psychologist who was asked to speak at functions all over the country. And he'd already done some work with two other high schools in Atherton. But if George was happy, everything was better.

"Tonight we celebrate!" he said.

"Can't wait," she said.

Sonja didn't know how to hang up the call, so she was relieved when it disconnected of its own accord. She stopped at a crossing to let some schoolkids pass. Sonja didn't want to celebrate. She'd be happy if they never celebrated again. It was probably just that she was exhausted. She thought about last night.

She and George had been eating oysters—*oysters!*—and drinking champagne outside on the deck. Shallow as it was, Sonja enjoyed the extravagance of it. Until she'd met George she'd never eaten an oyster. And she'd certainly never drunk real champagne.

"You're easily pleased, Sonja," George had said when she'd told him, again, how nice everything was. He liked being the one to provide her with nice things.

Afterward, they moved to the couch, ostensibly to watch a

movie, though Sonja fell asleep within minutes—champagne always had that effect on her. But she was startled awake when she
felt George's hands on her hips. The sky outside was dark and the
credits of the film were rolling on the TV. He pulled her to her
knees.

"George, what are you—"

But she knew exactly what he was doing. It was silly of her to
think that because she was asleep—because they'd had a very nice
evening—she'd be safe. When had those things ever kept her
safe before? She protested—sort of—in groggy surprise, but
he'd just held her tighter. There was no use fighting. She knew
George needed this. She just wished he didn't need it to be
so . . . aggressive.

It hadn't always been this way. When she and George were
dating, he had been a considerate lover. Before him, Sonja had
only had a few lovers, and they'd been more like boys than men.
Fumbling around, asking what felt good. George, on the other
hand, was authoritative. In control. It had been a huge turn-on.
And it wasn't just her sex life that had turned around with
George—her whole life became amazing. After living in an apartment on the wrong side of town for most of her adult life, suddenly Sonja lived in a beautiful home on two floors. She didn't
need to check her bank balance before she purchased anything.
She drank good wine and had discussions about politics and
medical science and the state of health care. And best of all, she
did this with George.

A few months after they were married, George went on a
business trip to Europe. He went on a lot of trips back then—
conferences, meetings, addresses—but this was for two weeks, the
longest they'd been apart since their wedding. He'd returned
home in the middle of the night. When Sonja heard the bedroom
door open, she started to rouse.

"There you are," she said sleepily, blinking to let her eyes
adjust. George was in the corner of the room, looking down at

her. At first she couldn't see his face. But when light from a passing car shone through the window, she noticed he looked a
little . . . different. "George?"

And then, suddenly, he was coming at her. That startled her
a little. He pulled back the blanket with one hand and with the
other, ripped the underwear from her body in one stinging movement.

"Ouch," she said. "Wow, aren't you . . ."

After that everything happened pretty fast. He took a fistful
of her hair and pulled so hard she felt light-headed—the next
day, her scalp was swollen; she hadn't known a scalp could *become* swollen. Then he lay on top of her with his full weight,
stealing her breath. By the time he slid out of his own pants and
slammed into her, she was silent and shaking. Her mind batted
around thoughts she was unable to process. Was this happening?
But this *couldn't* be happening. He was her husband.

When he was finished, Sonja was crying heavy fat tears. But
George didn't seem to notice.

"God, I missed you," he said, and fell asleep.

Sonja lay awake for hours, staring at the ceiling. Everything
hurt, and when she went to the bathroom, she was bleeding. It
felt acutely like she'd been assaulted but . . . was it possible? She
asked herself what she would say if it had happened to a client.
"What he did *isn't* okay. It was abusive. If you want to leave, I'll
support you."

As a social worker, it was clear-cut. As a woman, it was murkier.

The next morning George snuggled against her. "Good morning," he murmured. He was dozy and gentle and a different person
from the one he'd been the night before.

"George," she said. "About last night . . ."

There were already so many things wrong with her approach.
As a social worker she would have counseled her client to be upright when they had this discussion—a safe distance away, and
near an exit in case she needed to make a quick getaway. Sonja
was in bed with George. She'd slept the whole night there,

wondering if it would be the last night she spent in it, grieving the life she'd had with the man she adored.

Mourning her *abuser.* Another social-worker fail.

"Thank you," he said, nuzzling into her neck. "I was thinking about you the whole way home, on the plane, in the cab. I thought I was going to explode."

Sonja sat upright and stared at him. Put like that, it sounded romantic. Sexy. But it had been neither.

"Sonja," George said. He sat up too, suddenly on guard. "What is it? Are you okay?"

What is it? Was it possible he didn't know? He certainly seemed confused, half-awake, blinking to catch up. He was the very image of husbandly concern. She scanned his face, but he appeared to be genuine. Did he really not think anything was wrong?

She felt her conviction waver. If he didn't think anything was wrong, maybe nothing was? After all, an evening of rough sex after a trip away didn't necessarily constitute abuse. It probably happened between married couples all the time. The problem was simply that no one in George's world talked about it! She pictured her old school friends, what they would have said.

"Uh-huh. Jeff always gets so kinky after he's had a few! He gets it in his head that he wants to try some of that *Fifty Shades of Grey* stuff!"

"Adam's the same. I just go along with it . . . they love it and it gets it over with faster."

Yes. Sonja could hear them now. It was no big deal, just part of marriage. You had to give if you wanted to take. She was just letting her inner social worker run away with her.

"Everything's fine," she said finally, and slowly slid back down into the bed. But a tiny voice inside her asked: Was everything really fine? Or was she being weak-willed, skittish, making the excuses she'd heard other women make a million times before? *It's not so bad. He'll change. I love him.*

Sonja didn't have an answer. She also didn't have an answer to the more pressing question that had circled in her head that day, and had every day since.

If you are this weak-willed and skittish *with* George, what on earth will you be like without him?

TWO

There's nothing more calming in difficult moments than knowing there's someone fighting with you.

—MOTHER TERESA

18

ooking back, Alice could almost separate Zoe into two people: Zoe before and Zoe after. The funny thing was that Zoe had been a happy baby. A pudgy, giggly smiler. "Isn't she lovely," people would remark when they saw her. And then, invariably, their gaze would linger on Alice. She could practically see the questions lurking in their minds. With her dark hair and nearly black eyes, Zoe looked nothing like her. "Must take after her father," they'd say (and they'd be right, not that Alice would admit it).

Alice's mother had passed away while Alice was in her third trimester of pregnancy, leaving Alice grieving and alone. Her father managed to pick himself up and get on with his life, more or less. Paul continued drinking. Alice was the only one who seemed to be having trouble getting out of bed in the morning. Why? Wasn't she the one who had the most to live for? Alice had never been the prayerful type, but one night, when Zoe was five months old, she got down on her knees and asked for help.

The next day, Alice's father told Alice that her great-grandmother needed a live-in helper in her home in Atherton. Atherton was twenty-five miles out of San Francisco, and was a lovely family area. Alice looked at it as an opportunity for a fresh start. And it was. Her great-grandmother, Joan, adored Zoe, and while she wasn't much help physically, her sage advice was a great comfort. ("Forget what the book says," she'd say. "You're her mother. You want to pick her up, you pick her up.") Alice probably wasn't a typical mother during those years. While other moms were joining Mommy and Me, Charlie's Music Time, and signing up for swimming lessons, Alice was driving Joan to her appointments, grocery shopping, and looking after Zoe. But they were happy. This was their life.

Zoe was two when Joan passed away. Alice inherited her Atherton apartment and after a few months of grieving, started her business, and began to fill up her day with clients. Problem was, she didn't fill them with anything else. It had been a hard couple of years. Two deaths, a baby. At the end of the day, she pulled the blinds and snuggled up with her daughter, pretending the outside world didn't exist. Zoe was happy with the arrangement. As long as she was snuggled up close to her mother, that beautiful smile remained on her sweet little face.

By the time kindergarten approached, Alice had fallen into a rut. Any friends she'd had in San Francisco had given up calling. She hadn't been on a date since before Zoe was born. And Alice was determined to turn things around, for Zoe's sake. School would be the beginning of something for both of them. She would be the queen of the PTA. Carpooling, canteen duty. Driving a carload of giggly girls to McDonald's at the end of the school year, eavesdropping as they talked at full speed about whatever giggly girls talked about. Afterward, when their smiling mothers came to collect them, Alice would open a bottle of wine and they'd do some giggling of their own. She had seen it all so clearly.

But on the first day of school Zoe was hard to get going. It had taken ages to get her dressed and she barely ate a bite of breakfast. Alice had thought she'd be excited about school, but she'd been reluctant to talk about it—nervous, perhaps. She walked slower than usual on the way to school, and as they turned a corner and the school building came into view, she stopped walking entirely.

"Are you all right, Mouse?" Alice asked.

She followed Zoe's gaze to the large redbrick building that loomed before them. Students moved through the gates like a caterpillar, exploding into the playground with tanbark churning at their heels. Boys of about seven or eight rolled, entangled, on the grass while girls of a similar age demonstrated the way their shoes lit up in flashing lights when they stomped their heels. The parents stood in closed circles, glancing outward only to reprimand an unruly child before returning their gaze to the center. On first glance it didn't seem to be the most welcoming environment in the world. Which, Alice could admit, was a little disappointing.

Alice draped an arm around Zoe's shoulder. "Everything is a little scary on your first day. But once you get to know everyone, it will be great."

Inside the gates, signage directed them to classroom 1B, which was across the courtyard at the top of a flight of stairs. By the door, a woman attempted to pry a sandy-haired boy off his mother's leg.

"Excuse me?" she said to the woman. "Is this classroom one-B?"

"It is," the woman said. She spoke to Alice but her eyes were on the little boy.

"I'm Alice Stanhope," she said. "This is Zoe."

"I'm Mrs. Dawson," the woman replied. She finally succeeded in separating the boy from his mother, and he promptly began to wail. "Head on inside and I'll be there in a minute. Come on, now, Oscar—"

Alice regarded the woman, a little sadly. She was probably in her late fifties, with a helmet of brown hair and a stern jaw—the kind of woman, Alice thought, who prided herself on never wearing makeup and always telling people the truth, even when it hurt their feelings. In her imagination, she'd pictured a lively, smiling teacher—mid to late twenties—who'd greet Zoe (and maybe even Alice?) with a hug before leading her into the classroom by the hand.

"Go on, moms," she'd say. "Don't cry. We'll be fine, won't we kids?"

And they'd all shout "Yes!" and then the moms would go for coffee together and become firm friends.

Instead Alice led Zoe into the classroom. A few kids ran in wild circles around the tiny chairs and tables. One red-haired girl sat at a table, crying into her forearms. "Mom?" Zoe said. "My stomach hurts."

Mrs. Dawson bustled in, pulling the sandy-haired little boy by the arm. "Now then," she said to Alice. "Sorry about that."

"Zoe's not feeling well," Alice said. "Sore tummy."

Mrs. Dawson looked down at Zoe. "Are you nervous, Zoe?"

Zoe continued to look around the room, wide-eyed.

"I think everyone is a little nervous on the first day," Mrs. Dawson said, looking back at Alice. "Including Mom?" She lowered her voice. "Sometimes we can pass our nerves on to the little ones without meaning to. It's probably best that you leave us to it, Mrs. Stanhope."

Alice hated it when people called her *Mrs. Stanhope.* But she fought the urge to correct her and instead looked at Zoe, who was white as a sheet.

"Would it be all right if I stayed awhile? I think Zoe would feel better if—"

"We have a no-parent policy in the classroom, Mrs. Stanhope. It's really best for everyone. I promise, she'll be all right."

"Oh," Alice said. A no-parent policy. No matter how ridiculous that sounded—for a kindergarten class!—Alice was, first and foremost, a rule follower. It was one of the things she loathed most about herself.

She kneeled down beside Zoe. "I'll be right here at the end of the day. You'll be okay, right hon?"

"Yes," Zoe whispered.

Mrs. Dawson was standing over her, as though ready to strong-arm her out the door. Zoe looked on the verge of tears.

"I just—"

"She'll be fine, Mrs. Stanhope," Mrs. Dawson said. "We know what we're doing."

And yet, Alice found herself reluctant to leave.

All mothers found it difficult when their children started school, Alice told herself. That was all it was. She just needed to keep her mind busy until three thirty that afternoon, when Zoe would reassure her that it had been the greatest day of her life. And with that, Alice summoned all of her strength and walked out of the school grounds and back to her apartment, where she got into her car and drove to Mrs. Stephens's house. Mrs. Stephens had a doctor's appointment that morning. Alice drove her there and while she was waiting, she checked her messages. Her phone had been on silent so it didn't ring in the waiting room.

Eighteen missed calls.

She picked it up and listened to her voice mail. "Alice, it's Angela Dawson here. Please give me a call at 650-555-4102 as soon as you get this message. Zoe's been taken to the hospital."

Alice didn't remember how she'd got to the hospital, whether she'd driven Mrs. Stephens home first or if she'd just run out of the waiting room. What she did remember was the bizarre report when she got there.

"The tests were all clear." The doctor smiled at Alice.

"But . . . Zoe's teacher said Zoe was having chest pains," Alice said. "She hyperventilated. She couldn't *breathe*."

"We tested her for several things and everything came back clean. This is good news, Mrs. Stanhope."

"But . . . her teacher called an ambulance! It was very dramatic."

"In any case, I'm just glad she's feeling better now." The doctor closed the manila folder in front of him, then lifted it and tapped the edge against the desk. Alice's cue to leave.

Alice leaned back in her chair, her stance saying *I'm not going anywhere.*

"I'm not trying to downplay it, Mrs. Stanhope." He gave her a patronizing smile. "What happened to Zoe must have been very scary."

"It was. And I'm not leaving until I find out why it happened." Alice meant it. Mrs. Dawson had successfully bulldozed her out of Zoe's classroom when Alice's instincts had been telling her to stay. She wasn't going to ignore her instincts again when it came to Zoe.

The doctor's smile faded. "Look, sometimes these things just happen. We never know why. The good news is that Zoe isn't suffering from asthma, her heart and chest look fine, her blood pressure is good. Your daughter is perfectly healthy."

So Zoe went back to school a week later. And, despite Mrs. Dawson's no-parent policy, Alice had brought a chair and sat at the back of the room. If her daughter was going to have another attack of whatever it was, she was going to be there. But Zoe was fine. She followed instructions—sat on the mat for story time, did her cutting and pasting as she was supposed to. She was shier in this environment, not as likely to put up her hand or volunteer to help the teacher as Alice expected, but she was coping quite well. So the following week Alice decided to leave her to it.

Alice's phone was already ringing by the time she got to the car.

"Mrs. Stanhope, can you please come back? Zoe's hyperventilating again."

Back at the hospital, the doctor told Alice she had a perfectly healthy five-year-old girl. Which, of course, was positively unacceptable. "So you're telling me you have *no* idea what is wrong with my daughter?"

"Physically speaking, nothing is wrong with her—"

"But this is the second time she's had an attack," Alice interrupted. "I can't keep spending my days wondering if I'm going to get a phone call telling me that my daughter can't breathe."

Any form of cool that Alice had hoped to exhibit was gone. Her voice was full of emotion and, unfortunately, tears.

"Has Zoe been under any stress lately?"

"Stress?" Alice exploded. "She's *five!*"

"Any changes in the home? A divorce, a death?"

"No divorce. My great-grandmother died when she was two, I doubt she'd remember it." These questions didn't make any sense to Alice. What did any of this have to do with Zoe hyperventilating? "Please. *Please.* Help her."

The doctor sat forward. His movements were slow and deliberate, even the pushing of his glasses back against his face. It rankled Alice. Why was he so calm? Why was no one *worried?*

"Actually Alice, the clinical diagnosis of Zoe is likely to be anxiety."

Relief nearly bowled Alice over. "Anxiety?"

Anxiety was all right, wasn't it? Didn't Alice get anxious all the time? When she wasn't sure if she'd get the bills paid, when she thought she'd left the oven on after leaving for work?

"I think it's the most logical conclusion," the doctor said.

"But the hyperventilating—"

"A panic attack, most likely."

Alice stared at the doctor. A panic attack? She'd never had a panic attack over the bills.

"But . . . Zoe's happy. I mean, she was until she started school."

"Typically social anxiety does have a sudden onset. Many people report happy toddlers suddenly changing in childhood. Starting school is a common time for symptoms to start."

"Social anxiety?"

"It's similar to generalized anxiety disorder, but is characterized by excessive fears being linked to social situations—school, church, outdoor events, large spaces, that kind of thing."

"Is this my fault?" Alice asked. "For not taking her out more when she was younger?"

"We believe people develop social anxiety regardless of how they are socialized."

"Oh." Alice struggled to take it in. "So . . . how long will it last?"

"We don't know. If symptoms do continue, people see the best results with a combination of medication—usually SSRIs and/or benzodiazepines—and psychotherapy such as cognitive behavioral therapy. Alice?"

The doctor looked at her, standing now. She hadn't even felt herself get out of her seat.

"Benzodiazepines? Like Xanax? For my five-year-old?"

"We're getting ahead of ourselves. But they can be helpful. Depending on the severity of Zoe's anxiety. For some people this is a lifelong condition that needs to be managed."

Alice sat back down. Okay. They were getting ahead of themselves. That was what she wanted to hear. In a minute the doctor would tell her that drugs and therapy were only required in a small percentage of cases—that in most cases kids would snap out of it in a couple of weeks. *Zoe* would definitely snap out of it. Alice waited for him to say that.

He didn't.

19

Whoever was knocking on the door would have to go away.

In her apartment, with Kenny the cat on her lap, Zoe was trying to read *The Outsiders*. She had never been so grateful for locks. She wanted to stay behind the locked door and never go back to school again. Maybe she wouldn't go back for a few days. How could she, after the way Emily had looked at her? After the way she'd run out of there like a crazy woman?

She tried to concentrate on the words of her book, but her mind kept wandering to the Klonopin in the bathroom cabinet. How easy it would be to take one, to feel the delicious ooze of tension fading from her body. Too easy. After all, you didn't need to be a rocket scientist to get why so many people with social anxiety disorder became addicts. Alcohol, drugs, whatever it was—the option of escape was just too irresistible. It was why Zoe refused when Emily suggested they sneak a couple of glasses of her mom's wine. It was why she rarely took Klonopin. Life was hard enough for her. She didn't want to make it harder.

When she was a kid, Zoe used to hide in her mom's bed under the covers when she was feeling anxious. Sometimes her mom would come under too, for what felt like days. She'd bring popcorn or apples or toast. Sometimes they ate dinner in there. "Going to Comfytown," they called it. Zoe never felt more cozy and safe than when she was in Comfytown.

Unfortunately, she couldn't always stay in Comfytown. But when she did have to venture out into the big wide world, her mom still helped her to hide. Zoe remembered the time when she was six and her class performed "Old MacDonald Had a Farm" in front of the whole school. Her mom drove all the way to San Francisco to procure a two-man horse costume so Zoe could be onstage alongside her classmates and never have to be seen. Even now she sometimes, affectionately, called Zoe "my little horse's ass."

Zoe remembered the time she was ten, at school sports day, when she had a panic attack as she approached the starting line. Her mom burst from her seat in the grandstand. "What's wrong with her?" people were saying. Even in her stupor, Zoe was dying at being so cruelly exposed—while the entire school and their parents watched. *She's having a panic attack,* people would whisper. *She has anxiety.* The shame of such a humiliating defect.

"Asthma," her mom had said without missing a beat. "I forgot her Ventolin. I'd better take her home."

Zoe had lost count of the times her mom had said she had laryngitis (when she became dumbstruck in public) or was unwell (when she couldn't make it to an event at the last minute). If she were here now, Zoe knew, she'd make her feel better somehow. She'd put on a movie or some jolly music. Tell her a story about a time she'd humiliated herself a lot worse and get Zoe laughing. Maybe they'd even go to Comfytown. She was, Zoe realized, her only true friend in the world. The one who would never turn her back on her.

Kenny was purring now. If only she could share his bliss.

Someone was banging on the door again, more insistent now. Zoe lifted Kenny and let him nuzzle against her neck. She shrank back into the cushions. "Go away," she whispered.

20

Sonja had knocked twice on Alice Stanhope's door when the old lady on the folding chair finally piped up.

"Alice isn't home."

"I know." Sonja looked at her. "Actually, I was looking for her daughter."

"She came tearing up the stairs half an hour ago. Nearly knocked me off my chair."

So she was *home*, Sonja thought. She knocked on the door again.

"Oh, she won't answer it," the lady said. "Zoe never answers the door."

Sonja turned. "She doesn't?"

"Nope. She's agoraphobic or something."

"But . . . wasn't she was just outside? If you saw her run in."

The old lady squinted. "Okay, maybe not agoraphobic. But she's scared of people. People-phobic."

Sonja turned away from the door. "What makes you say that?"

"Like I said, she doesn't answer the door. If anyone talks to her she turns beet red and mutters something unintelligible. She doesn't have any friends. She and her mother are rather strange. A pair of hermits, those two."

Curious. And it didn't sound at all like the girl was fit to be home alone.

"Do you know them very well?" Sonja asked.

"As well as you know anyone these days. In my day people used to keep their elderly neighbors company. Not anymore."

Sonja turned back to the door, knocked again, harder this time. She listened at the door and thought she heard a faint shuffle. The old lady was right. Zoe was there.

"Zoe, it's Sonja, your mother's social worker. I'd like to talk to you. Can you come to the door, please?"

She put her ear to the door again, but this time there was silence. When she turned, the old lady was smiling a closed-mouth smile, eyebrows high in her hairline. "Told ya."

Just as Sonja was trying to figure out what to do, the door handle turned and the door opened a few inches.

"Hello," Sonja said, startled. "Are you . . . Zoe?"

"Yes," she said finally, as though she herself wasn't certain. Through the crack between the door and the frame, she looked younger than Sonja had expected. For some reason, perhaps the fact that she was happy to stay home alone, Sonja imagined her to be tall. Plucky. Full of adolescent attitude. But this girl was small. Timid-looking. She stared at the floor—not meeting her eyes at all.

Sonja fished a business card from her pocket. "My name's Sonja. I'm your mom's social worker." As she spoke Sonja heard the note of confidence in her voice that was absent in all but her professional life. She was glad that at least in some areas of her life she was in control.

"My mom's . . . ?" Now the girl's eyes did flicker to meet Sonja's and the color drained out of her face. "Is my mom okay?"

"She's still in surgery. But that's not why I'm here."

Her face registered relief, but was still hesitant. She was familiar-looking, Sonja realized. She had the bone structure of a doll, almond-shaped eyes and black hair. She also had a red mark on her right cheek. Sonja zeroed in on it.

"Do you mind if I come in and have a look around, Zoe, make sure everything is shipshape for your mother's release?"

Sonja sounded reassuring, she realized. Calm. Nevertheless,

for a moment it looked as if Zoe was going to refuse. She glanced at Sonja's business card again, and then over her shoulder, back into the apartment. Finally she took a step back, widened the door.

She'd failed the first test. Letting a stranger inside.

"Looks like you're getting a shiner there," Sonja said, as casually as she could. She stepped into the apartment, gesturing to Zoe's cheek.

"Oh." Zoe's gaze dropped. "I . . . I ran into a wall at school today."

"Ice helps," she said with a smile. "Is it okay if I . . ."

"Sure," Zoe said. "Look around."

Zoe remained in the hallway while Sonja did a loop of the apartment. It didn't take long—there wasn't a lot to see. The place was a little messy, but cozy. Photographs were dotted around in frames. It looked perfectly habitable.

"Why does my mother have a . . . social worker?" Zoe asked when Sonja returned to the living room.

The question stopped Sonja for a moment. It hadn't occurred to Sonja that Alice wouldn't explain all this.

"Well, the hospital put us in touch," she explained. "It's my job to take care of patients and make sure they have everything they need once they are released. For example, some people need help getting to and from appointments. Some people need to be put in touch with community services."

Zoe blinked. "Does my mom need that kind of help?"

Sonja hesitated. "I'm not sure yet. We'll know more after today."

"Oh."

Sonja didn't understand her bafflement. "Are you all right, Zoe?"

She shrugged in a way that Sonja read as *Yep. All good here.* But Sonja was getting the feeling that that was far from the truth. In Sonja's profession she'd learned to recognize "the feeling"— that elusive knot that appeared in your belly when something was not right. She had it now.

"So your mom tells me you're staying here alone while she's in the hospital?"

"Yeah." Zoe's voice was barely audible.

"Do you stay home alone much?"

"No." Zoe hovered at the window, looking out. "Mom's always here with me."

"Always?" Sonja smiled, but it was wasted because Zoe was looking out the window. "She never goes out with friends or away for a weekend?"

"No."

It was unsettling the way Zoe wouldn't make eye contact. Her cheeks were deep red, as if she'd just sprinted up some steps, or perhaps humiliated herself in front of a group of peers. Sonja thought again about the things the old woman outside had said about her. The mark on her face. "Zoe, I have to ask you a few questions, is that all right? There's nothing tricky."

Zoe concentrated on the floor. "I guess."

"Thank you. Do you have the numbers of any adults who live nearby that you could contact if you need anything?"

"Zoe shrugged. "I mean there's Dulcie next door."

Sonja waited, but that appeared to be it. "Okay. What about if the phone rings? Has your mom taught you what to say and what not to say to strangers on the phone?"

"I don't answer the phone."

Sonja wondered if she'd ever met a teen quite like this one. "And if there was a fire? Do you know at least two escape routes to get out of the apartment?"

Zoe just stared at the floor.

"All right," Sonja said finally. There was no doubt that this child was not fit to stay home alone. However, it wasn't Sonja's call to make. She needed to get in touch with Children and Family Services.

"You know, I have another client to see this afternoon, and I'm quite exhausted. Would you mind if I made myself a quick cup of coffee before I go?"

"Uh . . . I guess that's okay," Zoe said.

"The kitchen is this way, right?"

Sonja headed for the kitchen. Then, when she was certain Zoe wasn't following, she opened a few cupboards and the fridge. The pantry was reasonably well stocked, as was the fridge, but with food that required cooking—dry pasta, rice, chicken breasts. She'd expected to find food that could be reheated—lasagna, casseroles, a pie. The girl must be more competent than she looked. Then again, they often were, children of single parents. They had no choice but to step up and do their share of the cooking, the cleaning. Their parents needed the help.

Sonja got out a mug and flicked on the kettle. Then she slid her phone from her purse. She had the number for Children and Family Services saved in her contacts. She decided to call Chelsea, her contact there.

"What kind of treatment will my mom need after she's been released from the hospital?"

Sonja startled. Zoe was in the doorway to the kitchen, half in, half out. A cat was nestled like a newborn in her arms.

"I really don't know yet, Zoe."

Zoe's eyes, which were downcast, darted back and forth with thought. Her forehead was pinched in a serious frown.

"I know all of this is scary, but it's really better to take things one at a time," Sonja continued. "Each treatment is individual, and it's decided by the type of cancer they find."

Zoe's eyes widened, making her look even more childlike. "My mom has . . . cancer?"

It took Sonja a second to realize what she'd just done. "Oh. Zoe, I . . ."

The color leached out of the girl. Sonja took a step toward her, just as she took a step back.

"I'm sorry, Zoe. I thought your mom would have told you."

Zoe lowered her arms and the cat jumped from them. Her breath was coming in shuddery bursts. Within seconds, the hair around her temples was damp. It took Sonja a moment to realize what she was witnessing.

The girl was having a panic attack.

21

Kate lay on the couch in leggings and a T-shirt, a blanket across her knees. The TV was on and a book was beside her—she looked at neither. For days she'd stayed in this position, staring into space. Her baby was gone. *Gone.*

David was working from home, checking in on her regularly and bringing her endless cups of tea. They had been tiptoeing around each other for days, speaking to each other with careful courtesy. Hilary had stopped by last night with flowers and hugs. The kids were constantly checking if she needed anything. She was lucky, in lots of ways.

"Another tea?" David said, popping his head around the door.

She looked at the mug, still warm and full in her hands. "No. I'm good."

"How about some company?"

"Sure," she said, managing a smile.

Things were strange between them now. Bizarrely polite, like they were strangers, not people who knew the most intimate parts of each other. David relaxed onto the other end of the couch with a great exhalation and pulled her socked feet into his lap.

"I thought maybe we could go away for a few days," David said. "I spoke to Hilary, she's happy to take the kids for the rest of the week to give us some space."

"That sounds great but I need to go back to work tomorrow. Alice Stanhope, one of my patients, has had her surgery and it wasn't wonderful news."

David exhaled. "Look, Kate. I want to clear the air. I don't think you understand—"

"I do," she said. Because she *did*. This wasn't the first time she'd spent days lying, catatonic, on the couch after a miscarriage. David didn't want to see her suffer anymore. He worried about what it was doing to their relationship. He wanted them to get back to being happy.

"I just . . ." He shook his head; closed his eyes. "You deserve to be a mother. You, perhaps more than anyone. If I thought we had a chance . . . I mean, I wanted this for you so badly—"

For you.

"—but it's causing nothing but pain. I think that . . . if we were to focus on the good things between us . . . it might get better. We have so much. I realize it will take time. This is a huge loss. But we can have a different kind of life together. We can travel!"

She felt tears start to well up in her eyes, but she tried to smile.

"Too soon, I'm sorry," he said quickly. "But Kate . . . are we okay?"

No, we're not okay. The thought bounced out of nowhere, floated around in her consciousness, and burned with truth.

"Yes," she said, tucking the thought away again. "We're okay."

Kate had just drifted off to sleep on the couch when she heard Scarlett call her name. She opened her eyes. Scarlett hung over the back of the couch.

"Sorry to wake you," she whispered, "but it's your dad on the phone."

"Oh," Kate said, surprised. Her father wasn't one to call. He didn't stop by. If she didn't call and ask him to dinner every few months she wouldn't see him at all. She pulled herself into an upright position and took the phone. "Dad?"

"Kate. Did I wake you?"

It surprised Kate that someone who felt so distant from her could know such a thing, just by the sound of her voice.

"No," she lied. "I was awake. Is everything all right?"

"I just . . . David called me. He told me about . . ."

"Oh."

The miscarriage. It seemed impossible that something that never left her mind could come back to her like a slap. And yet it did. Over and over.

"I'm sorry, honey."

Honey. Kate couldn't remember the last time he'd called her that. "Well, you did warn me," she said. "Not to say anything until—"

"I shouldn't have said that." He sighed. "I don't know why I did. Sometimes I say things and I . . . I have no idea why."

Kate opened her mouth, then paused. It wasn't like her dad to be so forthcoming, particularly about his shortcomings. She felt herself soften toward him.

"Are you in pain?" he asked her.

"No," she said, even though that was miles from the truth. "Not anymore."

"Good . . . good."

The silence lasted and lasted . . . in a good way. Although the conversation was undeniably awkward, there was something wonderful about him trying. As Kate sat with the phone pressed to her ear, memories washed over her—memories of times like this, when her father had been unexpectedly tender. The time she'd fought with her best friend and he'd brought home ice cream. The time she got the top score for science and he called her grandmother to tell her how proud he was. The time he tried to give her advice on the first guy she liked who didn't know she was alive.

"Well, then," he said, clearing his throat. "I'd better let you rest. I just wanted to check in and say, you know, sorry."

"Thank you, Dad. It means a lot."

They said their farewells, but Kate found herself hanging on the line, wanting to say more. *How do you do it?* she wanted to ask. *How do you go from being someone who I feel I have no connection with to the only person in the world who can make me feel like I'm not alone? And why, dear God why, can't you be that person all the time?* She was still holding on the line a few seconds later when the call disconnected.

2 2

"K nock, knock," came the voice, and then the door opened. Zoe was sure she was in the middle of a nightmare. There was a social worker in her house. Her mom had cancer. She'd had a panic attack. Now, a second stranger was here.

"Come in," Sonja said.

This woman was around her mom's age, with a round face and cropped brown hair. She sat on the couch next to Zoe. "I'm Chelsea. I'm from the Department of Children and Family Services."

"Oh," Zoe said. What she really wanted to say was *What are you doing in my house?*

"I'm in your house, Zoe, because Sonja tells me you've been staying here alone while your mom is in the hospital, and she's worried that you might not be coping too well."

Zoe blinked. Shit. Clearly she *had* said it out loud.

"Are you all right, Zoe?" Chelsea said. "You seem a little shaken."

There are strange people in my apartment, Zoe wanted to say, but this time she managed to keep it on the inside.

"Ouch," Chelsea said, gesturing to Zoe's cheek. "What happened there?"

"I ran into a wall."

They clearly thought she was lying (because who runs into a

wall?). She was also blushing, which only made it look worse. But she wasn't lying.

Chelsea sat forward. "It must be pretty lonely here all by yourself. I know I get a bit scared when I'm home all by myself. Do you have any friends you could stay with? Relatives?"

Zoe shook her head. "I'm fine by myself."

"I'm sure you're very responsible," Chelsea said, "or your mom wouldn't have left you alone. But I wonder what would happen if something went wrong. What if you had an accident while you were here alone? If you, say, got an electric shock from the hairdryer?"

"I don't use a hairdryer," Zoe said.

"What if you burned yourself while you were making dinner then? What would you do?"

Zoe felt like she might cry. "I'd . . . call my mom."

"I see." Chelsea sucked the air between her teeth. "You know something, Zoe? I know a really nice lady who lives just a few blocks from here. She looks after kids who need someone to take care of them for a few days. I'm sure you could stay with her. Just until your mom gets out of the hospital? What do you think about that?"

"Thanks, but I'm good here," Zoe said.

The two women exchanged another look. "I'm sorry, Zoe, but we really don't feel comfortable leaving you here alone. If you don't have anyone to stay with, you'll need to go to emergency foster care."

"Emergency . . ." Zoe's heart began to thunder. "But I'm . . . fine *here*. Really."

"Zoe." Chelsea smiled. "Judy is really lovely. You'll like her."

Zoe blinked back tears. "Does my mom know about this?"

"As soon as she wakes up we'll tell her."

"She won't like it." Zoe felt whiney and petulant, like a child.

"Zoe," Sonja said. "Your mother is very ill. If she knows you're safe and happy, she can focus on getting better. Honestly, this is best for everyone."

Zoe tried to focus her thoughts but she couldn't. She couldn't do anything. Kenny the cat appeared at her ankle and she bent to scoop him up. "What about my cat?"

"We can kennel him for a few days," Chelsea said. "I know a great one not far away. I've used it for Lucy, my own cat."

Zoe hugged Kenny tight. She didn't care about Lucy.

"I'll take you over to Judy's," Chelsea said. "Why don't you go pack a bag? Everything will be fine Zoe, don't you worry."

Zoe closed her eyes. In a moment she would wake up and find that this whole thing—her mom's cancer, Emily, foster care—had all been a bad dream. She wanted her mom. She wanted her mom so bad.

The first thing Zoe noticed about Judy's place was that it didn't have a fence. It was a single-story place—not fancy by Atherton's standards, but it had freshly cut grass and a well-tended garden. Zoe didn't know if that was a good thing or not. Whenever she pictured foster homes she always pictured overgrown lawns and teenagers with tattoos, smoking cigarettes. This place showed no evidence of any kids at all.

Zoe and Chelsea had stopped off to take the cat to the kennel, and then visited a coffee shop "for a chat," which clearly meant "get the dirt on your mom." And the stupid thing was, Zoe *knew* this was the part when she was supposed to paint her mom as a veritable Mother Teresa meets Martha Stewart. She *knew* that. Problem was, when you can't look someone in the eye, you don't seem like a very reliable source. She ended up muttering things like "great mom," "good cook" to her lap, which no doubt made Chelsea think her mom was a psycho serial killer.

Chelsea knocked on the door and there was immediate movement inside. Zoe fought panic, even as her arms and legs began to tingle. Was this the kind of place she'd have to live if her mom died?

"Hello!"

The woman who answered the door was older than Zoe

expected—perhaps seventy. She was small and stout, in jeans and a blouse with gray hair cut into the universal cloud of fluff that old ladies seemed to favor. She smiled at Zoe with genuine warmth. "Welcome. You must be Zoe."

"Yes," Chelsea said when Zoe didn't respond.

"I'm Judy. Won't you come in?"

They followed her into a small sitting room, and Zoe sat next to Chelsea on a couch with fat floral cushions. A plate of cookies (oddly shaped enough to indicate they were homemade) sat in a dish on the table.

"Would you like a cookie, Zoe?" Judy asked.

Zoe shook her head.

"How about some tea?"

"No, thanks."

Judy was being perfectly nice, and Zoe didn't want to be rude, but there was no way she could eat or drink. It was taking all her energy just to keep it together.

"I hear your mom isn't very well, Zoe. I'm sorry to hear that. Hopefully she'll be better soon and you'll be back at home, taking care of her."

There was something like understanding in Judy's eyes. Zoe managed a small smile.

Chelsea left, after chatting with Judy for a few more minutes; then Judy offered to show Zoe to her room. Zoe stood and followed Judy to a small pink room with two single beds. They had matching floral quilts with pink pillowcases. There were a couple of pictures in frames, a pair of lamps, a poster of One Direction, and a pink iPod—Judy's attempt at getting young and hip, clearly. Zoe wondered if she swapped it for a blue iPod if a boy was coming to stay. One entire wall was covered in photographs of children and teenagers.

"You can take either bed," Judy said.

I want my bed, Zoe thought, tossing her bag onto the closest mattress. It was only when Judy nodded that Zoe realized she'd spoken out loud.

"Yes, there *is* something about your own bed, isn't there?" Judy said thoughtfully. "And there's definitely something about your own family. But I tell the kids who come here to think of my place not as an alternative home but an *extra* home. One of my boys who comes here regularly calls it 'coming to Granny's.'" Judy smiled. "I think it has a nice ring to it."

Zoe looked over at the pictures on the wall. "Are those the kids you've looked after?"

"Yes. Some of them are grown-up now, and doing really well. Some have children of their own."

"Why do you do it?"

Judy frowned, but in a good way, like she thought it was a very good question. "I suppose I want to do my part. There are so many people out there who are hurting. If everyone in the world did his or her part, then no one would have to be alone. We could all just be there for each other."

For some reason this made Zoe well up with tears. Judy patted her shoulder. Zoe was worried she might try to hug her, but instead she headed for the door. Judy, Zoe realized, seemed to have a knack for knowing what she needed. "I'm going to get dinner started. You just holler if you need me, okay?"

When she was gone, Zoe sat on the bed, feeling the eyes of the children who had been here before her. Some of them were doing really well now, Judy had said. Some of them had children of their own. Zoe knew she should find this comforting, but instead she wondered about the other ones. The ones who weren't doing so well. The ones for whom "coming to Granny's" wasn't enough. And she wondered, if something did happen to her mom, which one she would be.

23

As soon as Sonja opened the front door, she knew George was home. There was no evidence to this effect—she'd parked in the driveway, so she couldn't tell if his car was in the garage or not—but Sonja just knew. After years of marriage she was so attuned to his presence that she could tell before even opening the door. Sure enough, he was at the kitchen counter on his laptop. There were fresh flowers in the vase by the window. The house was clean and polished; the rich hardwood floors gleamed up at her.

It was a far cry from the single-fronted home she'd grown up in. Sonja's parents were working-class—a receptionist at a car dealership and a plumber—but Sonja had graduated to something bigger. A higher bracket. When she'd brought George home to meet her parents (separately, by then—they split up when she was nine) none of her family could conceal their surprise. "Good luck holding on to him," her dad had muttered too loudly. Her sister, Agnes, seemed surprised too, but at least she kept quiet about it. At their wedding, Sonja could admit she felt a little smug. *Bunch of nonbelievers*, she remembered thinking, looking back at them from the altar. She knew they attributed her lack of visits to her "being too good for" them and she was happy to go along with that. It was easier than the truth. That she was embarrassed. That, perhaps, she never had any reason to be smug.

"Hello," she said, dropping her grocery bags onto one end of the kitchen counter. She must have been on autopilot at the grocery store, because she didn't even remember what was in them.

"How was your day?" George asked, his eyes still on the screen.

"Well . . . I had to place a client's teenage daughter in foster care. That's never fun." She started unloading the groceries onto the counter. Eggs, marmalade, a cabbage. What on earth was she going to make with this?

"Why did you do that?" George asked.

"The girl was staying at home all alone while her mom was in the hospital," she said. "Which might have been all right. But then her neighbor told me she never answers the door, doesn't talk very much, and that she and her mom are very insular, they don't go out much. She also had a bruise on her cheek and a fairly unlikely explanation for why it was there. And then she had a panic attack while I was with her."

George shook his head. "They're not paying you enough, Sonja."

He looked back at the screen. Sonja noticed the glass next to his laptop, the finger of amber liquid. Silently she unloaded the rest of the groceries. Whenever George had been drinking, he had a tendency to underestimate his own strength. He also tended to become more aggressive after a few drinks; sometimes it even felt as though he *intended* to hurt her, as though he enjoyed it.

She'd heard all the popular sayings about marriage—how it was so much more about giving than receiving—but it was impossible to understand how much you had to give, and forgive, until you were in the situation. Sonja wanted her marriage to succeed. Then again, what did it mean to make a marriage succeed? Was it simply about staying together? Or was there something more she should be striving for?

Suddenly Sonja noticed George's gaze lingering on her. An uneasy feeling started.

"Come here," he said.

"George, I . . . I'm making dinner."

He cocked an eyebrow and glanced at the peculiar assortment of groceries. His expression said, *Really? You call this dinner?*

There wasn't a lot she could do at this point. If she'd thought ahead, she might have been able to fake an emergency at work and get out of the house. But it was too late now, George already had that look about him. His eyes were narrow and glassy, his body rigid. If there was such a thing as body language, it was saying, *I'm about to take what's mine.*

"Come here," he said again.

Sonja cringed internally. It would be worse because he'd been drinking. It was always worse. A few years back, after a half bottle of Scotch, he'd broken a bone in her wrist from holding her so tightly. It was an accident, of course. It was never intentional.

Sonja walked around the bench and stood in front of him. He grasped her waist and pulled her closer. She saw something in his eyes. A pulse of excitement.

"Lie on the bench."

"Can't we just wait until—"

He turned her around. Her stomach pressed painfully into the sharp edge of the countertop. Then he pushed her face down against the cold stone. The cabbage rolled onto the floor.

Marriage was all about giving, she thought. And George gave a lot. With his work, he'd changed so many lives for the better. He'd changed *her* life. It was only fair that he got something in return. With her hands gripping the counter, Sonja stifled a whimper. She could have stopped him if she'd wanted. She could have said no. But she didn't.

24

When Alice woke the morning after her operation, she couldn't find her phone. She needed to call Zoe. She was about to press her buzzer for the nurse when Dr. Brookes came in, trailed by Sonja. Today Sonja was wearing a silk shirt, tailored pants, and an immovable expression.

"Can I sit?" Dr. Brookes asked, and Alice hesitated. She'd been waiting all night for him to come in and discuss her prognosis, but suddenly she didn't want to hear it.

He sat anyway. "You sure you don't want anyone to be here?"

"Sonja's here," Alice said without looking at her.

"All right." Dr. Brookes let out a slow breath. "I'm going to get straight down to it. The bad news is the tumor in your right ovary is extensive. We also found tumors on your left ovary and the cancer has spread to the outside lining of the bowel, which puts you at stage three. I was able to debulk some tumors, though not all."

"Debulk?"

"Remove them."

"Okay!" Alice said, feeling a burst of optimism. "So you removed them?"

"*Some* of them. It's what we call a suboptimal debulking.

Unfortunately some of the tumors were inoperable, due to their location near organs."

"So . . . what happens now?"

"Now we hit hard with chemo."

Alice's heart sank. "Chemo?"

"Yes, I'd like to get you started as soon as possible."

Alice had known there was a strong likelihood she would need chemo, so she wasn't sure why this felt like such a shock. "And . . . after the chemo, then what?"

"With any luck you'll go into remission."

Beside her, Sonja scribbled furiously on a legal pad. When Alice looked at her, she lifted her head and gave the tiniest of nods. It made Alice feel a little better. For the first time, she felt glad Sonja was there.

"And," Alice said, "remission is—?"

"Remission is when we can't find any evidence of cancer."

Her mood lifted. "Okay. Good. Remission."

The pause, though short, was a presence in the room.

"Alice," Dr. Brookes said, "I always like to be optimistic. But you should know that only about twenty percent of women with stage-three ovarian cancer survive five years."

A shiver went down Alice's spine—powerful enough to make her jolt. But just as fast, something else happened. A memory. Of a bumper sticker she'd seen when Zoe was about a year old. She had been stuck in a line of cars in the supermarket parking lot while a tub of ice cream sat melting on the passenger seat. Alice looked around for another exit while simultaneously reaching back to pat Zoe's feet while she screamed in the backseat. Finally she'd opened the tub of ice cream and, with her fingers, scooped some into Zoe's mouth. The crying stopped immediately. That's when she noticed the sticker, on the rear window of the car in front.

I'M A SINGLE MOTHER, WHAT'S YOUR SUPERPOWER?

Single mothers, she realized, did have superpowers. Ovarian

cancer might have been the silent killer, but the silent killer hadn't banked on the superpowers of a single mother.

"Good," she said. "I plan to be one of those twenty percent."

Dr. Brookes smiled. "Glad to hear it. Now, I should have the pathology back before Friday and then we can come up with a plan of attack. I want you to know I'm going to give this my all, Alice."

"So am I," she said.

Once he was gone, Sonja put down her notebook and came to Alice's side. Alice was staring at her knees, tented in the bedcovers. She couldn't be bothered with Sonja. She was thinking about *cancer*. About 20 percent survival rate. About her superpowers. She was thinking about how she needed to find her damn phone.

"Sonja," she said. "Have you seen my phone? I really need to call Zoe."

Sonja was quiet long enough for Alice to look up.

"Alice," Sonja said, "there's something I need to tell you."

2 5

Kate stepped out of the car in the hospital parking lot and took a deep breath of secondhand cigarette smoke and damp asphalt air. *Don't look*, she told herself as she walked into the foyer. *Don't look at the babies.* But everywhere she turned there they were. Babies. Crying, burping, smiling. Clamped to its mother's hip or sitting contentedly on someone's lap. The yearning to hold a baby, to smell his or her milky breath, was so overpowering it almost doubled Kate over. Of course, babies were around the hospital every day, but this day, the day she returned to work, they seemed to be everywhere.

She caught the elevator to her floor, and as soon as the doors opened, she heard the shouting. She hurried down the corridor, following the noise. She found Alice Stanhope trying to lever herself out of bed while shouting at Sonja, who stood across the room from her.

"Alice!" Kate said. "What are you doing?"

Alice looked over at her and exhaled. "I'm discharging myself."

"What?" Kate put down her bag on the chair and went to Alice's side. "What's happened?"

"*She*"—Alice stabbed her finger toward Sonja—"put my daughter into foster care. She spent the night there. Sonja says she'll stay there as long as I'm in here. So I'm leaving. Right now."

Kate looked at Sonja.

"I met Zoe yesterday," she said, "and I had a number of concerns about her staying home by herself. I called the Children and Family Services and they agreed. Zoe couldn't name any friends or family members she could stay with so we placed her in a lovely foster home. She can stay there for a few more nights while Alice remains in the hospital and then she'll—"

"Zoe has never spent a full night out of her own home in her life," Alice interrupted. "It doesn't matter how *lovely* this home is, she will be traumatized. Besides, I haven't even met this person."

Kate wondered about this. A fifteen-year-old who had never spent a night away from home?

"She is perfectly safe at home," Alice continued. "Do you think I would take any risks with my own daughter?"

"Alice, she didn't have the details of any adults to call in case of an emergency. She had no idea how to escape in the event of a fire. She wasn't answering the phone at all, and she let me inside with only the slightest prompting. Then she had a panic attack," Sonja said.

"Because you told her I had cancer!"

Sonja blushed. "I apologize for that. Truly. I assumed Zoe knew and—"

"Why would you assume that?"

Kate listened as they argued back and forth, each exchange more heated. Both women made good points. There was no doubt that it would be traumatic for a teenage girl to be torn from her home, especially when dealing with the illness of her mother. But Zoe was clearly not fit to stay home alone. Finally when there was a lull, Kate said, "Where is Zoe now?"

"She's at school," Sonja said, exhaling.

"And after school?"

Sonja looked shamefaced. "Judy, her foster carer, will pick her up."

"Actually she won't," Alice said. "I will. Because I'm leaving."

"You can't," Kate and Sonja said at once.

"Well Zoe is *not* spending another night in foster care." Alice thought for a moment. "Look . . . what if we put a cot next to my bed, here? Zoe can stay here with me tonight."

Sonja was already shaking her head. There was no way the hospital would allow that. But she also saw from Alice's expression that she was about to lose her cool.

"What if Zoe stayed with me?" Kate blurted out. "I have the space. I mean, would that be better, for Zoe, than foster care? I don't live far away and I can bring her back here in the morning when I start my shift."

This silenced both women for a moment.

"That's very kind of you," Sonja said. "But we have protocol to make sure everyone is properly vetted, trained in things such as first aid, background-checked—"

"My husband and I have both had background checks," Kate said. They'd had to do that in order to do IVF. "Obviously I don't need first-aid training."

"Still," Sonja said, looking quite uncertain now. "It would need to be family or a close friend for us to consider this."

Alice, Kate noticed, was watching her curiously. Kate could tell she was considering her offer, even if only to spite Sonja.

After a minute Alice looked back at Sonja. "Kate's a close friend if I say she is."

Sonja started to speak but Alice was looking at Kate.

"One night," she said.

"Alice," Kate protested, "you need to stay for at least—"

"One night."

Kate nodded. It was, she figured, the best she could do.

But Sonja was still talking. "I'll have to speak to CFS about this," she muttered, turning to leave.

"Give them my regards," Alice called after her. She turned to Kate and raised an eyebrow. "And my good friend Kate's."

And it was the strangest thing: As Sonja walked out of the room, Kate had a surprising urge to laugh.

"David? It's me."

Kate was huddled in the kitchenette behind the nurses' station, her phone pressed to her ear.

"How's the first day back so far?" he said at the same time as she said, "Listen, I need to talk to you."

They both laughed. But inside Kate was wondering when they got so out of sync with each other.

"You go," David said.

"Okay well, my day has been . . . interesting so far. One of my patients, Alice, is a single mother, and her teenage daughter has somehow ended up in foster care. Alice is freaking out, understandably, and threatening to check herself out of the hospital, but she just had major surgery and there's no way she can do that. I know this sounds strange, but I . . . I offered to have her daughter stay with us tonight."

"Oh," he said, surprised.

"I know I should have checked with you first. I just wanted to help and it was the only solution I could come up with on the spur of the moment. Is it all right with you?"

"Well, I mean, sure," he said. After the miscarriage, he was probably willing to say anything to keep her happy.

"How old is she?"

"She's fifteen."

"All right. Scarlett's staying at Hilary's tonight but Jake will be here and he's bringing some buddies back to watch the game so there'll be some other young people around."

Kate paused. After what Alice had explained to her about Zoe, she got the sense that the fewer people who were at home, the better. But David had misinterpreted her pause.

"I know you're still down about this whole baby thing," he said. "I want to make it up to you."

There was something about the way he said it—*this whole baby thing*—that irritated her. Kate wanted to tell him that actually the only thing he could do to make it up to her was *give* her a baby. Instead she choked it back, thanked him again, and hung up the phone.

26

n second-period English, Zoe was trying to imagine a world without her mother. She'd imagined it so many times in her strange little movie-reel fantasies that it should have been easy. But now that it was real, everything was blurry. And the questions were never-ending. Would she stay in her apartment or would she have to move? Would she keep going to school or would she need to go out and get a job? Probably a job if she wanted to stay in her apartment. But what kind of job could she even *get*? She wouldn't survive two weeks even if she wanted to, which she wasn't sure she did. What would be the point of surviving without her mother?

This morning, as Judy drove her to school, she'd tried to tell herself that everything was fine, everything was over. But who was she kidding? Her mom had had surgery yesterday! Suddenly a horrible thought occurred to her. What if there were complications? She'd been thinking that it was the beginning of the end, but what if this was the *end* of the end? What if she was called out of class to be told her mother had passed away following a postsurgery complication? What if she wasn't even able to say good-bye?

"Okay, class, we are starting a new unit," Mrs. Patterson said. "Public speaking. So I've decided we're going to have a debate!"

There was a collective groan.

"Oh, why so glum? I happen to know a lot of you are very good at arguing. Anyway, you'll have a couple of weeks to prepare. I'm going to divide the class into two groups." She stretched her arms out in front of her. "This side is 'for' "—she gestured to Zoe's side of the room—"and this side is 'against.' Every person will have a speaking role, but some are bigger than others. If you have a large speaking role, you'll have less prep to do and vice versa. There will be the six speakers—three on each side. There'll be an adjudicator, who will help me decide the winners and then explain why they have won. There'll be a person to announce the debate. And each speaker will have a partner who will introduce them, and who will help prepare the speech and write rebuttals during the debate. Anyone who is left can stand up afterward and talk about who was their favorite speaker and why. Any questions?"

Zoe felt an overwhelming urge to vomit.

"So, who'd like to volunteer for the adjudicator role?"

A few hands shot up. Mrs. Patterson selected one of them.

"Good," she said, writing the name in a notebook. "Now, how about first speaker for the affirmative?"

Zoe wasn't sure what happened then. A moment of insanity? Whatever it was, it came to her all at once—like the desire to scream in an empty room or dive-bomb into the unbroken water of a pool. When she was a kid, she'd had similar compulsions. She'd be playing happily when all of a sudden she'd feel compelled to reach out and touch the wall or the edge of the fringed carpet. She'd tell herself that if she didn't touch the wall or carpet, the world would end right that second.

But this time, it was more than just a compulsion. It was about her mother. She had cancer. Not only that, she'd *lied* to Zoe about having cancer. Suddenly Zoe understood why. She'd lied because she didn't think Zoe could handle it. Which meant Zoe needed to become the kind of person that didn't need to be lied to. A strong person. The kind of person who could . . . participate in a debate.

She put her hand up.

"Zoe?" Mrs. Patterson said. "You'd like to be a speaker?"

Mrs. Patterson couldn't contain her surprise. Zoe felt her cheeks bloom red. She could feel people's eyes, but she focused forward.

"Yes."

"Well, that's great. Good for you."

Mrs. Patterson was being kind, but Zoe wanted her to move on to the next person. Stop smiling. *Next.*

Mrs. Patterson scribbled Zoe's name on her notepad. "And who'd like to be Zoe's partner? Hands up."

The absence of hands was practically a presence. A few chair legs squeaked. Cameron whispered something to Danielle, who giggled. Emily, two rows ahead, had already pushed her table up next to Lucy Barker's—clearly they were partners. Jessie Lee and Billy Dyer had their heads down, as Zoe would have if not for her momentary aberration.

"Come on, class. Who wants to be partners with Zoe?"

Zoe was certain that eventually the humiliation would form a knife and stick her through the heart. And still, the silence stretched on.

Finally, there was a sigh. "I will."

The voice was distinct.

"Harry," Mrs. Patterson said. "Good. You are partners with Zoe."

Mrs. Patterson wrote it in her notebook and moved on to the next role.

For the next fifteen minutes, Zoe kept her head forward, too afraid of making eye contact with anyone, especially Harry. She didn't know what to be more afraid of—the fact that she'd just volunteered to be in a *debate*, or the fact that Harry had volunteered to be her partner. Why would Harry—*Harry*—volunteer to be her partner?

"Okay then," Mrs. Patterson said when everyone had been assigned a role. "I suggest the speakers get together with your partners sooner rather than later. The topic is . . . wait for it . . .

whether students should call their teachers by their first names. I want to hear strong arguments! One partner will present the argument and the other will remain at the table, passing notes for rebuttals. Both participants will write the initial arguments as well as a full report about what you contributed to the assignment. Do you understand?"

"Yes, Mrs. Patterson," the class droned.

"Good. Well you can be dismissed a little early today so you can exchange numbers with your partners and make arrangements. I want well-written, well-rehearsed speeches, understood? Get practicing."

After class, by her locker, Zoe felt a presence behind her.

"So I guess we're partners."

All of Zoe's senses went on high alert, but she continued to shuffle books in her locker. "I guess we are."

Harry was quiet for a moment. She felt his eyes boring into the back of her head. After a few seconds she heard a sigh. "Listen, I'm sorry about what I said the other day," he said. "You know . . . 'Why else would I look at you'?"

Zoe died all over again. "It's no big deal," she muttered.

"Are you sure?"

"I'm sure." Zoe kept her nose in her locker.

"Oh-kay," he said skeptically. "But if it's no big deal, why won't you look at me?"

Zoe's cheeks bloomed red, which made turning around all the more mortifying. So she didn't.

"Suit yourself," he said finally. "So . . . how are we gonna do this? The debate, I mean."

It was the question Zoe had been asking herself since she put up her hand. She still didn't have a good answer.

"Well . . . I . . . I guess we'll come up with the main arguments in class tomorrow," she said. "And then we'll divide them between the three speakers. Then we write the speech."

Harry moved around to her right side, appearing in her peripheral vision. "Are you *really* not going to look at me? You know you volunteered to be a speaker, right? You have to stand up in front of the class? *Facing* the class?"

Zoe continued shuffling books in her locker, dying. "There are only two types of speakers," she said quietly. "The nervous and the liars."

It was her favorite quote. She'd always wanted an excuse to say it to someone. But at the same time, she'd laid herself bare—giving away any notion that she was keeping her back to him to torture him or pay him back for what he said about her.

"Mark Twain, right?" Harry said after a moment.

"Yeah." In her surprise Zoe forgot herself and looked at Harry.

"Okay, point taken," he said. "Don't look at me. But we're going to have to write the damn thing sometime. How about tomorrow? I have an appointment right after school, but I'll be home by four P.M. Come to my place. I live in West Atherton. I have a closet that you can keep your head in the entire time if you like."

For a millisecond Zoe nearly laughed. Then she remembered that she couldn't go to Harry's. She'd probably have a panic attack right there on his doorstep! The whole thing was ridiculous. She was going to make a fool of herself.

But, because she just needed the conversation to be over, she shrugged and said, "Fine. Tomorrow after school at your place."

She'd figure out a way to get out of it later.

Zoe was on her way to math when she heard her name in the corridor. She assumed she'd misheard, that someone had called "Chloe" or "Joey," but when she spun around, Mrs. Hunt, the school principal, was looking at her.

"Can you come with me a minute, please?"

Mrs. Hunt wore a strange smile that might have been conceal-ing anger or even sadness. Zoe's stomach plummeted. Her mom.

"I . . . I have to get to class," Zoe stammered, overcome by an urge to flee.

"It's all right," Mrs. Hunt said. "I'll give you a pass."

So Zoe had no choice but to go with her, into her office.

"Have a seat," Mrs. Hunt said when they got inside. Zoe did. Her hands were shaking and she found herself holding her breath. "Zoe, your mother called me and told me about her cancer. I'm so sorry."

Slowly she started to breathe again. Her mom must have been alive to make the call. And yet she was surprised her mother had thought to call the school to tell them this. Especially since she hadn't done Zoe the same courtesy.

"Thank you."

"I want you to know the school will support you through this. My door is open for you any time, and so is Mrs. Logan's."

Mrs. Logan, the guidance counselor. Zoe had seen her once during her first semester, a standard visit after her mother had explained about her social anxiety disorder. Mrs. Logan was the brand of therapist that just sat there and waited for you to talk. Perhaps not the best strategy for someone with a pathological fear of talking to people.

"Thank you," she said again. She should have felt relieved. Her mother wasn't dead and she wasn't in trouble for skipping school. Still, she felt wary.

"Zoe, I also mentioned to your mother that we have a thera-pist working at the school at the moment who has extensive experience with teenagers. I wondered if you might like to talk to him."

"Oh, thanks but . . . I think I'm okay."

"You don't have to talk to him about your mother's diagnosis if you don't want to. You could talk to him about anything. Issues with friendships. Problems at home. Anything at all. He's right next door, you could see him right now—"

"Thanks," Zoe interrupted. "But I'm fine."

"All right," Mrs. Hunt said, standing. "But if you change your mind, just say the word."

Zoe let herself out of Mrs. Hunt's office. As she got a pass from the desk she stole a glance into the next office, where a man sat in a swivel chair, typing. He was pretty old, maybe sixty, with grayish black hair. Perhaps feeling her gaze, he glanced up as she walked past his door.

Zoe felt a strange pulse of energy.

"Here's your hall pass, Zoe," the secretary said.

"Oh," she said. "Thanks."

She shoved the pass into her pocket and let herself out of the office. But as she took off down the hallway she had the weirdest feeling that she was being watched.

27

Everyone was in a hurry that afternoon. Kids charged through the school gates, backpacks slung over one shoulder, walking briskly or running. Eager to get home. Zoe was just as eager. She was almost at the gate when Sonja appeared beside her.

"Zoe?"

Zoe's breath vanished. "Uh . . . yeah?"

"I'm here to take you to the hospital."

Zoe took a step away from Sonja, even as she reached for Zoe's bag. "Can I help you with this?"

"It's okay," Zoe said, moving farther away. She wanted to ask what had happened to Judy, but she couldn't seem to find the words. Thankfully Sonja imparted this information voluntarily.

"Your mom has made alternative arrangements for you," she said, and Zoe felt a wave of gratitude. Her mom was going to take care of things. Everything was going to be all right.

"My car is over here."

Sonja's car was ridiculous. Zoe wasn't exactly a gear-head, but you could tell, even from the smell, that it cost. Cream leather seats, shiny brown dash, and a perfume smell that gave Zoe an instant headache. On TV and in movies, social workers always seemed to drive beat-up cars and smoked and had purple hair and a long list of atrocities committed against them, which had driven them to the job in the first place. Sonja seemed to defy every one of the stereotypes.

"Well," Sonja said once they'd been on the road a minute and it was obvious Zoe wasn't going to speak. "How was last night?"

"Fine."

"And you liked Judy?"

"Yes."

Sonja tapped the steering wheel with pale pink fingernails. Her little finger, Zoe noticed, was chipped, the nail torn to the nail bed. It was an unexpected chink in her perfect armor.

"And how are *you* doing?" Sonja said. "You were quite upset yesterday."

Zoe turned to look at Sonja and met her eye. She quickly looked away again, but not before she saw something else in Sonja's eyes. She actually *cared*.

"I'm okay," Zoe whispered.

The small talk was painful. Zoe pretended to look out the window as if she were fascinated by the streets she walked along every day. If Emily were here she'd be babbling about anything—hair products, the assignment she got today, the leather seats of the car. The fact that Zoe couldn't find a single word to say was just lame. She was lame.

When they reached the hospital they walked in silence through the lobby and into the elevator. The awkwardness was painful, but Zoe was buoyed by the fact that she would soon see her mom. The prospect of relief from the last twenty-four hours was making her woozy. Her mom was going to fix everything.

"Which room is it?" Zoe said when they came out of the elevator.

Sonja gestured and Zoe began to run. But when she rounded the corner to her mom's room, she stopped dead. There was a nurse in there, changing a bandage around her mother's middle. The bandage was caked in dried blood. A lot of blood.

"Oh," Zoe said.

Her mom rolled her face toward the doorway. "Mouse!"

She looked awful. Tired and puffy and not like herself. Her hair, usually bouncy blond and tousled, was limp and desperately needed a wash. Her skin was pale and entirely free of makeup. She looked like a different person.

Somehow, Zoe managed to smile. "Hey."

"Come in," she said. "Are you all right?"

"I'm fine," Zoe heard herself say. She felt surprisingly awkward standing there, like she was talking to a stranger and not her mom. She stepped forward and gave her a brusque kiss.

"I had no idea they were going to put you into foster care," her mom said. "If I had known I—"

"Why did you tell me it was gallstones?"

Zoe hadn't known she was going to blurt it out until the moment she did. But the betrayal stung. Her mom had always been the one person who told her the truth, no matter how difficult.

"I'm so sorry, honey. I should have told you the truth."

"Why didn't you?"

"I . . . I wanted to find out exactly what we were dealing with before I worried you with it."

Zoe heard what she wasn't saying. *I didn't think you could handle it.*

Zoe was aware of the nurse in the room and Sonja was close behind her, and she knew she was dangerously close to crying. But she had to ask. "What *are* we dealing with?"

"Ovarian cancer," her mom said. "But the doctor has removed most of the tumors and we're going to start chemo soon. He knows what he's doing. We have the best team possible working on me. I'm going to survive, hon."

Zoe watched her mom, wondering if she was telling her the whole truth now.

"So what was it like?" her mom asked eventually. "The foster home."

Zoe shrugged. "It was all right."

"Well, I've arranged something else, if it's okay with you."

"What?" Zoe asked, suspicious.

"There's a nurse here, her name is Kate. She offered to have you stay with her tonight. And tomorrow, I'll make them discharge me. It's not ideal, but . . . it's just for one night. You'll like Kate. She's young and pretty. She's a lot like . . . well, you."

Zoe fought to hold in the tears. Another night in a strange house. Her nerves had been stretched taut all day. She'd been just hanging on until she saw her mom and she took care of everything. But her mom wasn't taking care of everything. Which meant she needed to keep it together.

Her mom reached for her. "Honey, I know how hard this is for you. If there was anything else I could do—"

"Will I . . . will I have my own room?" she managed.

"You'll definitely have your own room. Kate told me. She's very nice."

Zoe didn't care if she was nice. She wanted to go home with her mom. Her normal mom, not this strange, puffy, sick version. She wanted to go back to her apartment and for everything to go back to normal. She wanted to be alone so she could cry, really cry. Instead she managed to say, "Okay."

"Kate will be here soon so you can meet her. And honey, tomorrow, everything will be back to normal, okay? I promise."

Her mom looked at her, smiling, desperate to instill a sense of calm in Zoe. But all Zoe could see was her mom's puffy face, her stomach wound, and the dried blood. And that look in her eyes that said she'd just lied to her. Again.

2 8

As they pulled through the wrought-iron double gates and into Kate's driveway, Zoe's eyes bulged. Kate's house was gigantic. The driveway was wide and tree-lined and her whole apartment block would have fit on the front lawn. It was entirely different from Judy's house, but it still terrified her. Would she have to eat dinner with Kate's family? What if they wanted to ask her lots of questions about her life? What if they wanted to talk about her mom? They were being kind, having her to stay, and Zoe didn't want to be rude—but sometimes, for Zoe, being rude was inevitable.

She and Kate hadn't made much conversation on the way home, but it was okay. Like her mom said, Kate was nice. The kind of nice where she only had to look at you and you felt warm—that kind of nice. She asked closed-ended questions (Zoe's favorite) like "You okay?" and "Ready?" and then nodded with a smile as though they were on the same page. She was pretty too. Her hair was a dark brown long bob, her eyes were blue, and Zoe couldn't see a single pore or blemish on her skin. Also, she was cool. She wore Converse with her uniform and her nails were painted a purplish red.

She wanted to ask Kate who she lived with—a husband, she assumed, but who else? Toddlers? A baby? She didn't seem old enough to have kids any older than that. In a way Zoe hoped she would have a kid. Kids and old people (with the exception of Dulcie) were among the few members of society that Zoe felt comfortable conversing with. They didn't judge or look too closely. If you talked to them and made them feel special, you were theirs for life.

"Okay," Kate said. "Here we are."

They'd stopped off at Zoe's apartment to pick up a few things, and now Kate picked up her bag and carried it toward the house.

"It's okay, I'll get it," Zoe said.

"Oh, sure. Here you go."

Zoe meant to be helpful, but it just came out rude. Why was she so awkward? Why couldn't she be normal, charming, conversational? For some reason she wanted Kate to like her. Unfortunately, the more Zoe wanted to impress someone, the less impressive she generally was.

Kate handed her the bag. The foyer was the size of Zoe's apartment.

"Yeah," Kate said, seeing Zoe's face. "I can't get used to it either. What's the point of all this space for a foyer?"

Kate smiled and Zoe relaxed a little. Until a voice called out from somewhere in another room. "Kate? Is that you?"

"Yes," she called. Then to Zoe she said, "Come on, come and meet everyone."

Instantly Zoe's palms became slick. "Everyone?"

"It's just my husband, David, and my stepson, Jake. And maybe a couple of Jake's friends."

Kate started to walk but Zoe remained bolted to the floor. Kate paused in the doorway and looked back at her uncertainly.

"Hey!" a man said, appearing beside Kate. He kissed her cheek, then held out his hand to Zoe. He grinned. "You must be Zoe."

Zoe took his hand, cringing about the dampness of her own.

"I'm David," he continued. "Don't mind us, watching the game. I don't suppose you're a 49ers fan?"

She shook her head.

"Damn, I could have used the support. Hey you're not a Raiders fan, are you? If you are, you're about to get your ass whupped." He chuckled.

Zoe stared at him. He was the dad Zoe had seen so many times on films and on TV. The dad who wore sweatpants with reading glasses. The dad who tossed burgers at school sports day, and who, on vacation, sent the family into the hotel while he went out into the rain to get the bags.

"I don't really follow sports," she admitted.

"Do you eat nachos?" he said. " 'Cause we've got plenty of those. Come on, come on." He took her bag and draped his arm lightly over her shoulder, guiding her in the direction from which he'd come. A cheer came from a room nearby, reminding Zoe of the proximity of other people.

"Actually, I'm not hungry," she said, planting her feet.

David shot a glance at Kate, then let his hand slide off Zoe's shoulder. "Oh. You sure? There's other stuff, too, if you don't like nachos. . . ."

"Why don't I show you the guest room, Zoe?" Kate said. David nodded slowly and Zoe could see that he'd just recalled that Zoe's mother was sick. He was probably attributing her strange behavior to that. It was nice, to have an excuse for once.

"Thanks though," Zoe said to him, then followed Kate up the stairs.

It was a little surreal to find that the guest room had its own bathroom. A full bathroom, made of stone that twinkled like it was ingrained with diamonds. It had a bath and separate shower and two sinks! The bath was deep, with jets. It looked impossibly inviting.

"Feel free to have a shower, or a soak in the tub," Kate said. "Some of my toiletries are in the cupboard under the sink. Help yourself to anything."

Once Kate left, Zoe sank onto the bed. She had longed to be alone for the past twenty-four hours, but now that she was, she wasn't sure she wanted it anymore. As she sat all alone, the pain of her mother's illness finally pierced her. Was this her future? Living in strangers' homes—kind strangers who quickly realized the truth about her, and were disappointed?

Zoe thought about her mom for a moment, lying in her hospital bed. She'd be freaking out. Zoe fished her phone out of her bag and sent her a quick cheerful text. Even if she *had* lied to her about her cancer, Zoe didn't want her worrying while she was in the hospital. When she was finished Zoe went to the bathroom cupboard. There was a wicker basket inside with shampoo, conditioner, body wash, some nail-polish remover, and expensive-looking moisturizer. Zoe dug into it. A few bobby pins were scattered across the bottom of the basket, and a new disposable razor.

She sat on the edge of the tub. Her mother wasn't fooling anyone with her talk about everything going back to normal. Zoe knew ovarian cancer wasn't one of the "good" cancers. One of the side effects of being a worrier was that she spent a lot of time researching things. Her grandmother had died of ovarian cancer just before Zoe was born. It was the silent killer, she recalled now. The one that didn't show symptoms until it was too late. And if there was one thing Zoe knew, it was that she wouldn't survive in this world without her mother.

Zoe took off her clothes and slid into the empty bath, turned the taps on. Then she reached for the razor. She stared at it, turning it over, observing the glint of the light on the blade. If she were a different kind of person, she'd take the blade, press it against her wrist. But she wasn't a different kind of person. Was she?

When Zoe was nine, her mom took her to the zoo. Zoe, of course, hadn't wanted to go. "Zoos are crowded," she said. "I might get lost."

"I won't let go of your hand," her mom said.

"But I don't like zoos."

"You love animals."

"I love seeing them *on TV.*"

The funny thing was, Zoe wasn't agoraphobic. She liked the outdoors. Sometimes early in the morning or late at night she would ask her mom if they could "go get some fresh air." No, it wasn't the outdoors she was afraid of, or the animals. It was the people.

They got to the zoo an hour before it opened so they could get in first (Zoe couldn't handle standing in lines) and spent a few minutes in the gift shop trying on giant animal heads. Zoe actually cracked a smile when Alice put on the lion's head. "You are so silly, Mom," she'd said, giggling. Her mom was so pleased that she went to buy it, but when she checked the price tag—sixty bucks for a novelty lion's head!—she changed her mind.

Half an hour later, when a line formed behind them, Zoe had forgotten the lion's head and was starting to freak out. Some girls her age approached with their mothers. Zoe felt their eyes on her, staring. Judging. After a while it became unbearable.

"Mom, everyone is looking at me."

Her mom glanced around. "No they're not, hon."

"They *are.* I want to go home."

"We can't go home," her mom said. "I've already bought the tickets."

"Mom, *please.*"

Zoe's face was hot, and sweat poured from her underarms. Her mom looked bewildered. Zoe hated herself for asking—she knew the tickets had cost a lot of money—but she had to get out of there.

"Fine," her mom said finally, stalking out of the line. Zoe was right on her heels. But she was walking in the wrong direction.

"Are we going home?" Zoe called after her uncertainly.

"Nope."

"Mom!"

Her mom marched into the gift shop and grabbed the lion's head off the stand. She winced as she handed over her credit card and, a minute or two later, she slipped it over her head and returned to the line.

"Mom, what are you doing?" Zoe asked, astonished.

"No one is looking at you now," she said, winking at Zoe through the eye slits. "They're looking at *me*."

29

That evening, as she lay in her hospital bed, Alice was worried. Had she done the right thing, letting Zoe go back to Kate's? After all, she didn't know the faintest thing about Kate, other than that she was a nurse with a soothing bedside manner. Her husband could be a pedophile, an abuser! Sure, Kate said she had been background-checked. (Briefly Alice wondered why she had been, but manners had stopped her from asking. Manners! Who cared about manners—this was her daughter!) Then again, there were plenty of criminals with clean records. Weren't there?

She took a deep breath. *Get it together, Alice.*

Alice was not a conspiracy theorist. Growing up, she had been schooled in the idea that people were, by and large, good. If something went missing, it probably hadn't been stolen, you'd most likely lost it. The government was not in cahoots with pharmaceutical companies to make you ill so they could make money. The world *these days* was much the same as it had always been— with good people and bad people. She had always felt strongly about this. She still did. But fifteen years ago, she'd been exposed to the bad. Worse, she'd *invited in* the bad. She thought now of that strange, horrible night. The glass of red wine she'd gulped down. "I *insist*," she'd said.

She dragged her phone from her bedside table and saw that Zoe had already sent her a text.

Hey Mom everything is fine. I have a room with its own bathroom! Hope you're okay. Zoe.

Alice put down her phone. *Everything is fine.* Why did Alice not believe that? After all, things always seemed like they were fine— until they weren't.

30

"re you sure Zoe's all right?" David asked, climbing into bed beside Kate. He had a book in his right hand and his reading glasses perched on his nose.

"Actually I'm not," Kate said. Zoe had spent the entire evening in her room and hadn't even answered the door when Kate knocked to tell her dinner was ready. When Kate had let herself in, she'd found the door to the bathroom door closed, so she'd left her plate on the bed.

"Poor kid," David said. "What will happen to her if . . . her mother doesn't make it?"

"I have no idea. Usually there are oodles of family members around. I guess if no other family members come out of the woodwork, and if she's under eighteen, she'll go to a foster family."

"And if she's over eighteen?"

"Then she's on her own."

"Jesus." David closed his eyes. "Can you imagine Jake or Scarlett on their own?"

Kate put a hand on his. "It would never happen to them. There are too many people who would want them. You and me, Hilary and Danny, uncles, aunts, cousins . . ." As she said it, Zoe's fate seemed especially unfair. How did Scarlett and Jake have so many people and she had none? "Maybe I should check on her again?" she said.

David touched her shoulder. "Wait."

She paused.

"Can we talk a minute?" he said. "I feel like things aren't right between us."

Kate hesitated for a moment before returning her legs to the bed.

"Can I just say I'm sorry?" he said, removing his reading glasses. "I know how hard all of this has been on you. I want to help you, but I feel like we're just . . . out of touch with each other. I want to give you everything you want, Kate. It kills me that I can't give you this."

She drew herself over to him, taking his hands. She had a feeling that this was the opening she'd been waiting for. "You *can*, David. If we don't give up, we can still have it. I know it hasn't been easy, but don't you always say 'nothing worth having is easy to get'?"

He let out a long, slow breath. All at once Kate got the feeling this wasn't the direction he wanted the conversation to go.

David rubbed the bridge of his nose between two fingers, his eyes settling in the middle distance. "Think of it this way. What if you wanted to run a marathon even though every time you ran it caused you enormous pain? What if each time you set out on a run you ended up hospitalized and immobile for weeks? Would you expect me to support you then?"

"No," Kate said. "But the situations are different."

"*How?*"

"Because you've already run two marathons!" she cried. "And, since I'm the one who is willing to put in the training, you owe it to me to at least let me try for one."

David stared at her.

"I'm sorry," she said. "That wasn't fair."

He sighed. "I don't want to argue, Kate."

Kate looked at him. His face was full of compassion, full of determination to work this out. But there was something else in his face too. Resolve. He'd made his decision.

"Neither do I," she said, even though it was the opposite of the truth.

Kate knocked gently on Zoe's door. "Zoe? Are you awake?"

There was no movement inside. She was probably asleep. The kid had had a rough day. Kate turned back toward her room, then hesitated. She was responsible for the girl, at least for tonight. She should probably at least sight her before going to bed. She knocked again, a bit louder. "Zoe?"

Still nothing. Kate felt a flap of panic.

"Zoe?" This time she yelled it, flinging open the door. The room was empty, the bed made. The lasagna Kate had left her was on the desk, untouched. In a millisecond she went from concerned to hysterical. What if something had happened to her? What if . . . she'd done something to herself? Most of all . . . *What had she been thinking, inviting her here?*

"Zoe?" she cried. The bathroom door was closed, a thin line of light beaming out from the crack at the bottom. Just as it had been two hours earlier when she'd dropped off the lasagna. Kate lurched toward the bathroom door, but a moment before she got there, it opened.

"Hi."

Zoe stood there. Her hair was wet and she wore a pair of dark sweatpants, a T-shirt, and socks.

"Oh," Kate said. "Hi. I was just . . . checking you were okay."

"Sorry. I was having a bath." She looked at the floor, but Kate could see that her face was red and tearstained. Kate herself had had many a long cry in the bath.

"You're not hungry?" Kate said, gesturing to the lasagna.

"No." She blushed. Poor sweet thing was shy just having a conversation.

"I can make you something else?"

"It's okay," Zoe said. "Thanks though."

"Well, let me know if there's anything I can do for you," Kate said. "Even if you just want to talk."

"I will."

Kate started to turn, but Zoe reached out and touched her arm. "Thank you . . . for . . . you know, letting me stay at your house."

"Oh." Now it was Kate's turn to feel shy. "Well, we're happy to have you."

Zoe hesitated. "Is my mom going to die?"

In her job, Kate was a believer in absolute truth. But this situation was different. It wasn't her truth to tell. She opened her mouth, unsure of the words that were going to come out.

"I thought so," Zoe said before Kate could answer, and she walked back into the bathroom and closed the door.

31

Zoe stood at the unfamiliar gate with her finger poised. She knew she should just press the buzzer. If she turned back now, there was every possibility that she'd be caught. A car could drive up or someone could come out to check the mail, and find her hovering there. Explaining that would be worse than just ringing the damn bell.

That morning, for the second day in a row, Zoe had woken in a strange house. She'd barely slept a wink the night before. Right before she'd nodded off she'd received a text message from her mom saying she needed to stay in the hospital for a few more days. This worried Zoe, not only because it meant she couldn't go home, but also, what did it mean for her mom? Were things worse than she was letting on? This morning she'd remained holed up in her room until the last possible minute before she had to leave for school, eager to avoid any sort of family breakfast routine. Kate had knocked, but she seemed to accept that Zoe was not hungry and didn't force her to come down.

School had been as awful as she expected. It had been easy to avoid Emily—as she seemed to be doing her best to ignore Zoe. In fact, no one paid Zoe any attention. It was a relief, of course, but as always, somewhere deep down inside, it hurt. She didn't register on anyone's radar. What did that say about her?

Now, sweat bloomed under her arms. Idly she wondered what on earth she was doing here. She'd had every intention of canceling—making up an illness or injury—but as the school day went on, she realized her alternatives were as bad as going to Harry's. She could go there . . . or go to Kate's. She lifted her finger one more time and, before she could think better of it, pressed the button. A moment later the gate buzzed.

Harry's house was nearly as big as Kate's—with a sweeping path winding up to the front door. By the time Zoe made it to the double doors, a tiny girl with coils of blond hair stood in the open doorway. A grand staircase rose up behind her.

"Huwo."

The girl was maybe two or three, dressed in a ratty Tinker Bell costume and carrying a wooden spoon wrapped in a tea towel. She frowned as if Zoe's presence was highly inconvenient. "Tum in." She sighed. "You're about to miss da so."

"Um, what?" Zoe said.

"You're about to miss the show," Harry translated, jogging down the stairs in jeans, a gray T-shirt, and bare feet. His T-shirt showed off his torso—which was narrow but toned. Zoe felt a frisson of something deep down. Wow.

"The show?" Zoe said.

Harry scruffed the little girl's hair. "Actually, Maggie, Zoe is here to see me. We have homework."

"No!" The little girl's face morphed into pure fury. "You have to wats da so!" She launched herself at him, catching his upper arm.

"Dad?" Harry yelled, with Maggie hanging off his biceps. "Need some help here."

Zoe followed Harry through an archway into a living room that belonged in a design magazine. The floors were black, polished concrete, and art hung on every wall. On the white, streamlined couch was a man who looked exactly like Harry—except older. His right leg, in a cast, was stretched out in front of him, and the television was on. When he saw Zoe he became instantly animated.

"Well, hello there!" he said, his eyes darting to Harry. He tried to stand but then gestured at his leg and gave up. "I'm Leigh, Harry's dad. I'm not usually here during the day, but as you can see I'm recovering from knee surgery."

Zoe smiled at the floor, blushing. "Hi."

"Dad, this is Zoe," Harry said. "We've got homework. Please tell Maggie we don't have time to watch the show."

"No!" she screamed.

"I'll watch the show, Mags," Harry's dad said.

Maggie continued to scream, but Leigh wasn't listening, he was looking at Zoe. He seemed unexpectedly delighted to see her, which made no sense to Zoe. Surely Harry had people over all the time?

"So do you kids want to work in here or—"

"We'll go to my room," Harry said quickly, and before Zoe had time to protest, he was guiding her toward the staircase. Harry's room? She'd never been in a guy's room her entire life!

They walked to the top of the stairs in silence. So far Zoe had managed to avoid saying a word to Harry, but now the silence was deafening. Her palms became slick. *Say something!*

"So did you have your . . . appointment?" she blurted out. "After school?"

Harry blinked, surprised. "Oh. Yeah."

Zoe had hoped it would kick off some more conversation— he'd tell her that he'd been to the dentist and needed a retainer, or to the PT for an injury—but that appeared to be the end of that. Silence descended again. They walked past an enormous window and Zoe fantasized about diving out of it. At the same time, another part of her, a braver, more hormone-driven part, wanted to go into Harry's room.

"In here," Harry said when they reached a door at the end of the hallway.

Harry's room was as big as Zoe's apartment. Despite its size, it was plain and boyish and a little bit messy, with a desk and chair, and an unmade king-size bed against one wall.

"Make yourself comfortable," Harry said, easing himself onto the bed. Then he paused. "Sorry, did you want a drink or something?"

"No," Zoe murmured, though her throat was bone-dry. She sat on Harry's desk chair. "I'm good."

"Okay then," he said. He reached for his laptop on his bedside table and arranged it in his lap. "Where do we start?"

Zoe felt oddly distracted. Harry looked different like this, in his room. More relaxed or something. Maybe it was the T-shirt he was wearing? He looked really . . . hot. Really really hot.

"Zoe?"

"Oh, um . . ." She tried to gather her thoughts, but her brain was not complying. Harry and his newfound cuteness had thrown her off. The ridiculous thing was, she *knew* where to start. Last night, she had watched Emma Watson's UN speech about feminism. It was simple, uncomplicated—like most powerful speeches. It followed a standard sort of structure that by now Zoe was familiar with. Open with some anecdotes, delve into some history, perhaps a few statistics. Move on to the present and end, of course, with hopes for the future. It wasn't rocket science, at least the writing of it wasn't. So why couldn't she bring herself to speak?

She looked at Harry and then quickly away again. Had he always been this cute?

She felt him watching her. "Man, you *are* shy, aren't you? The closet is over there if you want to put your head in?"

"No," she said, her cheeks pooling with color.

Harry raised his eyebrows. *Really?* Clearly she wasn't fooling anyone. He frowned, thinking hard. It only made him look cuter.

"What if you closed your eyes? Would that help? Maggie gets freaked out at birthday parties that have kids' entertainers, but if she closes her eyes she really enjoys it."

Zoe thought she might actually die, right there in Harry's room. Harry would have to track down her mom, in the hospital, to give her the body.

"Okay, I'm not saying you're like a three-year-old," he said quickly. "I just saw a parallel. The point is, we need to do something. I can't do the debate without you—you're smarter than me! But we can't get to the smart, if we don't get rid of the shy."

He gave her wink, and Zoe fell in love with him just a tiny bit. Or at least enough to try closing her eyes.

"I guess I can . . . try it," she said. She closed her eyes.

"Cool," Harry said. "So where shall we start?"

For a moment all Zoe could think about was Harry's wink. But after a moment, she began to recall the Emma Watson speech.

"We need to open by introducing our argument," she said, "then offer some anecdotes, some history, and some statistics if we have any. Then we talk about the present and end with the future."

Zoe heard Harry's fingers on the keyboard—fast, urgent keystrokes.

"I think our argument should be centered around the fact that we are a country of equality," she said. "If students are called by their first names, why should teachers be different?"

"Good point," Harry said, typing faster.

"The second speaker is going to talk about how calling teachers by their first name promotes trust between teacher and student, which in turn, leads to students asking more questions and getting better outcomes. They will quote some direct studies to support this. And the third speaker will . . ."

The blackness against her eyes was like a cool compress to her self-doubt, and Zoe found herself able to think surprisingly well. Usually when she spoke in front of someone her entire consciousness was focused on herself, and more debilitatingly, what others were thinking about her. This time she was thinking about the debate. And funnily enough, she was thinking of things *other* than the debate. Like Harry. Although he was several paces away, she was hyperaware of his presence in the room. The tap of his fingers on the keyboard. His smell—deodorant and chewing gum. When he shifted on the bed, or reached for something, she could practically feel it. He paused occasionally to make the odd—usually good—point, but other than that, Zoe did most of the talking. After about forty-five minutes she heard the metallic thunk of the laptop closing.

She opened her eyes.

Harry was on the edge of his bed, his body a mirror to hers. Their knees faced each other, inches apart. Zoe wanted to look away, she *knew* she should, but somehow she couldn't. She felt something. A pulse. And she had the distinct feeling that Harry felt it too, because they both immediately dropped their gaze and began to fidget. And any reprieve she'd had from her anxiety vanished, just like that.

"Good job," he said, running a hand through his hair. "I think we're done."

Zoe's cheeks, judging by the heat in them, were fiery red. She was looking at a hangnail, so she didn't notice Harry reach out. He touched her flaming cheek. "Red," he said matter-of-factly.

"Yeah," she said in the same tone.

"So I guess you're *seriously* shy?"

She shrugged. "I guess I am."

"So why volunteer for the debate?"

Zoe hesitated. It wasn't that she didn't know, it was more that she didn't think Harry—or anyone—could possibly understand.

"Have you ever wanted to do something so badly but your body won't let you?" she said.

Harry was silent for a long time. "Actually I have." He gazed off, thinking deeply. "Sometimes you think if you want something bad enough, your body will *have* to go along with it."

"Exactly," she said. "But so far, for me . . . it's not working so well. My body has a mind of its own. The blushing. The sweating. The shyness. You know."

Harry stared at her for so long Zoe thought she might explode with mortification. "Well," he said. "I think it's cool that you're trying."

Zoe dropped her gaze, suddenly overwhelmed. "Oh wow," she said, looking at her watch, "is that the time? I've, um, really got to get going."

She stood, tripping over a shoe on the floor but catching herself before she fell flat on her face.

"Zoe—"

"Sorry, I'll see you at school," she said and bolted. But as she descended the stairs, amid all her feelings of horror and humiliation, she realized she actually felt pretty good.

32

Theo waved his hands theatrically in front of Sonja's face. "Sonja? Anybody home?"

"I was listening," Sonja said snippily. But she wasn't. She'd always thought team meetings were pointless. She felt for the clients of her colleagues, of course, but she didn't see how it was a good use of her time to be updated on ill people she had nothing to do with.

"Update on Alice Stanhope?" Theo prompted after a few seconds.

"Oh. Right. Well, she'll be released from the hospital tomorrow. She's refused Meals on Wheels, but her daughter will be back with her, so she won't be completely alone. I'll take her home and make sure she has everything she needs."

The truth was, Sonja was feeling guilty. She still wasn't sure what she could have done differently with regard to putting Zoe in foster care, but she had put her concerns to rest about Alice. Clearly Alice was a good mother. She certainly hadn't been responsible for the bruise on Zoe's face. The only thing Alice was guilty of was, perhaps, being a struggling single mother without much support.

"Will she be having further treatment?"

"Chemo, starting in a couple of weeks. I'll be in touch with her about transport. And I'll attend appointments with her as a support person."

"All right," Theo said, looking at the notepad in front of him. "That's it for updates. Now, the Donaldsons are having trouble understanding the costs for Tom's surgery. Can someone give them a call?" He glanced up. "Sonja?"

"I can do it," Dagmar said. Dagmar was fresh out of college and a little too keen for Sonja's liking. Always watching what everyone else was doing, and talking about "best practices." Sonja was tempted to let her call the Donaldsons, but it wouldn't look good in front of all these people, and Sonja understood all about keeping up appearances.

"It's okay," Sonja said, reaching for the file. "I'll do it."

The meeting ended with Theo delivering his mandatory speech about how they did a tough job and they all needed to support each other. Then, one by one, people filed out of the room.

Sonja remained where she was, flicking through the Donaldsons' file, though her mind was elsewhere. Everything ached. Her legs, her arms, her breasts. Her *mind*. She'd spent the whole night berating herself. What was wrong with her? Some women would probably love the unpredictability of sex with George. It was spontaneous. Exciting. Creative. Perhaps if she weren't such a frigid old bore, she would have thought so too.

The truth was, for years, she'd been waiting for George to leave her. Waiting for him to find a younger, fitter model. Someone who could match his libido. In a way it would be a relief, even if the shame would destroy her. The girls she went to school with—the ones who'd whispered about the new Range Rover she'd driven to the last reunion—would delight in the news of her abandonment. *Goes to show*, they'd say, nudging each other. *Money can't buy a good marriage.* (*Neither can poverty!* Sonja would point out, if they were ever brave enough to say it to her face.) Sonja had a brief longing for her sister, Agnes. Once, she would have been able to discuss this whole thing with her. But she'd shut Agnes out for too long. She had a feeling that ship had sailed.

Besides, for the most part George was a gentleman. That was what she loved the most—the gallantry. The times when he'd hold out her coat for her to slip her arms into. The times that he called her "darling." The nights spent on the couch watching *House of Cards* or *Breaking Bad*. Recently, after they'd watched the film *Midnight in Paris*, he'd looked at her with something resembling fondness and said, "Remember when we went to Paris? Why don't we do that again? Just hop on a plane?" They never did hop on a plane, but she took it as evidence that things could have been worse.

"Everything okay?"

Sonja hated herself for jumping when Dagmar appeared in the doorway.

"Oh," she said. "Sorry. Do you need the room?"

"No." Dagmar rolled over a wheelie chair and sat in it. "Actually I just wondered if you were okay. You seemed a bit distracted in the meeting."

Sonja frowned. "Did I?"

"What happened to your wrist?"

Sonja glanced at her wrist. It was sore, perhaps bruised from last night. She'd worn her wrist brace to cover it up. "Oh, you know . . . tennis."

"You're limping a bit today too," Dagmar said.

Sonja wanted to tell Dagmar to mind her own business. Instead she said, "Arthritis in my hip. You'll understand when you're old." She smiled.

"I'm probably overstepping," Dagmar guessed correctly. "But Theo was just saying we need to look out for each other. And I've been wondering."

"Wondering what?"

Dagmar shrugged, raising her eyebrows with an expression that said *You tell me.*

Sonja continued to look baffled, partly because it was the game, and partly because she *was* baffled. How old was Dagmar anyway? Twenty-one? Was she actually having this conversation with her?

"Sonja. You're constantly peppered with small injuries, you're jumpy and defensive, you're always distracted . . ."

"No, I'm not," she said. Was she? "You think I'm being *abused?*"

"*Are* you?"

"No!" Sonja laughed.

It *was* funny. Dagmar thought she was being abused. But Dagmar just gave her a surprisingly all-knowing look. "You know that if you need someone to talk to, it would stay between us. I can tell you about your options."

It was too ridiculous. They were the exact words Sonja used with clients who'd been hospitalized with injuries consistent with domestic violence. Sonja herself might have given Dagmar the verbiage when she started with them. Next she'd go into the "Abuse isn't always clear-cut" part.

"Abuse isn't always clear-cut, you know," Dagmar continued. "And there are lots of different kinds. Verbal abuse. Sexual abuse. Physical violence. Any way that someone controls you is abuse."

Sonja shook her head. But her mind caught on the words "sexual abuse." She'd recited the spiel so many times but she'd never really thought about it. *Sexual abuse.* What was that, exactly? Then again, what difference did it make? She wasn't one of those women who was admitted to the hospital with broken bones and black eyes (well, the broken wrist, but that had been an accident). She was simply submitting to her husband's advances. It wasn't as if she couldn't refuse. She *could,* any time she wanted.

It wasn't abuse.

Unfortunately she'd paused for too long. Dagmar looked victorious. "You're better off alone, Sonja. It might not feel like it now. He might have threatened you, told you he'd hurt you if you tried to leave, but if you want to, you *can* get away."

Sonja wanted to tell her that George hadn't threatened her. That the truth was, she didn't want to get away. She liked having a warm body beside her while she slept. She enjoyed the money— or at least, not having to worry about it. And his intelligence! When he delivered a keynote, people hung off his every word, and afterward people stood around, just trying to get close to him. That was the kind of presence he had. She liked being married to someone like that.

"If you're not ready to leave, there are still things you can do," Dagmar continued. "Reach out to friends and family so you know you're supported. Most victims of abuse wind up isolated— through their own or their partner's efforts. It's important that you remain connected to loved ones so you have options if you do decide to leave."

It was preposterous. Sonja wasn't going to leave George. Still, she thought about her family. When was the last time she called her sister, Agnes? More than a year ago, at least.

"And when things start to get ugly—make sure you speak up. Tell him you don't like what he's doing and if he continues, you will leave. Even if you won't leave *him*, you can leave the room or the house, if appropriate."

"I appreciate your concern, Dagmar. But George is not abusive. Honestly, you've got your wires crossed."

Dagmar's expression didn't so much as flicker. "At least document it, then. The wrist. The hip. Take photographs and e-mail them to someone you trust. Or to yourself. With dates and an outline of what happened. Then you'll have it. In case you ever need it."

Sonja opened her mouth to tell Dagmar, again, that she was wrong about what she was suggesting. But when they locked eyes something passed between them and then she didn't feel the need to say anything at all.

33

Kate was feeling resentful even before David walked in that evening. She couldn't help it. As she stirred the dinner she tried to talk herself out of it. *It's Jake's birthday*, she told herself. *Let's just have a nice evening.* She pictured her anger sitting in her belly, a bitter seed, and then imagined removing it with her hands and flinging it out to sea, like she'd been taught to do in a meditation class once. But even after flinging it, it continued to burn just as hot in the pit of her stomach.

The irony was, this was how new mothers seemed to feel. When her cousin Stella had her baby, Kate recalled her saying that she couldn't even look at her husband without wanting to punch him—something about his presence in the room just set her off. It was natural, Stella had explained, for new mothers to feel like this. It was the body's way of preventing another birth before it was ready. Kate suspected it had more to do with hormones and the sleep deprivation, but oh how Kate yearned for those hormones and that sleep deprivation. Being angry with her husband for giving her a child was far preferable to being angry with him for *not* giving her one.

"Hey," David said when he got home. He was home early from work, a quarter past six. "Is it just us?"

"For now," she said. She was wiping down the bench, not

meeting his eye. They were speaking civilly, like they always did, but there was an undercurrent. "Hilary, Jake, and Scarlett are on their way. Hilary is bringing a cake and I've made spaghetti Bolognese."

She was trying hard to be pleasant and it was uncomfortable and awful. Yet letting it out simply didn't feel like an option.

"That's really what he wants for his birthday dinner?"

"He's a man of simple tastes," Kate said. *Like his father,* she wanted to add, but it sounded too friendly, too conciliatory. And she was not feeling conciliatory.

She wasn't sure why she was so riled up. It hadn't been an unpleasant day. She'd spent the morning at the hospital and none of her patients had taken particularly bad turns. Even Alice seemed to be recovering well from the operation and should be discharged tomorrow. She'd spent the afternoon grocery shopping for Jake's birthday dinner. Usually Kate loved the suburban humdrum of grocery shopping. She even enjoyed family dinners. Jake and Scarlett were good kids (how could they not be, with parents like Hilary and David?), and when they all got together she always felt a strange sort of pride at how harmoniously their blended family worked. In the early days, when she, David, Hilary and Danny and the kids gathered around the dining room table, Kate had always imagined the high chair that would one day be pushed up against the table. The chubby face that would be covered in red sauce. The big brother and sister who would lovingly talk about how annoying their li'l bro or sis was. The "annoying" kid who would be the apple of the family's eye.

Kate had had such a clear picture of it all. And now that the image had been denied her, Kate felt cheated. It was, she realized, her own fault—marriage wasn't meant to be conditional. But hadn't she, during the last two years while she'd been playing the role of doting stepmother and new wife, been doing it on a silent promise of something to come? Hadn't she signed up for a life that she'd only be happy with if certain conditions were met? She must have, because now that she understood David's conviction that they should not have a child, she couldn't seem to summon that old affection for Hilary, Jake, and Scarlett. Instead, she found herself entertaining different thoughts. *Who are these strangers in my living room? These children who aren't my own, this motherly figure who was once married to my husband? What happened to the things I'd assumed would once be mine—the big belly, the Lamaze breathing, the fluffy toys? The child who at certain angles looked like me and at other angles looked like David's aunt Maude? What happened to that?*

"Zoe's staying again tonight," she said to him, stirring the sauce. "She had an assignment to work on with a friend after school, but she'll be here soon." Kate paused when he didn't say anything.

"Tonight? But it's Jake's birthday."

Kate turned around. "Her mom is staying in the hospital for one more night. I didn't know what else I could do." She watched his face. "I mean . . . is that all right?"

"I guess it has to be," he said finally.

David took the spoon from her. He began to lift it to his mouth, then appeared to think better of it and just stirred it instead. It was strange, feeling so awkward with the man who shared her bed.

"Zoe's a quiet kid, isn't she?" he said after a few seconds.

"She's shy," Kate said, oddly protective of her. "But she's a sweet girl." Kate took the spoon back. "I got a call from the clinic today." She paused, letting that sink in, or perhaps, psyching herself up. "We don't have any embryos left and they want to know if we were planning to do another stimulation cycle to harvest more eggs."

The silence that followed felt charged. Finally, a sigh. "I'd been clear on this, Kate."

"I thought I had, too," she replied.

David was silent, which was a good sign. He was a thinker. He would understand that it was unreasonable of him, making this decision unilaterally. He might still worry, but he'd have to reconsider it if he understood how important it was to her.

"Kate, I just feel like this would be . . . prolonging the pain," he said finally. "Haven't we already implanted three embryos? Now to start the stimulation cycle again from scratch? Do you really want to go through all that again?"

"Yes," she said.

David closed his eyes. "Well, I don't."

And that was it; they'd both finally come out and said it. Whoever said the truth was cathartic must never have been in their situation.

"So what do we do?" Kate said.

The question hung between them—a guillotine blade, ready to cleave them apart.

"Do you want us to, uh . . . come back?"

They both looked at the doorway, where Hilary, Danny, Jake, and Scarlett stood. A purple helium balloon with the number 17 on it bobbed above their heads.

David sprang into action first. "No, don't be silly. Come in, guys."

They stumbled into the room. It was hard to tell how much they'd heard, but from the way they were acting, they knew they'd walked in on an argument. Kate hustled to straighten up, to look nonchalant—everyone would be more comfortable if they covered it up, pretended it never happened. Kate knew the rules. At the same time she suddenly saw the utter ridiculousness of it.

"Yes, come in," Kate said, pasting on a giant smile. She stepped forward to hug Jake. "Happy birthday!"

34

Zoe sat in Kate and David's sunroom. She'd let herself in the back door when she'd found the front door locked. There had never been any discussion of a key and there was no way she was going to ring the bell—what if David or one of his kids had answered? She'd planned to creep into the kitchen, say a quick hi, and then rush up to her room, but then she heard the voices. Lots of them. There was some sort of gathering in the back room.

Now, she sat on a wicker chair, trapped. She had no intention of walking into a room full of strangers so instead she stayed put, thinking about Harry. Wishing she was back in that bedroom with him.

"Oh," Kate said, coming into the room. "Sorry. I didn't know you were home."

"I let myself in the back door," Zoe said. "Sorry, I should have—"

"No, it's fine. I should have given you a key." Kate pushed her hands back through her hair, uncharacteristically flustered. She wore skinny jeans with a white T-shirt, under a casual multicolored kimono. Zoe wondered if she put a lot of thought into what she wore or if it was just a talent of hers, looking effortlessly cool.

"I was just . . . taking a minute. It's Jake's birthday, we're having a gathering. Did you want to join us?"

"Thanks, but I'm okay."

Kate nodded slowly, perching on the arm of the wicker sofa. "Did you see your mother today?"

Zoe shook her head.

"She's doing better, Zoe. She'll be fine to come home tomorrow."

"Will she be in pain?" Zoe asked.

"She'll have to rest for a week or so," Kate said. "No heavy lifting. She should stay in bed, or on the couch."

"I'll download some Leo DiCaprio films," Zoe said. She thought of the time they'd watched *Gatsby* and her mom had actually moaned when Leo came onto the screen. "Mom loves Leo."

Kate smiled. "Who doesn't love Leo?"

Zoe shrugged. She didn't tell her that she thought Leo was old and a little wrinkly.

"So did you finish your assignment?" Kate asked her.

"I . . . think so."

"What's it about?"

"A debate. My side is arguing that we should call teachers by their first names. I'm the first speaker."

"You're a speaker?"

Kate's eyebrows shot up, which confirmed how ridiculous the whole thing was. She'd have to make something up. An illness or something. It wouldn't even be a lie. The whole idea was making her ill.

"Wow, well done you," Kate said. "I'm terrified of public speaking."

"You are?" For some reason this surprised Zoe.

"Uh-huh. I did a speech on my wedding day and I was so nervous I had three glasses of champagne right before. I forgot half of what I was going to say and then I hiccupped my way through the other half. It was a disaster. David still teases me about it."

"I'm scared of public speaking too," Zoe admitted.

"Oh. Are they making you do it?"

"Not exactly."

Kate nodded thoughtfully. "You know what I do when I'm scared of doing something? I just don't think about it. On our honeymoon, David really wanted to go bungee jumping. I told him I'd do it, because I wanted him to think I was fearless but the truth is, I was petrified." She laughed. "We jumped off a bridge in New Zealand and even as we walked up it I told myself we were just having a nice stroll."

Zoe laughed. In her world, nothing went unanalyzed. The idea of doing something terrifying without totally unpacking it, using affirmations, and psyching up for it first, just felt . . . impossible.

"Obviously you have to prepare for your debate," Kate said. "But maybe don't think about the fact that you have to deliver it just yet. Take it one step at a time. Write the debate. Practice it. But just tell yourself you're going to deliver it alone in your bedroom or something."

Zoe suddenly wondered if Kate *could* see through her. Was it *that* obvious she was a loser who did speeches in her room?

"Anyway," Kate said after a moment. "I'm sure you don't need advice from me."

"It's good advice," Zoe said.

Kate smiled. And for a few seconds, even in the silence, Zoe felt surprisingly comfortable. It wasn't like her to be comfortable in silence, or with a stranger.

"I like this room," Zoe said, finally, partly to fill the silence and partly because she *did* like the room. It was small, but with lots of windows and a view of the garden. It gave Zoe the feeling that she could see everything without anyone seeing her. "It's a good place to hang out . . . be by yourself, you know?"

"Yes," Kate said. "Well . . . I guess I'll leave you in peace, then."

"I didn't mean you had to leave," Zoe said quickly, exasperated with herself. She'd just had a nice conversation with Kate and it sounded like she was trying to kick her out. The irony was that, strange as it was, she wanted Kate to stay. "Sometimes I say things because I . . . I don't know what else to say . . . and my words just come out wrong."

Kate frowned. She focused on something off in the distance, like she'd just remembered something. "I'm sure you're not the only one who does that."

"Feels like it sometimes."

"I'll bet." Kate smiled, looking back at Zoe. "Well, I really do need to get back to dinner. Are you sure you won't join us?"

Zoe shook her head.

"Okay." She headed for the door, then paused and looked around, seeing the room as if for the first time. "You know what? This room *is* a good place to be by yourself."

Zoe smiled and Kate left the room. But when she was gone, Zoe realized that while it was a good place to be by herself . . . it was an even better place to be with someone else.

35

Alice was home, finally. Sonja insisted on seeing her up to her apartment, which Alice allowed, even if she was ignoring her entirely. Children and Family Services had confirmed this morning that she was a "fit" parent and Zoe would be returned to her today, no thanks to Sonja. Inside, Alice went straight to the window and pulled open the curtains. Sonja was carrying her bags, something Alice would have ordinarily refused, but she didn't today. Let her carry the bags.

"Kate will be here in ten minutes," Sonja said. "With Zoe. And your cat will be dropped off shortly. Can I get you anything?"

"No."

"I can stay for a while, if you like," she said. "We can go through your insurance papers. Or we could talk a little about how best to discuss this with Zoe."

It was almost as though Sonja didn't *want* to leave.

"I know how to discuss this with Zoe," she said, looking out the window. She added "Thank you," but it was more of a thank-you-very-much than a genuine thank-you.

"I was wondering about Zoe's father," Sonja said tentatively.

Alice spun to face her. Sonja actually took a step back. "Why were you wondering that?"

"Well, I just . . . I wondered if he could be of any help to you. Or Zoe?"

"No," Alice said. "He couldn't."

Sonja seemed to be contemplating whether to say anything more. For a social worker, she really did seem to be quite unsure of herself. "I understand that Zoe doesn't know who he is. I just wondered if that is a good idea. I mean . . . in case—"

"In case what?" Alice held her eye defiantly for a moment, and then she exhaled. "Zoe is better off alone than with him."

"All right, well, if you're sure—"

"I'm sure, Sonja. Good-bye."

Alice turned back to the window, but Sonja didn't leave right away. Even with her back to her, Alice could feel her there. For a moment Alice wondered if behind her strange immovable face, Sonja was more fragile than she seemed.

"Sonja, I—"

Alice turned around just as the door closed with a gentle click.

Alice was still standing at the window when the car pulled up. She waited for the door to fly open and Zoe to come tearing out of it. The car ride would have been excruciating for her. Alice had asked Sonja to organize a cab for her, but (of course) that was against the rules.

Zoe's door opened a crack but she stayed put in the car. Alice strained to see into the car. Zoe was looking at Kate, her head nodding, her mouth moving. *Talking.* Perhaps not starting a conversation but at least answering questions. It was . . . unexpected. Zoe barely talked to *Alice* when they were in the car! Seeing her talk to Kate, Alice felt a surge of pride, followed by another feeling that she couldn't quite define. But both those feelings were quickly forgotten when Zoe finally emerged from the car, locked Alice in her gaze, and began to run, full-pelt, up the stairs toward her.

———

Once, when Paul was drunk, he asked Alice if she ever resented Zoe for coming along and ruining her life. Zoe was three.

"You used to have a life," he slurred. "Friends. Prosperence." ("Prosperence," Alice decided, was a mash-up of "prospects" and "prosperous," so she didn't bother to correct him.)

She should, of course, have been outraged at the question—the very idea of asking a mother if she resented her child—but it was hard to invoke that sort of feeling about something Paul said, particularly when it was something so utterly laughable.

The truth was, Alice herself had been unprepared for how much she would love Zoe. She liked kids well enough, admired their honesty, among other traits. But she hadn't understood the way she'd become addicted to Zoe's smell, the feeling of her nestled against her hip, the way she would call spaghetti "sketetti." Most of all, she didn't understand how addicted she'd become to the way Zoe *loved her*. Sometimes Alice wondered if she liked that a little too much. Sometimes she wondered if Zoe had ruined her life, or if it was the other way around.

A week after being released from the hospital, Alice sat on the couch, leafing through her mail, while Zoe sat on the floor, folding laundry. In some ways it felt as if nothing had changed. Apart from the great wound on Alice's belly, and a diary full of chemo dates, things had effectively returned to normal.

Zoe looked up at her, holding a white shirt.

"Kate has a shirt like this," she announced.

"How nice," Alice said, trying for a smile. In the past week Zoe must have mentioned Kate's name a dozen times. Not a ridiculous amount, Alice conceded, but a lot for Zoe.

Kate did a speech at her wedding and got the hiccups.

Kate has a little sunroom that's nice to sit in.

Kate has a giant house.

Kate. Such a pretty, inoffensive name, and Alice was starting to find it quite irritating.

"It would look really good with a chunky necklace," Zoe said, "or with a sweater over the top, you know, layered?"

"It would," Alice agreed. She wanted to add that she wore layers all the time. That Kate didn't actually invent layering. But that would have sounded mean-spirited. Alice was relieved when there was a sudden knock at the door, so they could finally stop talking about *Kate*.

"It'll be Dulcie," Alice said, shifting forward in her seat. "Give me a pull to standing, would you, Mouse?"

Alice reached out her arms, but Zoe beat her to it, heaving herself off the floor in a flash. "I'll get it."

Alice was stunned into silence. Zoe *never* answered the door. Even now she didn't look entirely comfortable. Her hands shook and her cheeks were already flaming. But she was crossing the living room and wrenching open the door. Was she dreaming?

"Oh, it's you," came Dulcie's voice. "Here, my grocery list. And tell your mother I don't want the generic brand of canned tomatoes. But not the fancy ones either, too expensive. I like the ones with the yellow label and—"

"Actually," Zoe said, her voice wavering slightly. "My mom isn't well. She's been in the hospital. She can't even do her own grocery shopping, let alone anyone else's."

There was a pause.

"Well, what am I supposed to do?" Dulcie said.

"You could go yourself," Zoe suggested. "Or you could pay the grocery store to deliver. Or you can leave your list with me and I will do it when I can. But right now I'm looking after my mother."

"When you *can*? But I need these things—"

"You heard your options. Push it under the door if you want me to do it. Bye, Dulcie."

Zoe closed the door.

"Did you . . . did you actually just do that?" Alice said.

Zoe blinked as if she couldn't quite believe it herself.

"What just happened there?" Alice said.

A little smile started. "I just didn't think about it," Zoe said. "That's what Kate does, when something scares her."

Alice could actually feel her daughter's sense of accomplishment radiating from her.

"Cool," Alice said, giving her a high five. At the same time, she conjured up an image of Kate's pretty face in her mind and then imagined slapping it.

36

Zoe was going to debate practice. Or maybe she wasn't. She hadn't decided yet. The debate was in a week. Their team had organized an after-school meeting to "practice" their debate, but from what Zoe could tell, it was actually to "write" the debate, because except for her and Harry, no one had actually done it.

Apart from in class, she hadn't seen Harry all week. For some reason, she found herself avoiding him. At lunchtime she sat outside, alone. In class she kept her head down. Once she'd even ducked into the restroom when she'd noticed him coming down the corridor toward her. It wasn't that she didn't want to see him. The problem was, she had absolutely no idea what to say when she did see him. She couldn't flirt, that was for sure. She could barely be around him without blushing. And so, she decided, it was better not to see him at all.

Now she stood at her locker, clutching her index cards. The meeting had started twenty-four minutes ago, and for the past twenty-four minutes Zoe had stood with her head in her locker, frozen with indecision. The stupid thing was, she *wanted* to go to the meeting. She *wanted* to be part of the debate. She just wanted to go as an invisible person.

She took her bag out of her locker and walked toward the

gates. This was ridiculous. She was going home. But at the last minute, as if tricking herself, she took a sharp left into the classroom where the meeting was being held.

Eric stood at a laptop while people talked over one another. A few people looked up when she walked in, then quickly down again. Harry stood at the back. Just like that, Zoe's breath disappeared. She turned, ready to duck out again, pretend she'd taken a wrong turn.

"Hey, Zoe."

She froze in the doorway, then turned back. It was Ella Brennan. Zoe didn't even know that Ella knew her name.

"Hey," she said, so quietly that even *she* couldn't hear it. She walked a little closer to the group, feeling Harry's eyes. Being in the *same room* with him sent tingles up and down her body. Not the tingles of discomfort she usually had around people. A different kind.

"So," Eric said to the group. "What are we going to close with?"

A few people called out ideas, most of them juvenile. The rest talked among themselves or thumbed their iPhones. Clearly the group had lost their mojo.

Eric struggled to get the group's attention. "*Guys?* Come on! We need a closing!"

Jim yawned. Ella put her phone away, but looked unenthused. Everyone else shuffled uncomfortably. Zoe stood on tiptoe, trying to get a look at the laptop. She scanned the notes that had already been taken. When no one else offered anything else, she took a deep breath.

"We could close by appealing to the teachers," she said in a small voice. "Focus on how they must feel, being the 'Mr.' and 'Mrs.' all the time. I mean . . . surely they'd prefer to be humanized by being called by their first name?"

A few people turned to see who was talking. Zoe tried to shrink down, make herself smaller.

"Good idea," Eric said. "The other team won't think of getting the teachers on their side. And Mrs. Patterson is choosing the winner. We want to get her on our side."

Zoe felt so pleased she forgot not to look at Harry. He was already looking at her, smiling a little. Any breath she had left was suddenly gone.

"Anything else, Zoe?"

She jumped at her name. Her hands were shaking so much she had to clasp them together. "Um . . . well, we can talk about how teachers are people," she suggested. "You know . . . their parents took the time to give them a name and stuff. So we should use it."

"Wait," Jim exclaimed. "Teachers are *people*?"

A few people laughed but Eric rolled his eyes and kept typing furiously. Zoe could feel the heat in her face, the sweat beading on her forehead. But it occurred to her that, in this instance, it might just be worth it.

When Eric finished typing he turned to Zoe, his palm in the air. It took Zoe a moment to realize he was looking for a high five. She obliged, seconds after she should have, feeling ridiculous.

Afterward, out in the hallway, Harry fell into step beside her. Zoe tried to speed up, but there was no getting away from him. Finally she focused on walking in a straight line, which as it turned out, did require her concentration.

"So where've you been these last few days?" he asked, halfway down the corridor.

"Why?" Zoe said. "Were you looking for me?"

She didn't mean it to be cute or sassy (when had she ever been either?) but, by some miracle, it came out that way. Harry responded with a satisfying burst of laughter. Then he flicked her a sideways glance. "I *was* looking for you," he said. "Just so you know."

Zoe's heart was racing even before the double doors swung open, and giant bodies filled the room. The football team. They seemed to fill the entire corridor, many of them high-fiving Harry as they went. Zoe shrank down and moved as far as she could toward one wall. In an instant she wanted to be invisible again.

"Hey, Harry."

"Missing you out there, man."

"How's the knee?"

"Not bad," Harry replied. "Good practice?"

There were a few more high fives and then the guys disappeared into the locker room, leaving nothing but a faint scent of body odor behind. Harry, she noticed, looked a little wistful.

And then, they were alone again.

"So . . . what happened to your knee?" Zoe asked shyly.

"Can you keep a secret?" he asked her.

Zoe nodded dumbly.

"Nothing."

Zoe blinked. "What the heck does that mean?"

They'd reached the door now, and Harry pushed it open and stood with his back to it. As Zoe slipped past him, he grinned. "Why don't you try to figure that out while I walk you home."

"Sure," Zoe heard herself say, to her utter surprise. And as they headed down the steps together, side by side, Zoe felt almost like a normal teenager.

37

Preparing to have chemotherapy, as it turned out, was like preparing for a wedding (or what Alice had heard about it), jam-packed with appointments. Except instead of having spa appointments for spray tans and leg waxes, Alice had medical appointments. A few days ago, she'd had her PICC line put in—a tube that would remain in her arm for the next few months, making it easy for them to attach the IV during chemo. She'd visited her dentist to check her teeth for signs of infection. She'd undergone blood tests. Everything looked good. So today, three weeks after her surgery, was the day.

When she heard a knock on the door, she looked at her watch. Sonja was early. She was driving Alice to chemo today. Alice was less than enthusiastic about the idea, but she didn't have a lot of other options.

She dropped her feet onto the ground leisurely. Let Sonja wait. But before she was even out of her chair, there was another knock, and then a voice called out, "Alice? Are you there?"

Alice suspected she was hearing things—a side effect of the cancer perhaps. Still, she called out uncertainly, "Paul?"

"Yeah, it's me."

She opened the door and stared at him.

"I'm sober," he said. "I can't promise about tomorrow, but today I'm here to help, for as long as you need me."

Alice looked at his clean clothes, his wet hair. He looked almost like a . . . caring family member. "Seriously?"

He nodded. "I'm sorry I haven't been here earlier. But I'm here now."

Tears built treacherously in Alice's eyes. "So you are."

"Well," Paul said. "What can I do?"

Alice thought for a moment. "Do you . . . still have a driver's license?"

"Miraculously, I do."

It was, indeed, a miracle. Alice smiled at the thought of calling Sonja to tell her that she would not be required to drive her to chemo. Then she grabbed her keys off the hook in the kitchen and tossed them at Paul. They fell to the floor with a clatter. Alice prayed it wasn't an omen.

"Pick those up," she said, grabbing her purse. "You're taking me to chemo."

Paul double-parked in front of the outpatients' area. As Alice was getting out, she noticed Kate out in front of the building in her uniform and sneakers.

"Good morning," she said.

Alice stared at her. "Do you meet everyone outside?"

"No," she admitted. "But on the first day of chemo, I try."

Alice felt irrationally annoyed that Kate was giving her no reason to hate her.

Kate looked over at Paul, still behind the wheel, with a painful look of optimism. "Is this—"

"My brother," Alice said. "Paul. He's going to park the car and meet us up there." She nodded at Paul and he drove away. She wondered if she'd see him again today. Doubtful, she decided.

"Okay," Kate said. "Let's go."

They entered the hospital side by side. On the way, Kate's phone rang but she immediately silenced it. It was as though Alice were the only person in the world. No wonder Zoe liked her so much.

When they arrived in oncology they stopped briefly at a desk for Kate to grab some documents and Alice surveyed the waiting area. A group of three women in their fifties or sixties—sisters perhaps—giggled quietly. A young girl, probably no older than twenty-five, lay with her bald head in (what must have been) her mother's lap. A blond woman flicked through a magazine while her husband dozed beside her.

After a moment Kate appeared with a folder and steered Alice to a large communal room at the end of the corridor. Along each wall was a row of beige vinyl armchairs of which about half were occupied. Green curtains hung open between each chair. Support people sat beside their charges, reading magazines or talking to nurses, while the patients stared at iPads or portable DVD players. Alice watched a bosomy nurse theatrically sneak some cookies to the husband of a patient.

"These are the fancy ones," she whispered, loud enough for the whole room to hear. "They're s'posed to be for patients only. Don't tell anyone or I'll lose my job."

"This is you," Kate said, leading her into the far corner. Alice was grateful to be tucked away. There was something about being in this big long room alone that made her feel exposed.

"The nurse will come over soon. She will attach the IV to your PICC line and start with some saline solution. Then, once your chemo cocktail arrives from the pharmacy, she'll start that. You might start to feel tired, maybe a bit woozy. Make sure you tell your nurse if you're feeling faint, nauseated, or tingly."

"And then what?" Alice asked.

"And then the fun part." Kate held up an iPad. "I've put some movies on here for you. *Titanic. Gatsby. Romeo and Juliet. The Wolf of Wall Street.*"

Alice stared at her. "But . . . how did you—"

"Zoe told me." She smiled, then added, "Who doesn't love Leo?"

Alice wondered why this sweet gesture suddenly sat like a bad prawn in her belly.

"Oh, and I'll take that," she said, swiping Alice's phone from her hand. She tucked it into her pocket. "You can have it back when you're done."

"Are phones not allowed?"

"Well, they are. But I want you and Leo to have a good time. And patients report they are far more relaxed if they're not checking their phone every five minutes."

"But what if Zoe—"

"I'll answer it. If it's important, I'll bring it to you," Kate said, dumping the iPad in Alice's lap. "Watch Leo. Iris will be here to hook you up in just a minute." The nurse who had handed over the contraband cookies turned and waved at the sound of her name. "You'll love Iris," Kate said. "She's everyone's favorite. And I'll be back to check on you throughout the morning."

"You're leaving?" Alice said, suddenly vaguely panicked.

"Just going to my office at the end of the hall. If you need me, you tell Iris, I'll come right back."

Alice suddenly felt very small in her large leather chair, waiting for poison to be intravenously tubed into her bloodstream. Kate paused and came back to her side. "You know what? Why don't I wait awhile?"

Alice wanted to tell her *No, it's fine, you go on back to work.* Instead she smiled and accepted the offer from the woman that she wanted so much to hate.

Once Alice was attached to the IV, Kate returned to work and Alice started thumbing over her iPad. Then she noticed Paul squeaking across the large room toward her.

"You're back!" she exclaimed.

"Of course." He was swaying a little. "How are you feeling?"

"Not bad. No nausea yet." Alice sniffed the air. Paul smelled of some kind of spirit—bourbon or maybe whiskey. "Paul. Are you drunk?"

"No. I mean . . ." He looked guilty. "A little."

"Why did you come back here?" she asked. "It's not like you'll be able to drive me home in your state."

"No," he agreed. "But I ran out of money and didn't have anywhere else to go. And I thought you might like someone to talk to while you had your treatment."

Alice stared at him. She and Paul had been close once, but since he'd discovered alcohol, their relationship had fizzled to the odd phone call for money or visit to drop off food. The idea of making small talk with him—while he was drunk—was oddly unsettling.

"Um," she said finally. "Well, what did you want to talk about?"

Paul looked pleasantly surprised—clearly he'd expected to be thrown out. He glanced behind him and located a chair, which he pulled up to Alice's.

"Whatever you want," he said.

It was a nice gesture, leaving it to her, but it was too broad, and she didn't have the brain capacity right now to narrow it down. "You decide," she said.

"All right," he said. "There *is* something I've always wondered about."

This should be interesting, Alice thought. She'd never thought Paul wondered about anything, these days, other than alcohol. "Go on."

"It's just," he continued. "You never did tell me who Zoe's father was."

Right at that moment, Alice had her first wave of nausea.

38

am calm, confident, and in control. I am calm, confident, and in control. I am calm, confident, and in control. Zoe silently recited the affirmations on the stage while her legs bounced under the table. She felt a thousand eyes on her (even though there were probably only twenty-five people in the room), but none of them were Harry's. Beads of sweat ran from her armpits down her sides. Where *was* he?

Since last week, they'd made some progress in their unconventional friendship. She still tried to duck away when she saw him coming in the corridor, but she'd always hoped he'd catch her first, and he usually did. Conversation was still mortifying, but Harry did most of the talking. Whenever they were in close quarters Zoe felt an almost exquisite agony—like she'd die if he took even a step back from her, and she'd die if he didn't. Sometimes, when she caught Harry looking at her, she'd allow herself to wonder if he felt the same way, but she knew that was just her own wishful thinking. Once, when Mr. Bahr called on her in class and she was disintegrating under the spotlight, Harry leaned so far back in his chair he fell backward and the entire class cracked up laughing . . . at him instead of her. For the first time in ages she felt like someone knew she existed. More than that, someone *cared*. She still had no idea why he was pretending to have a knee injury, but she liked the feeling that they were sharing some kind of secret.

Yesterday the whole debate team had gone to the library to have one last practice of the debate. Zoe was so nervous she couldn't even return Harry's smile when she walked in. Later, when she read from her index cards, she barely lifted her head, but she managed to croak out the speech. Even she couldn't deny the victory in that.

Afterward Harry said to her, "You were awesome."

"We're going to be graded on eye contact," she replied dryly.

He thought for a moment. "So just look at me."

It was beyond weird that she thought that might work.

"It will be fine," he said. "You can do it."

It was a new feeling, having someone believe in her. Her mom did, of course, but that was different. Her mom believed in her because the idea of Zoe being humiliated was too painful for her to consider. But Harry, he believed because he actually thought she was good. Her team was *relying* on her. There was something about that. Something hard to refuse.

There were seven of them onstage now, six speakers and the adjudicator, and the rest of the class was in the audience. Zoe focused on the back wall like she'd planned, pretending she was there all alone, but every now and then she glanced into the faces, looking for Harry's. Still no sign of him.

"Okay, class, welcome to our debate," said Jim, who was the adjudicator. A burst of adrenaline shot through Zoe. "The topic is 'Should we call teachers by their first names?' Can I have one person from each team come up and introduce each team member please?"

As each team member was introduced, Zoe scanned the rows again for Harry. He wasn't there. Zoe's skin began to prickle. He was supposed to be introducing her!

"Harry?" Jim said, scanning the rows as Zoe had just done.

Everyone looked around. Finally Jim looked at her. "Where's Harry?"

She must have mumbled something like "I don't know" or maybe just said nothing at all, because Jim turned away from her and looked at Mrs. Patterson. "What should we do?"

"Can someone else from the team introduce Zoe?" she asked.

Eric jumped up and introduced her without so much as a blush or a moment's hesitation. Every other introduction was just as fluid, just as fast. And then introductions were over and they were all sitting down again.

"And now," Jim said, "I'd like to invite our first speaker for the affirmative, Zoe Stanhope, to please take the floor!"

There was clapping, and Zoe's heartbeat started to thrum in her ears. She stared at the door, waiting for Harry to come flying in, apologizing for being late. But the doors remained closed. The clapping died down and the class looked at her, all of them expectant. Zoe tried to push her chair back but her feet didn't seem to work properly. Potential disasters popped into her mind, one after the other. What if her skirt was hitched into her underwear? What if she blushed? What if she panicked? A tingle started around her chest and suddenly her bladder felt full.

I am calm, confident, and in control. I am calm, confident, and in control.

She managed to hoist herself into a standing position, but stayed where she was, behind the desk. "Uh . . ." she started, into the cavernous room. "Thank you all for being here today . . . students, and um . . . Mrs. . . ." Her mind went blank. What was her teacher's name again? She looked down at her cards, but her neatly printed handwriting was suddenly blurry. "May I begin by . . . ," she started from memory, and then a card dropped from her shaking hands. "Whoops," she said, squatting to pick it up. She dropped another. Her face burned red. Why had she agreed to do a debate? Was she crazy? From a squatting position, Zoe glanced around, catching Mrs. Patterson's eye, noting a faint sense of worry on her face.

The silence in the room was loud. So loud.

She stood again. In the crowd, she saw Emily, her expression unreadable. No one else could meet her gaze. Someone coughed, then someone else. Zoe's breath started to be sucked from her lungs. She knew she should speak—saying something was still a hell of a lot better than saying nothing—but nothing would come and all she could think was that she couldn't breathe and that she really needed to pee. She closed her eyes, but then all she could think was that now she was a freak with her eyes closed. So she opened them, her knees pressing together, her face pinched and hot, trying not to cry. Trying to breathe.

Finally Mrs. Patterson spoke: "Zoe, do you need a break? Maybe we can start with the . . ."

The door suddenly burst open and there he was. Harry. He did a quick scan of the room and then his eyes locked on her. She saw him register the scene and the reflected panic in his face. She'd seen the same look on her mother's face so many times before. But this time it was worse. Because it wasn't her mother. And because this time her bladder chose that moment to release, all over the floor.

39

Alice wasn't sure why she decided to tell Paul the truth. Perhaps it was the fact that he was toasted and likely to forget anyway? Or perhaps it was the fact that she'd always wanted to tell someone? Perhaps it was the fact that they didn't have anything else to talk about? But for some reason, as she was hooked up to an IV line feeding poison directly into her bloodstream, Alice started to talk.

"Remember," she said, "when I decided I wanted to be a therapist?"

"Rings a bell," Paul said, though she suspected it didn't. The truth was, it was just one in a line of professions that she'd been certain were the career for her. Journalist, PR professional, nanny. Back then, everyone told her she was a "people person." So why not help people, she'd thought, and found herself a job as a receptionist at a psychology clinic, to see what it was all about.

Alice's new boss, Dr. Sanders, was in his mid-forties. Good-looking, for an oldie, with an air of authority that Alice had never encountered before. It hadn't taken Alice long to realize that Dr. Sanders was a superstar. He was revered all over the country for expertise in adolescent psychology—he had published two books on the subject and was a regular on TV as a consulting psychologist. The phones rang hot, wanting him to give keynote presentations at conferences or seminars. Clients came out of his office smiling—kids who, Alice knew, had suffered sexual assaults, loss of parents, debilitating mental illnesses. Parents phoned up daily, so desperate for a session with him they were willing to wait a year for any appointment.

Alice worked hard for Dr. Sanders. He was an old-school kind of boss, never made his own coffee, never typed up his own notes. Everyone in the office called him "Dr. Sanders." He commanded a certain respect.

Alice wasn't sure when she started trying to impress him, but it didn't take long before she started going above and beyond the call of duty of a receptionist. Once, after he mentioned he liked his coffee from a certain coffeehouse on the other side of town, she made a special trip on a Saturday to pick up a jar for the office. She'd work Saturday morning if he asked her to, because the part-timers, according to him, had no idea what they were doing. It was addictive, the way he looked at her. That look of gratitude when she'd fielded a call for him—making elaborate excuses when his mother, aunt, or sister called. No wife ever called, at least not when Alice answered. He didn't talk about personal things at work, but Alice noticed he didn't wear a ring.

She did think about him sometimes. It wasn't that she had a crush on him, exactly—he was too old for that. But occasionally, she wondered what it would be like to be with him. It was like wondering what it would be like to be a housewife in the 1800s—she was fairly certain she wouldn't like it, but she wondered all the same. It was his calm, powerful nature, she supposed, that got her wondering.

One night, right as Alice was leaving the office for the evening, he called. He'd headed home an hour or so earlier to prepare for an interstate conference the next day and had left some documents at the office. It was too late to book a courier.

"Would you like me to drop them to you?" she'd said.

"I wouldn't want to trouble you," he said. He always said things like that.

"I insist," she assured him. "I'm on my way."

The truth was, she was being nosy. Someone like Dr. Sanders was bound to have a fabulous house. And Alice was naturally curious.

He was on the phone when he answered the door and he ushered her inside. Alice hadn't expected to be invited in and she felt a little thrill as she stepped across the threshold into the vast home. She followed him across a parquet floor into a paneled living room, glancing around wildly to check the place out. He gestured for her to sit, then wandered off, the phone still pressed to his ear. Alice glanced at the open bottle of red wine on the table. There were two glasses there, one of them clean. Was it for her? Surely not. Maybe he was expecting company? A date?

"Sorry about that," he said a moment later, putting his phone onto the coffee table. He looked at the untouched glass, then at her. "You're not having a drink?"

"Oh, I . . . I wasn't sure it was for me," she said, suddenly self-conscious.

"Who else would it be for?" he said.

Alice shrugged as he picked up the bottle. For the next few moments the glug of wine leaving the bottle was deafening in the silence, and it might have been the sheer awkwardness of it but Alice felt a sudden urge to flee.

"Can I ask you something, Alice?" Dr. Sanders asked, sitting down next to her and handing her the glass. He twisted his body to face hers, his elbow resting casually against the cushions.

"Uh . . . sure."

"Do you enjoy working for me?"

"Yes," she said uncertainly. "Of course. It's a great job."

"What do you see for the future?"

Suddenly Alice understood. It was a performance review, of sorts. The realization relaxed her a little.

"Well, since you've brought it up," she said, "I've been thinking more and more that I might like to become a therapist."

He smiled. "I think you'd make a wonderful therapist. But I was actually asking what you see for the future personally, not professionally."

"Oh." She felt suddenly on guard again. She didn't expect to have this kind of discussion with Dr. Sanders. "Well, you know . . . I hope I'll get married one day. Have children."

"The usual."

"It's not very original, I guess," she admitted.

"Perhaps not. But I suspect there's a reason everyone wants to do it."

The silence stretched on. Alice took a gulp of wine. She waited for Dr. Sanders to say something, but he didn't. His expression was unfamiliar, and a little unsettling.

"What about you?" she asked finally. "Would you like to have a family . . . or, I mean, do you already have one?"

"Not yet," he said. "But I'm hoping I'll be a late starter. I'd like to have a family one day, very much. I just have to meet the right woman."

They'd edged into strange territory now, and Alice's urge to flee intensified. So when Dr. Sanders leaned forward and took her glass to put it on the coffee table, Alice felt relieved. She assumed that he was going to thank her again for coming and wish her good night. But then she saw something different in his eyes. She only had a second to register it, before he touched her face and pressed his lips—all dry and whiskery and passionless—up against hers.

She reared back. "Whoa!" She didn't know what else to say. The horror must have been evident on her face.

Dr. Sanders remained silent. But his face, Alice noticed, had changed. His eyes grew narrow. His lip curled. Alice should have stood then, but his hands were still on her face. Were they gripping slightly tighter than before? Whatever it was, Alice felt like something had changed. It was like she'd been . . . pinned in place.

"I should go," she said, but there was uncertainty in her voice. She had an instinct to make a run for it, but it was too ridiculous. She didn't need to run from Dr. Sanders. She'd look like an idiot.

His face was still mean. "Why did you come here?" he said quietly.

Alice tried to remember. It took far too long to draw up the memory. "I . . . to drop off your documents."

"No," he said. "Why did you come here?"

Something about the way he asked made her question herself. Had she come here for another reason?

"I . . . I don't know," she said helplessly.

"Yes, you do." His grip tightened on her jaw. "You do."

The next thing she knew, Alice was on the floor, trapped by his weight. He let go of her face and took her two hands in his one, holding them high above her head. "Dr. Sanders," she rasped. "Please."

It was nonsensical, but she was still holding on to one last shred of hope that it was some kind of joke. It was cleared up when he hit her, once, across the face.

"You know why you came here," he said, his voice different somehow.

She started to cry. "Please," she said, her voice no more than a breath. "No."

There was a strange absence to his eyes. As he wrenched up her skirt she wanted to scream, but she couldn't summon the breath.

Afterward he seemed, not apologetic exactly, but concerned. He handed her her underwear. She was still wearing the rest of her clothes, though her shirt and bra had been pushed up to her neck and her skirt was around her waist. She tugged everything down. She was still wearing her shoes.

"Are you all right?" he asked.

For some reason she couldn't fathom, Dr. Sanders seemed interested in her response.

"Yes," she said, the biggest lie of her life. "Can I . . . can I go?"

"Of course," he said, moving out of the way. "See you at work."

She saw something in his eyes then, and that's when she realized how crazy he actually was. He actually expected that he would see her at work. But he didn't.

Dr. Sanders never saw her again.

Paul, remarkably, was still awake when Alice finished recounting the tale. And he looked comfortingly horrified. "That fucking . . ." His face contorted. "I'll kill him."

"That'd be great."

"Jesus," he said. "I thought that the guy cheated on you or was married or something. Not *that*."

The surprising part about it was that Dr. Sanders had pursued Alice. She'd assumed he'd be thrilled when she disappeared from his life—making it easier to pretend it never happened. But when she didn't show up at work the next day, he'd called and left a message for her. And he continued to call for the next three days while he was out of town. Alice became so anxious about it, she'd got a new number. Then it occurred to her that he'd have her home address in the company records.

"I packed up my apartment, moved in with Mom and Dad," she said.

"That was then?"

It had been a dark time. Her mom had just been diagnosed with cancer—and Alice had told them she was moving home to be closer to her. Her parents had thought it was out of the blue.

"What happened to the job?" her dad had asked.

"I quit," she'd said. "You were right. It wasn't for me."

Her parents had been skeptical but they assumed, as Paul obviously had, that it was over a boy. A heartbreak. Something that she would recover from, given time.

For months Alice replayed the evening—and all the months leading up to it—on a loop, wondering what she might have done differently. Wondering what her role had been. And worrying that she would run into him. She worried so much she made herself sick. She gained weight. Her periods stopped.

Later than she should have, she realized why.

And then . . . her mother died. The funny thing was, if not for that she might have terminated the pregnancy. But there was something about losing her mother that made her want to hold onto the life she had inside her. It was almost as if her mother's death had assured Zoe's life.

A few months later when her great-gran needed a carer, it felt like the perfect solution. She could get out of San Francisco. She wouldn't have to worry about running into Dr. Sanders whenever she left the house. She could start over, with her baby.

Which is exactly what she did.

40

David had made lunch reservations. It had been forever since he'd done that. He used to do it all the time in the early days, when the prospect of getting through the entire workday without seeing each other was simply too difficult. The funny thing was, until recently Kate had *still* found it hard getting through the day without David. Every night when she arrived home she automatically quickened her pace, already anticipating the sight of him—at the grill in shorts or helping Scarlett with her homework at the dining room table. Unfortunately it had been weeks since she'd felt this sort of anticipation. So when he'd suggested lunch, she'd been cautiously optimistic. Perhaps things were turning around? Maybe he'd even reconsidered things on the baby front?

She was putting on her coat before heading out to meet him when her phone started ringing. Actually, not her phone. Alice's.

"Alice Stanhope's phone, this is Kate speaking."

"Oh uh . . . hello. This is Rosalie Hunt, Zoe's school principal. May I speak to Alice?"

Kate hesitated. Alice was probably just getting into her first movie. She didn't like the idea of disturbing her if she didn't have to.

"I'm sorry, she's not available right now. Can I help you?"

There was a short silence. "Who am I speaking with?"

"Kate Littleton. I'm a . . . family friend."

"Well . . . this is a little awkward. I really do need Alice down at the school right away. It's quite urgent."

"Is it Zoe?" Kate asked. Her heart had quickened a little. "The reason I have Alice's phone is in case anything came up about Zoe."

"Well unfortunately something *has* come up. Zoe has had an . . . incident at school today. And she appears to have left the school premises."

"She ran away?"

"We just can't locate her right now. But if we don't find her soon, we'll have to contact the police. Is Alice able to come down?"

"Unfortunately not." Kate looked at her watch. "Not for a few hours, at least."

"I see. Well, is there someone else who can help? Anyone who knows Zoe, who might know where to find her? I'm afraid we're a little bit stumped."

Kate imagined Zoe's horror if the police were involved. "I can come down," she heard herself say.

"Thank you," she said, sounding relieved. "Come right to my office. I'll see you soon."

Kate had no idea where to find Zoe, but at least there'd be someone there waiting for her if she did turn up. The idea that no one would be there for the girl after her . . . incident, whatever it was, was just too much for Kate to bear.

Kate briefly considered telling Alice, but decided against it. She had at least two hours of chemo left and the last thing she needed was to be strapped to her chair worrying about her daughter that whole time. And who knew, maybe Kate could sort the whole thing out and she'd never have to know? She drove like a fiend to the school, parking illegally right out front.

Now she sat in the principal's office.

"Thank you for coming down. I'm Rosalie Hunt."

"What happened?" Kate asked.

"Zoe's class had a debate this morning."

"Zoe told me about it," Kate said. "She was quite nervous."

"Apparently so. She's not typically one to take part in this sort of thing, so her teacher was thrilled that she volunteered for a big role. She appeared to be doing well with it, attending group meetings, and she turned in a stellar written portion. But once she got in front of the room, Zoe froze. Couldn't find her words." Rosalie exhaled, long and slow, through her nose. "It seems she had some sort of panic attack. And then, well, she . . . urinated on the floor."

Kate's hands found her cheeks. "No."

"Obviously we're very concerned. I don't suppose you'd have any idea where she might have gone?"

"None. But . . . I'll find her."

"If you do I'd suggest taking Zoe home right after so she doesn't have to run into any of the students. And then . . . probably a few days at home would be best."

"Yes. Yes. Of course."

"Students do recover from these kinds of things, but it won't feel like it for Zoe. Make sure you—"

Kate didn't hear the rest. She was already on her way out the door.

41

t didn't take Kate long to realize she was completely out of her depth. She'd called Zoe using Alice's phone, but she didn't pick up. She'd searched the school grounds, visited Alice's apartment, the nearby park, the mall. Now, she was stumped.

What had she been thinking? What did she know about where Zoe would go? Alice would finish chemo in just over an hour, and Kate's hopes that she would never have to know what had happened had long since diminished. Alice would certainly need to know that her daughter had urinated all over the floor at school. And the next thing she'd need to know was why Kate had come barreling down here without telling her what was going on first. The funny thing was, Kate didn't have a good answer.

Why *had* she done it?

She knew she should head back to the hospital now, but instead she continued crawling the streets in her car, looking for a teenage girl whose life was in tatters. She had just headed down a street that she had traveled down twice already when her phone rang.

She snatched it up. "This is Kate."

"What happened to you?"

It was David. She tried not to sound disappointed. "Sorry?"

"Our lunch date?"

It came back to her then. "Oh no! David, I forgot."

Silence.

"Why didn't you call me from the restaurant?" she asked, turning down a side street. There was a person walking along the side of the road and she craned her neck. A middle-aged woman.

"I assumed you'd been held up at the hospital," David said. "Then an hour went by, and I had to go."

She thought of him sitting alone at the table, waiting for her to turn up. "Oh gosh. Honey, I'm so sorry. I was on my way there, and then . . ." Kate noticed a girl sloping along the side of the road, a blue sweater around her waist. She drove up beside her. "David . . . I'm sorry, can I call you back?"

More silence.

"David? Are you—?"

But he was already gone.

Kate hung up the phone and put down her window. "Zoe?"

The girl glanced over at the car. It was Zoe, all right. Her face was red and tearstained.

"It *is* you." Kate released the breath she must have been holding for the past hour. "I've been looking for you everywhere!"

Zoe looked bewildered. "You have?"

"Yes!" Kate pulled to the side of the road and jumped out of the car. She gave Zoe a quick hug, which she neither engaged in nor threw off. "The school called your mother while she was in chemo and I took the call. They told me what happened. Are you . . . okay?"

Zoe started to nod, even as she dissolved into fresh tears. "It was just . . . it was my turn to speak and I . . . froze. I couldn't move, couldn't speak. My hands were sweating and my heart was racing. And I . . . I was concentrating on breathing and I didn't even feel it happen. It used to happen when I was a little kid, but not in years. The entire class saw me pee my pants."

Kate nodded, registering that this was, perhaps, the longest sentence she'd heard Zoe say. "What did you do?"

"I bolted."

"And you've just been wandering the streets since then?"

She nodded. "I wanted to go home but . . . Mom's just had chemo and I couldn't go home to her like this, not today. My best friend hates me, so I couldn't go to her place. And I don't have anyone else, so I really don't have anywhere to go." She looked at Kate and her face crumpled again. "What am I going to do?"

Kate looked at her small, tearstained face, and her heart broke a little. *I don't have anyone else.* The words were as wretched as they were factual.

"You're coming home with me," Kate said, tucking the girl tightly under her arm as if her sheer proximity could erase that one, tragic truth.

Kate called the school principal to let her know she'd found Zoe, and now Zoe was tucked up on a chair in the sunroom wearing a pair of Kate's sweatpants.

"Your mom should be finished with her chemo by now," Kate said. "Why don't I take you to the hospital? I'm sure once you speak to her—"

"I can't tell her this."

"Zoe—"

"She shouldn't have stress, right, when she's having treatment? I read that on the Internet. It's bad for the cancer."

Sometimes Kate hated the damn Internet.

"Your principal said you should have a few days at home," Kate said. "So your mom is going to know something is up. I really think you should tell her what's going on."

"No," she repeated.

Kate didn't think she'd heard Zoe sound so firm. She had a sudden flash of Alice saying the same thing about Zoe when she was diagnosed with cancer.

"You need to talk to someone, Zoe," she said. "Before you go back to school—"

"I'm not ever going back there. Ever."

"Well, I agree you shouldn't go for a few days," Kate said carefully. "As for 'ever,' you don't need to make a decision about that right now."

Zoe lifted her head suddenly and Kate saw that her eyes were filled with tears. "I really wanted to be a good speaker," she said. "And now I never will be."

Kate moved closer and let Zoe fall against her. She wanted to tell her something positive—like if you wanted something badly enough, it was bound to happen. Problem was, in her heart of hearts, Kate didn't know if that was true.

42

Sonja lay on the couch in her pajama pants and socks and a big comfy sweater. Her feet were in George's lap and the television was on. This was her happy place.

"Should we start the next season of *Dexter*?" she asked, sitting up and reaching for the remote. She'd been dreaming of this all day as she rushed around at work. Escapism.

George gave her a sidelong look that sent a chill through her.

"I thought we could do something else."

Sonja's stomach clenched. Surely not? She was still tender from the evening before. In the past, after a night like that, she'd be safe for a few days at least. These days it felt as though she was never safe.

"George," she started in a wobbly, unconvincing voice. "I'm not really in the mood."

But George was already rising up over her, pushing her onto her back. At least it was the couch, she thought. No sharp angles or surfaces. But even as she had the thought, his hand tangled in her hair, and she realized what was coming.

Suddenly Dagmar's words came back to her. *When things start to get ugly—make sure you speak up. Tell him you don't like what he's doing and if he continues, you will leave.*

"George," Sonja said. "Please don't."

Too late. He yanked—sending a blinding pain into her scalp, so strong that she involuntarily bucked him off. He rolled onto the floor. His shock was so complete that she was able to slide out of his grasp and off the sofa, just out of his reach.

"I asked you not to do that," Sonja said. "I don't feel like it, and you were hurting me."

George's eyes widened slightly. It had just rushed out of her, but now that she'd said it, she wanted to choke it back in. It had sounded so prim. She watched him take it in for a moment before cocking his head.

"Are you serious?" he said.

Sonja hesitated, then nodded.

His lip curled slightly at one side and Sonja's heart started to thud. In his lap, she noticed his hands were curled into fists. George had never hit her—at least not in anger. There had been the odd slap, or spanking, during sex. He'd held her down too roughly. But he'd never outright hit her.

He stood.

"What is going on with you, Sonja?" he asked quietly.

She took a tiny step backward. "Nothing. I . . . just . . . really want to watch *Dexter*."

He was quiet, as if weighing something up. And, for the first time ever, she admitted to herself that she was scared of him. Scared of her husband. His breath was high in his chest. All these tales she'd told herself about her being in control of the situation were just that. Tales. She was, she realized, entirely at his whim.

Finally he nodded. "All right then."

"All right . . . what?"

"All right. We'll watch *Dexter*."

Sonja watched him. His expression was hard to read. "*Really?*"

"Of course. If you're too tired."

George straightened up and reached for the remote control, while Sonja looked on. It felt like a trick. It was simply too hard to fathom that he'd just accept it and move on.

"Well," he said, looking up at her. There was the faintest trace of impatience in his voice. "Are you joining me?"

"Yes," Sonja said. "Yes, okay."

But as she slid onto the couch beside him, Sonja was tense. She had a feeling that this wouldn't be the end of it. Yes, she'd won this time. But sometimes the enemy you knew was better than the one you didn't.

43

When Kate arrived home after dropping Zoe at her apartment, David was waiting for her on the doorstep. His top button was undone and his tie was loose. When he saw her coming, he rose to his feet.

"What are you doing on the doorstep?" she asked.

"Need to make sure the gardeners are doing their job."

He smiled. She took the smile for what it was: a peace offering.

"I'm so sorry about lunch," she said. "I should have—"

"It was just lunch, Kate. I know you have a lot going on. Come inside."

He put his arm around her and led her into the front living room. For once the place was devoid of teenagers. Hilary's brother was getting married in Mexico and they'd all headed off early that morning. Kate and David had even been invited—David, of course, still played golf with his former brother-in-law. They'd toyed with the idea of going but had decided against it after the miscarriage.

"Why don't we open a bottle of wine?" Kate suggested. One of the few upsides of not being pregnant was a drink after work. Today she needed one.

"What a good idea. I'll go to the cellar."

Kate kicked off her shoes and fell onto the couch. Beside her on the side table was a candle and she lit it, then nestled into the cushions. David returned a moment later with two chilled glasses.

"Well," he said. "This is romantic."

She smiled up at him. He put the glasses on the coffee table.

"It's so quiet," he said. "I can hear myself think."

"It's lovely," Kate agreed. "The whole place to ourselves."

She let that comment hang for a moment, until he gave her a familiar look. And she turned to him.

It was nice, the sex. After the last two years, it even felt a little gratuitous. For so long (though David didn't always know it) she'd been aware of exactly where she was in her cycle—and was always more keen during the "hot spots." After they'd started IVF, sex had been something controlled—not for a few days before or after an embryo transfer. It had been forever since they'd had the inclination and just gone for it. And the beauty of infertility, of course, was that there was no need to scramble for a condom.

The best thing about it was that, for a few minutes, Kate felt like they were them again. Without fertility issues or embryo discussions or ex-wives or kids. Afterward, in the postcoital glow, Kate felt a small burst of courage.

"David, can we . . . talk?" she said.

In her arms, she felt him stiffen. "Kate—"

"What? You said the other night that we should talk about it. Can we?"

Slowly David disentangled himself from her and sat up. "It depends what you mean by talk," he said warily.

"I realize I can't force you to try again for a baby," she said, also sitting up. "But you can't force me to stop wanting to. And until we resolve it, we have a problem."

"You mean until we have a baby, we have a problem?"

Something about the way he said it irritated her.

"If you want to put it that way, yes," she said.

David wiped his face with his hand. His face was a hard frown, his eyes sharp. It surprised her. "So that's how you're going to play it?" he said.

"I'm not playing anything, David."

"Is this what this was all about?" He looked around the room. "The wine? The candles? The sex?"

"No," she said, taken aback. "I can't believe you said that."

David stood. "Jesus. Are we really talking about this again? I've actually forgotten who we are when we're not talking about a baby, Kate."

"David—"

"I just . . . I can't do this anymore."

Kate's breath caught. "What do you mean?"

"I might . . . see if I can get a ticket to Mexico after all. Go see the kids. I think some time away would be good."

His voice was softer now, which somehow made it worse. It sounded as though he was making a thought-out decision rather than lashing out, saying something he'd regret later.

Kate couldn't believe it. Four years of marriage, countless fertility treatments, and this is what they had come to. She knew she could end this now, once and for all. Just tell him, *Okay, let's forget about having a baby.* If she did that, she'd have her husband back. She'd have the life she loved back. But she couldn't bring herself to say the words.

"Have a good time in Mexico," she said instead, and she stepped around him and headed up the stairs.

44

Zoe sat on the couch, looking at her phone. Emily had called twice, probably to laugh at her. Zoe didn't want to speak to her. Speaking to her would mean news from the outside world, and news from the outside world, she was certain, wouldn't be good. Eventually she put her phone on silent and shoved it in a drawer. She'd been back in her apartment for half an hour when her mom got home.

"Hi," Zoe said. "How was chemo?"

She was surprised to see that her mom looked pretty normal. Much the same as she'd looked that morning, perhaps a little tireder. She dropped onto the couch beside her. "It was okay."

"Did it hurt?"

"No. It was like donating blood."

It was weird, but she seemed remarkably upbeat. Not the fake upbeat she did when she was trying to make Zoe feel happy but . . . actually happy.

"Was it boring?"

"Actually Paul came with me."

Zoe stared at her. "*Paul, Paul?* As in, my uncle Paul?"

She nodded. "He showed up here this morning and offered to drive me. Weird, huh?"

"Really weird." She looked at her mom. "Are you hungry? I can fix you something . . ."

"I'm fine, honey."

"Do you want a—"

Zoe trailed off when there was a knock at the door. Their reaction, when Zoe thought about it, was comical. They both sat up, frowned, and stared at each other. Zoe could see her own thoughts reflected in her mother's face. Had they ordered something? Had Dulcie had a fall? (She rarely came by after dark.) The idea that someone would come, unbidden, to their door was simply unfathomable.

"You get it," her mom said finally, which was a surprise. Chemo must have had more of an effect on her than Zoe thought.

Zoe opened the door. Immediately she wanted to close it again.

"Hey," Harry said.

Zoe's humiliation came back like a punch. The debate. Peeing herself. Harry's face, as he watched the whole thing. She wanted to die, literally, right here, right now.

"I tried calling," he said, "but you didn't pick up."

Zoe stared at him. "How did you know where I lived?"

"Emily told me. She was worried."

"Emily was *worried?*"

He glanced past her, into the apartment. "Can we talk?"

Zoe didn't want to talk. She wanted to slam the door and hide—or better yet, move to a new neighborhood. But her mom had appeared at the door beside her and was staring at Harry with such amazement that it was almost funny. Almost.

"Um, okay," she said.

She opened the door further, letting Harry in. Her mom continued to stand there, the three of them forming a weird triangle. Zoe tried to imagine what her mom was seeing. Harry—a guy!—arriving on her daughter's doorstep. It was as ridiculous as if Santa himself had shown up.

"Uh . . . Mom?"

"Sorry," she said, a fraction too slow on the uptake. "Yes. Right. I was uh . . . about to lie down." She gave Zoe a meaningful look, which might have been trying to convey either excitement or terror, then reluctantly disappeared.

Zoe waited until her mom's door had shut before turning to Harry. He was already sitting on the couch. As surreal as it was, Zoe didn't feel as uncomfortable as she would have expected, having Harry in her apartment. It was almost as if, after what she'd done today, any other humiliation was small fry.

"It wasn't as bad as you think," he said before she could speak.

"Sure." Zoe sat on the floor, her eyes in line with his knees.

"We continued with the debate. I did your part. Most people just felt really bad for you. And FYI, Amy totally choked on her part too. Stumbling all over the place and her hands were shaking."

"Did she pee herself?"

"No. But Jimmy farted and blamed it on a squeaky chair leg."

Zoe felt like she should smile but she couldn't muster it. They fell into silence.

"Listen, I figured you'd be feeling pretty bad after today," he said. "I wanted to come and make you feel better."

"That's sweet, but I don't like your chances."

"Steel yourself then," he said, and Zoe did. If there was one thing she was good at, it was steeling herself. "I have Crohn's disease."

Zoe blinked. That wasn't what she was expecting.

"What's—"

"—Crohn's disease? It's a chronic inflammatory disease of the gastrointestinal tract." He said it like he was reciting it from a dictionary, then added, "I know. Sexy right?"

Zoe was stunned silent.

"It's why I'm not playing football any more. It's why I often have to step out of class. And it's why I was late to the debate today. I never know when it's going to flare up."

Zoe wasn't sure at what point she started looking Harry in the eye. "Will it . . . will it kill you?"

"Unlikely. But there's no cure. It's a lifelong illness that has to be managed. This summer the doctors removed a foot of my small intestine. They thought it would give me some reprieve from symptoms for a while, but less than two months on, I'm having flare-ups again."

"So you can't play football with Crohn's?"

"Technically you can. But let's just say you don't want to be in the middle of a game or a practice when you have a flare-up. Anyway I've lost a lot of weight since I was diagnosed last year, and I get epic joint pain now, which makes it hard to play."

Zoe had no idea what to say.

"It isn't the most glamorous of illnesses. The guys knew I was having surgery this summer, so I said it was for my knee. My dad just had knee surgery—it gave me the idea." Now Harry looked shy, which was a first. "Anyway, like I said, I understand embarrassment. Believe me."

"I have social anxiety disorder," Zoe blurted out. After Harry's admission she felt an unstoppable urge to be free of her own burden. "With panic attacks. Usually a panic attack makes me feel like my heart is going to explode and I can't breathe and stuff. But today it made me . . . pee. I also never know when it's going to happen, but I knew today would be a risk. I just didn't know how bad it would be."

"That sucks."

"Yep."

"I definitely have it worse though," Harry said after a moment.

Zoe scoffed. "Please. No you don't."

"Sure I do. You only pee yourself. I shit myself. Fairly regularly."

Zoe stared at him. "You . . . ?"

"Uh-huh. I have to carry spare underwear at all times."

Zoe took a moment to digest that. Suddenly she understood where Harry disappeared to during class. What his appointments were for. Why it was easier for him to study at home. Why the fake knee injury.

"Well . . . at least no one knows what's wrong with you," she said. "I can't even have a normal conversation with anyone without blushing."

"I. Shit. Myself," Harry repeated, deadpan. "I think it's best if we just stop this conversation and agree that I have it worse."

Zoe started to giggle. It was the most unusual conversation. But for once, unbelievably, she didn't feel awkward.

"Well, my mom has cancer," she said. "So I think I still win."

She was saying it in a jokey way, but mid-delivery she realized it wasn't really very funny. The smile disappeared from Harry's eyes.

"Your mom has cancer?" He sat forward and rested his hand lightly on her knee. Despite the context, Zoe felt her heart race a little.

"Yep. She's acting like it isn't so bad, but I don't believe her. I think . . . I think she might be going to die."

Her voice broke on die, and Harry slid off the couch onto the floor beside her. "Wow, that's . . . ," he started, then sighed. "Fine. You have it worse."

Zoe surprised herself by laughing. Harry laughed too, but respectfully. Zoe looked at him. His eyes, so full of concern. How had she not realized how perfect his face was before?

He watched her contemplatively for a moment, and Zoe felt her breath quicken. "So, now that I've told you that I shit myself, would it gross you out if I kissed you?" He stroked the side of her face with his thumb.

Zoe smiled. "Surprisingly, it wouldn't."

He smiled back, taking her face in his hands.

And then, they were kissing.

When Harry left, Zoe stood in the doorway of her mother's bedroom. She waited for her to pop up and beg for information. *Who was that boy? Why didn't I know about him? Do you like him?* But her breathing was slow, rhythmic. Asleep. She looked tiny in her big bed, just a little mound with a blanket pulled up to her chin. It was hard to believe that this woman, whom Zoe had seen drawn up to full height, arguing with any doctor or parent, anyone who dared to say anything about Zoe, was reduced to this tiny heap. Zoe lay on the bed and shuffled up until they were spooning. Still, her mom didn't so much as rouse. She had a sweet, unfamiliar smell that she could only assume came from the chemo, and it made her sad. She longed for her mom's usual scent.

She fell asleep thinking about Harry. When she woke again, two hours had passed. The room was near black. Zoe's arm was still across her mother, except now it was drenched in sweat.

"Mom?" she whispered. "Mom? You're soaked through."

Zoe brought a hand to her forehead. She was warm, but not roasting hot.

"Mom?" she said again.

She finally roused. "What?"

"You're wet."

Drowsily, her mom examined her shirt, which was stuck to her chest. She blinked hard, confused, then relaxed back into her pillows. "Oh, it's just the hot flashes. I'm fine, honey."

"Your sheets are soaked."

"So they are." She yawned and started to rise into a sitting position. "I'll change them. You go back to sleep."

"I'll do it, Mom."

"Don't be silly, honey."

Her mom dropped her bare legs to the floor, but before she could stand, Zoe grabbed her arm. "Mom, stop. I'm doing this."

Perhaps out of exhaustion, she nodded. "All right."

Her mom sat on the armchair while Zoe stripped and remade the bed. Zoe put towels down on her mother's side, over her pillows, and a stack of towels beside the bed. It felt good, she noticed, being the strong one.

"Are you in pain?" she asked as she moved her mom back to the bed.

"No," she replied, obviously a lie.

"Did the doctor give you any pills to take?"

"There's some in my purse."

Zoe fetched the pills and a glass of water and fed them to her mother before laying her down on top of the towels. She covered her in blankets and then, once again, lay down beside her. Her mom was cold now, and Zoe hugged her tight. Maybe she didn't have her mother's smell anymore, but she did, for the time being, have her mother. She wondered how long she would have her.

Her mother—forever in tune with her, even like this—must have sensed her thoughts. "I'm not leaving you, Zoe," she said quietly.

"No," Zoe said, brushing away a tear. "I'm not leaving *you.*"

45

Kate stood in the kitchen of her enormous, empty house. It had always felt too big, but now with no one else in it, it felt ridiculous. Five bedrooms, only three of which were used, two of them only part-time. When Kate moved in, the rooms had felt like a promise. She'd thought they'd be filled soon. Now they were just a reminder of what she'd never have.

She'd gone to bed at nine the night before, half an hour before David left for the airport. After several hours of trying to sleep she'd finally given up and turned on the television, flicked through a few books. At one point she even drew herself a bath. Around 5 A.M., she finally drifted off to sleep.

She knew she'd messed up yesterday. Not because she'd planned to ambush David as he thought, but because she'd turned into something she didn't want to be. A nag. A broken record. The problem was, she didn't know what else to do. What did you do in a marriage when you didn't agree? With an issue like a baby, there was no compromise—one person won, the other lost. So how did the loser go on without becoming bitter? Without blaming their partner for what they had missed out on? Until recently Kate had been so smug about her marriage, so smug about the lack of conflict, the wonderful communication. But sometimes all it took was one big obstacle to break down even the most harmonious of marriages.

Around 10 A.M., when Kate went to check the mailbox, she found Zoe sitting on her doorstep. For some reason, Kate's breath caught.

"Hi," Zoe said, stumbling to her feet. "Sorry . . . I . . . I didn't know where to go."

"Zoe. Does your mom—?"

"I didn't tell her." Zoe couldn't look at her. "I couldn't. She was so sick, Kate."

They stood there for a moment, on the doorstep. Zoe looked so small, so lost. Kate didn't know what to do. She wasn't sure it was a good idea to let Zoe inside when Alice knew nothing about her daughter's whereabouts—but what else could she do?

"Okay, well . . . come in."

Zoe shot inside, which was probably a good thing as Kate was already wavering about her decision. What would Alice say when she found out? Kate was overstepping the boundaries and she knew it. At the same time, she was tired after a night of hardly any sleep. And, she had to admit, she was happy to see Zoe.

"So," Kate said when they found themselves, unsurprisingly, in the sunroom. "The first chemo treatment knocked your mom around a bit, did it?"

"She woke up last night so drenched in sweat I had to change her sheets."

"Night sweats can be a side effect of chemo. Your mom is lucky she has you to look after her."

Zoe nodded. She looked so sad sitting there it just about broke Kate's heart.

"And how are *you* feeling?" Kate asked.

Zoe pulled her legs up in front of her and rested her chin on her knees. "How do you think?"

"Do you want to talk about it?"

"No."

Kate thought for a minute. She'd always found that talking to patients—about anything—led to better outcomes. Sometimes it would take an hour of talking about the weather before they finally came out and asked the question they'd been wanting to ask: How long have I got? So she decided on a change of topic.

"Would you mind if I ask *you* a question?"

Zoe looked at her. Despite herself, she seemed a little intrigued. "Okay."

"The other day, you said, 'Sometimes I say things because I don't know what else to say . . . and it just comes out wrong.'"

"Yeah."

The truth was, Kate had been thinking about it in the context of her father. Hadn't he said something similar? That he didn't know why he said things?

"I've been thinking about that," Kate said, "and I wondered: How can anyone know what you mean? I mean, when even you can't articulate it?"

Zoe shrugged as though it were a silly question. "Because of my actions. If I like a class, I always turn up for it . . . even though I might accidentally insult the teacher when I hand in my homework. Or if I hate a class—aka gym—I'll avoid it at all costs. If I want to be friends with someone, I might try to sit near them, even if I don't have the guts to talk to them. If I know someone is sad, I might try talking to them—even though I'll probably end up blurting something out that makes it worse."

"Actions," Kate said, as if it were wildly complex instead of simple and obvious.

Zoe smiled with a little shrug. "They speak loudly, I hear."

Kate thought of the things her dad had said over the years that had disappointed her. And then, of the things he *did*. Raising her, when he could easily have handed her off to a relative. Showing up to dinner whenever she invited him, awkward as it was. Calling her after her miscarriage to say he was sorry. Zoe was right. Actions spoke loudly.

"I probably shouldn't have come here without telling my mom," Zoe said finally, proving Kate's theory that keeping communication going was always a good idea.

Kate looked at her. "Why didn't you tell her? Do you think she'd make you go to school?"

"No," Zoe said.

"So why not tell her?"

"She doesn't need to worry about me on top of everything else."

"That's sweet of you," Kate said. "But I'm not sure hiding things from her is the answer."

"What is the answer?"

"Honestly," Kate said, "I have no idea."

They smiled at each other. Kate felt a tiny bit better.

"I really do love this room," Zoe said after a few moments.

Kate nodded, suddenly remembering what Zoe had said last time she was in there. "It's a good place to be by yourself, right?"

Zoe blushed and it occurred to Kate that this might be her cue to leave. Zoe probably needed some peace and quiet, some time to process everything. At the same time, Kate found herself reluctant to leave. For the first time in months, she felt comfortable right where she was.

"I know I said that," Zoe said slowly. "But what I meant was, it's a good place to be by myself . . . with you." She rolled her eyes at herself. "God, does that even make any sense?"

Kate smiled. "Actually," she said, "it makes perfect sense."

46

Sonja stood in the doorway to the living room, watching George on the couch. She was worried. Since she'd denied his advances last night, something had changed between them. This morning he'd come downstairs fully dressed and declined her offer of breakfast, saying he'd grab something on his way out. Tonight, after a quiet dinner, he'd taken himself off to the couch to watch the news without a word. As unsettling as the sex was, being ignored was worse.

"Do you want to go to bed?" she said now, touching his hair. With her eyes, she tried to make her intent clear. It wasn't that she desired sex, as much as she couldn't remain on tenterhooks forever.

"You go ahead," he said, keeping an eye on the screen. "I'll be up in a bit."

As she climbed into her empty bed, Sonja felt a little baffled. She wanted to set the clock back to the night before and let George do what he wanted to her. Let him squeeze her breasts. It couldn't hurt worse than being rejected. It couldn't hurt worse than being alone.

Sonja must have fallen asleep, because when she startled awake, the room was near black and the clock blinked 3:45 A.M. She could feel George beside her, perhaps just coming to bed.

"George?" she said. "Is that you?"

She rolled over and blinked up at him, smelling whiskey. In the dim light she saw him smile. Then he wrapped his hands around her throat.

Sonja tried to rear back, but she was pressed against the mattress and there was nowhere to go. She could feel his thumbs pressing against her Adam's apple. Panic set in. She began kicking her legs and arms. She couldn't move, couldn't breathe.

She held eye contact, making her eyes round and serious, trying to communicate that it had gone too far. But, although he was looking at her, he was unseeing. He didn't look like George at all. He looked like a monster.

Finally, he let go.

Sonja quickly rolled away from him, gasping and retching. Air wheezed in and out of her lungs, making a horrible rasping noise. She turned to look at George and noticed that the smile had slid from his face. This wasn't about sexual gratification, she realized. Not anymore. It was about power. And George had to be the one to have it.

47

A week after her first chemo session, Alice was struggling. She wasn't sick to her stomach, but she felt woolly-headed, sweaty, like she had the flu, and she was bone-tired, as if she could sleep for days. For a week her evening routine had been the same. Each night she'd curl up with Zoe and a cup of tea, Alice watching the television, Zoe absorbed in her book.

"Can I get you some pills?" Zoe asked each night, code for *You don't look so good.*

"Sure," Alice would reply, code for *I don't feel so good.*

Now Zoe was at school, which meant Alice was on her own. She hadn't worked since before chemo—she'd had to hire another two part-timers while she was out of action. Yesterday one of them had dropped off a stack of get-well wishes from the clients, as well as a bunch of flowers from Mrs. Featherstone. Alice was touched. She had, of course, sent cards to her clients when they'd been in and out of the hospital. But she hadn't understood how humbling it felt to be on the receiving end.

Alice pulled a blanket around her shoulders. Her brochure said she should call the hospital if something didn't feel right, but according to the cancer-forum ladies, chills were a normal side effect of chemo. The cancer-forum ladies were people she interacted with online and who had screen names like Hope4me and LongLife and Survivor! (Alice's screen name was CancerSucks.) The strangest thing about chemo, the forum ladies agreed, was the red pee. The nurses had explained to Alice that because the dye in the chemo was red, her pee would be red too, until it flushed out of her system. The good news, the forum ladies all said, was that you could tell when the chemo was through, because your pee returned to its normal color. Calling it "good news," Alice thought, was a stretch, but she supposed they were all in short supply of good news.

There was a knock at the door just as Alice got comfy on the couch.

"Go away," she whispered.

But whoever it was just knocked again. Groaning, Alice hauled herself upright and toward the door. When she swung it open, Paul was standing there. He was wearing the same hoodie and jeans he'd worn the last time she saw him.

"Hey," he said. "How're you doing?"

Alice's mind spun. It was one thing making the effort to show up *once*. People made the effort once all the time. Volunteering to serve the homeless on Christmas Day, for example—who didn't love doing that? But how many people showed up to serve the homeless the day after Christmas as well? Not many, Alice guessed. Because once you'd paid your dues you could go back to living your life feeling that you'd done your bit.

Why wasn't Paul doing that?

Alice stared at him. "What are you doing here, Paul?"

"I just . . . I couldn't stop thinking about what you told me," he said. "About Zoe's father."

Alice turned and headed back into the apartment. "Come in," she called over her shoulder. She fell onto the couch with another violent shiver.

Paul shut the door and joined her in the living room. "I just wish I had known. Did Mom or Dad know?"

Alice pulled the blanket tightly around her. "No, not the details. I just told them what I told you."

"That he wasn't father material?"

"Yes." Alice was stunned. That was *exactly* what Alice had said. She hadn't realized Paul had been paying attention.

"Alice. I'm your big brother. I could have . . . done something. I could have tracked him down and punched his lights out."

A lump, big and fat and gnarly, grew in Alice's throat.

"I've been a shit brother," he continued. "But I'm going to step up. I promise."

It was so little, so late. And no help to her at all. But hearing him say it brought Alice dangerously close to tears. As for stepping up, she believed that, at least in this moment, he meant it.

"Thanks, Paul." She gave another involuntary, violent shiver. "Is it . . . is it cold in here?"

"Actually, I was about to take off my sweater." Paul put a hand to her forehead. "Jesus, you're roasting!"

She pushed his hand away. "Hot? I'm freezing."

"You're on *fire*, Alice."

She shivered again, as if to prove him wrong. Then she realized that fever and chills were not an either/or. And according to the forum, a temperature was something you *did* call your doctor for. "Let me find my thermometer," she said. "If it's over a hundred point five, I'll need to go to the hospital."

"Forget the thermometer," he said.

"No, really. The forum said—"

"Fuck the forum," he said. "We're going to the hospital."

Alice felt unexpected tears well in her eyes. "All right," she said. "Just let me get my coat."

The truth was, she probably did need to go to the hospital. And there was something about someone else taking control of the situation that was simply too hard to resist.

48

Zoe was going back to school. At least, she was walking in that direction. Who knew what would happen when she got closer. But she was doing as Kate taught her and not thinking about it. It had been a week since the debate. It would be hard to go back . . . but people did hard things every day. Lord knew, her mom had it tough this last week, after chemo. She'd been pretty sick, but she was managing.

As she got closer to the school, the street swelled with students, hoofing their way toward the school gates. Zoe's heart began to race. A few people glanced in her direction but she focused on her feet. She didn't want to see the exchanged glances, or hear the whispers. *That's her. That's the girl.* High school had been bad enough before she became the girl who peed her pants.

Was she actually going to do this? She needed to make a decision, and fast. The gates were approaching. She could keep walking, or she could go in. She took a breath, steeled herself. Then she headed in.

There was a collective gasp as she approached the front steps. She looked up long enough to map a course around the kids who sat there (several who'd been part of the debate) and then, with her head down, took the steps two at a time. She'd just reached the double doors into the building when she heard an explosion of giggles followed by a shriek from someone else and a *Shhh!* from a third party.

You can do this, Zoe told herself. *Just don't think about it.*

In the hallway, conversations hushed as she passed. Zoe scanned the halls for Harry, but when she couldn't find him, stared straight ahead. She slowed as she approached another group, waiting for someone to let her past. She noticed Seth in the circle, along with a few others including Cameron Freeman in the center. Cameron noticed Zoe and a faint smile appeared.

"Ooh no, I forgot what I was supposed to say . . . ," he said in a squeaky, girly voice. "Um . . . oh . . ."

There was a sound of plastic hitting the ground, then the slosh of water against the linoleum floors. The crowd jumped back. Cameron had dropped his water bottle. "Oops!" he cried. "I couldn't hold it."

Cameron laughed hysterically. Seth gave him a shove. "It's not funny, man," he said. Zoe stepped over the water and kept walking.

At her locker, she noticed Jessie Lee smiling at her. Jessie Lee had dyed the front of her hair purple now. The rest was black and cut so she looked like a shaggy rock star. She wore a black tank with a giant red tongue on the front and two strands of long, fake pearls.

"Zoe," she said. "You're back."

Zoe nodded.

"I'm glad."

"Thanks."

Jessie Lee raked her hair back out of her eyes, but it immediately returned to its original position. "You know, once, in junior high, I stepped in dog shit and then walked it into the classroom. By the time I'd realized, Mr. Schmidt had noticed and was making everyone check their feet. Someone saw it was me and announced it to the whole class. Everyone called me shit-shoes for months."

Zoe remembered Jessie Lee being called shit-shoes. She hadn't known why. Jessie Lee had acted as if it hadn't bothered her.

"No one says it anymore," Jessie Lee continued. "Eventually people move on. Find someone else to torture. We all have to take our turn. Share around the suffering. It's pretty funny, really. Shit-shoes."

"I wonder what they'll call me," Zoe said.

"Dunno. Pee-stage doesn't have quite the same ring."

Unbelievably, Zoe laughed. Just a little.

"Zoe?"

Zoe turned to see Emily bustling up behind her. And just like that, *wham!* the panic was back in the center of her chest. "Hey. What's up?"

Emily's neck was craned and her gaze was fixed on the puddle on the floor. "Who did that?"

"Oh . . . you know . . ."

"It was Cameron," Jessie Lee said.

"Fucker," Emily muttered.

Zoe basked in that for a moment. It might have been the love-liest thing Emily had ever said to her.

After a moment, Em looked back at Zoe and sighed. "Zo, I feel terrible. About our stupid fight . . . about everything. I tried call-ing you, like, a gazillion times, but you wouldn't pick up."

"I didn't want to know what everyone was saying about me," Zoe said.

"Ha! As if anyone would say anything with your resident body-guard hanging around."

"My . . . what?"

A twinkle appeared in Emily's eye. "Harry?"

"Harry is my bodyguard?"

"He's been telling everyone that if they said anything about the debate when you come back today, they'd have to deal with him." She grinned. "Clearly Cameron didn't get the memo."

Zoe couldn't help it, a huge grin spread across her face.

"Does this mean things are happening between you two?" Emily asked coyly.

Zoe felt the heat on her face. But this time, she didn't care.

"He's a good guy," she said finally. "Even if he is not very punctual."

The playfulness drained out of Emily's face. "So, I guess I'm asking . . . will you have me back?"

"Of course I will," Zoe said. But before they could even hug, a commotion erupted down the corridor. Zoe turned in time to see Harry shove Cameron hard enough to make him skid through the puddle of water and land on his ass.

"Sorry I'm late," Harry said, striding down the hall toward her.

"Why don't you tell me what happened? From the start."

The school-therapist guy sat with his legs crossed, one ankle at the opposite knee, a notepad and pen in his lap. A coffee table sat between them. After what had happened at the debate, Mrs. Hunt had insisted that she see him and, as Zoe wasn't especially keen to go to first period, English, she decided to go along with it.

"I peed myself," she said.

The humiliation at the retelling was nearly as bad as the event. Worse, maybe, out of context. She imagined his thoughts. *How revolting, a fifteen-year-old who couldn't control her bladder!* But he just nodded, as if that humiliating, horrific incident were irrelevant.

"Yes," he said, "but . . . I'm more interested in what was going on to cause that to happen?"

Talk about getting straight down to it.

Zoe balked at telling him about mother's cancer. She wasn't ready for that. But she thought she could, maybe, tell him some other things. Her fight with Emily. The debate.

"Can I close my eyes?" she asked.

He looked surprised, but then he said, "By all means."

She did, and immediately she felt more comfortable. This guy had a way of looking at her that was a little unsettling, but perhaps that was true of all therapists? When she'd knocked on his door a few minutes ago, he'd seemed busy, but then he'd immediately closed his laptop and said, "Please, come on in." Now, she suspected, he was regretting his enthusiasm.

"So tell me a little about your anxiety issues," he said.

He said it just like that, a statement. Zoe supposed she should be impressed that he'd figured her out at a glance, but instead she just felt exposed.

"Well . . . I have social anxiety disorder. With panic attacks."

"And yet you were part of a debate," he said quietly, almost to himself.

"I know it seems weird—"

"Unexpected," he corrected, like a good therapist.

"The thing is . . . I've always kind of liked the idea of being good at public speaking. Which is crazy, because obviously I'm not even good at, you know, private speaking. But the day I volunteered for the debate it was kind of like . . . my body took over. My mind told me that if I didn't put my hand up, something bad would happen. Like a—"

"Compulsion?"

"Yes," she said. "A compulsion."

There was something about the way he just said it, without inflection or judgment. Or pity. It was simply a fact. It gave her the courage to continue. "I get these compulsions sometimes. And I can be a bit . . . OCD. Sometimes I think I'm saying something on the inside but I say it out loud. And regular things freak me out, like eating in public or talking in class."

He was quiet for a moment. "Sounds like you've got a lot going on inside that head of yours. Must be exhausting."

Zoe nodded. It was strangely validating to hear him say it.

"Can you tell me what strategies you've tried to help with these things?" he asked after a few moments.

She told him about her short stint with a therapist and how she'd convinced her mom to let her stop. She told him about the affirmations and the not-thinking-about-it trick that she'd picked up from Kate. If he had feelings about this, he kept them out of his voice.

"Medication?"

"I was prescribed Klonopin," Zoe said, "but I don't really take it. I'm scared of getting addicted."

"And . . . closing your eyes? That's one of your strategies?"

"Yes. A friend of mine suggested it. It helps. I don't worry as much about what people are thinking."

There was a long silence.

"Is it a bad strategy?" Zoe asked, after a moment.

"There are worse ones. Self-harm, for example. But there are better ones too. And we're going to talk about them in just a minute."

Zoe wasn't sure why, but she felt a burst of optimism. If it was possible that there was something he could do—something that would make her life better—she wanted to know what it was.

"Can you open your eyes now, Zoe?" he said.

She did. He put his notepad and pen on the coffee table. "Okay. Firstly, can I just say what a remarkable job you've done holding it together. Social anxiety disorder can be an incredibly difficult condition to live with. Many people with the disorder fall into a serious depressive state. And by depressive, I mean unable to go to school, do homework, perform basic household chores. And you are not only keeping up with your regular routine, but you are actively trying to challenge and improve yourself by taking risks and employing strategies that help you. Honestly, I'm a little flabbergasted. I've never heard of anyone with social phobia volunteering to be part of something as public as a debate, at least not without a lot of support and medication. You should be applauded."

Zoe felt her eyes unexpectedly fill with tears. "I shouldn't be applauded. I'm terrified all the time. I'm terrified of what people think of me. I'm terrified of my mom dying. Mostly I'm terrified of feeling like this for the rest of my life."

"What if I told you that you don't have to feel like this the rest of your life?" he said. "Zoe, have you heard of a treatment called exposure therapy?"

"Uh . . . is that . . . like electric shock therapy?"

"Not at all. Exposure therapy is when you actively challenge your fears, one at a time, until you are not afraid of them anymore."

"Like the debate?"

"Well, yes, but we would start on a much smaller scale. The idea of exposure therapy is that you start by tackling something that is scary, but not so scary that you can't be successful. Most important, you tackle each thing in a controlled way, with support."

Zoe wasn't sure she liked the sound of exposure therapy. "But . . . the debate—"

He held up a palm, silencing her. "When you did the debate, you didn't have me on your team." He smiled a little.

His arrogance was, in a weird way, reassuring. As was the prospect of having a "team." Zoe felt fear and hope sparring inside her.

"I would say that the debate scenario might be something we could build up to, say, after a year of incremental exposure therapy," he said, "but for now, we'll do much smaller things. The good news is that we know you have guts. That will serve us well in exposure therapy."

Zoe swallowed. "So . . . what would I have to do? In this *exposure therapy*?"

"It's up to you. You clearly have a fear of speaking in public, maybe we can try something related to that, like asking a question in class? Or you could try to challenge another fear, like eating in public? Even one French fry. Would that be doable?"

Zoe stared at him. "But how would eating a fry help me?"

"It might not help you much," he admitted. "But if the next week you ate two fries, and the week after you ate a chicken nugget and two fries, and the week after you ate two nuggets and two fries . . . you get the idea. In six months you might be able to eat an entire meal in public, and that would make a difference to your life, wouldn't it?"

He raised his eyebrows and Zoe had no choice but to nod.

She suddenly realized why this guy was so good. You had to improve under his guidance. Even your feelings were too scared to disagree with him.

"So," he said. "Shall we make a deal? By the next time we meet, which I think should be in a week, you will have either eaten in public or asked a question in class. Can we agree to that?"

"Yes," she said, "we can."

They both stood.

"Thank you for seeing me, Dr. Sanders," she said, reaching out to take his outstretched hand. She shook it, cringing at her clammy palms. His hands, she noticed, were dry and surprisingly cold.

49

At lunchtime, in the cafeteria, Zoe was looking for Harry. Instead, she found Emily.

"Hey," Zoe said, approaching her table. Emily was sitting with Lucy Barker and Jessie Lee. "Saved you a seat," she said.

Zoe hesitated. With one eye, she continued to look for Harry. She stood in a thoroughfare and she had to squish up against the table to let people past.

"If you're looking for your boyfriend," Emily said, knowingly, "he's gone."

"Harry's gone?"

"Aha, so he *is* your boyfriend!" She snapped her fingers in delight. "Man, I'm so jealous."

"Where is he?" Zoe asked.

"He was suspended," Lucy Barker said, clearly delighted to impart this particular piece of information. "For hitting Cameron this morning."

"*Hitting* Cameron?" Zoe exclaimed. "He pushed him."

"Whatever it was, Harry's been sent home."

Zoe ignored a loud whisper of "That's her!" as someone passed her. She was too busy thinking about Harry. She'd been looking forward to—and anxious as hell about—the possibility of sitting beside him in the cafeteria.

"Are you going to sit down or what?" Emily said. "We have so much to catch up on!"

Zoe remained standing. It was hard to describe how it felt to have someone in her corner. Harry had stood up for her. He'd gotten into trouble for it. She thought of what Dr. Sanders said. And she had a feeling she'd just gotten another new member on her team.

"Can we catch up later?" she said to Emily. "I have somewhere else to be."

Zoe was skipping school, something she'd never done. She felt a knot of anxiety at the idea of getting caught, but she tried to block it out. What's the worst that could happen? she muttered to herself. Just don't think about it.

"So you're my bodyguard?" Zoe said when Harry answered his door.

Harry grinned. "Apparently I am. You'd better be impressed because my parents grounded me for two weeks."

"I'm impressed," she said, blushing.

He widened the door. "In that case, won't you come in?" he said, in a fake-formal voice.

She ducked under his arm, into the house. He followed her into the lounge room and fell backward onto the sofa. Zoe hovered awkwardly.

"We're alone," he said, sliding over to make space for her. She sat beside him and his arms went around her. Then he looked mock-confused. "Am I correct that the school day isn't over yet, Miss Stanhope? I didn't pick you as one to play hooky."

"Neither did I," Zoe said. Harry held her so casually that she found it hard to look at him.

"Are you okay?" he said, becoming serious. "Did something happen? Did anyone else say anything to you?"

"No," she said.

He sat up. "Then what is it?"

"Nothing." Her cheeks, she knew, were pink.

"But you're acting weird."

She rolled her eyes. "In case you've forgotten, I have social anxiety disorder."

"I realize that, but . . ." He seemed genuinely surprised. "I didn't think you'd be shy around me, you know, after everything."

"Harry!" she said. "I'm even more shy around you after everything."

Her cheeks burned. She was afraid to look at him, afraid of the feelings that she would undoubtedly feel if she did. And at the same time, she wanted to feel those feelings.

"What are you thinking?" she asked him, finally.

"Just that if talking makes you uncomfortable, I can think of something else we can do."

She looked at him. He smiled. And for the next hour, all Zoe worried about was Harry's parents coming home from work early.

50

Paul had just made Alice a cup of tea that she wouldn't drink. He'd been doing all kinds of useless things like that today. Passing her books she didn't want to read. Fluffing her pillows. That she *really* didn't get. Weren't pillows naturally fluffy? Sure, in times gone by when they were stuffed with feathers and twigs they probably needed fluffing, but Alice's pillows, which were made out of some sort of wonderful foam that shaped itself to her head, did not.

Still, Alice was grateful to Paul. At the hospital she was told she had an infection—which explained the fever and why she'd been feeling so crappy. She'd been admitted for intravenous antibiotics and Dr. Brookes had wanted to keep her overnight for observation, but Alice had refused. She had Paul to look after her at home, she'd said, and he'd nodded, nobly if a little uncertainly. Who knew her brother could be so useful?

She'd just got comfortable on the couch with the remote control when the phone rang.

"Hello, Stanhope residence," Paul said, and then his eyes drifted to Alice. "Yes, just a moment. Al?"

He passed her the phone.

"Alice Stanhope."

"Hello, Ms. Stanhope, this is Rosalie Hunt, Zoe's principal."

"Is Zoe all right?"

"Well, that's why I'm calling. I understand she was back at school this morning, but I checked today's register and it seems she didn't attend any of her afternoon classes. I wanted to check everything was okay."

"She didn't attend afternoon classes?"

"No, not according to my records."

"Well . . . perhaps she wasn't feeling well?" Alice suggested, to herself as much as Mrs. Hunt, although that didn't totally explain it. If she were ill, surely she'd be home by now?

"Yes, I'm sure it's something like that. I just thought it was worth double-checking, especially after last week."

Alice gave herself a couple of seconds to scan her brain, but she couldn't come up with anything. "What happened last week?"

"The debate?"

She spoke as though Alice should know what this meant. Should she?

"Er . . . when Zoe . . . urinated on the stage?"

Alice thought she might faint. She let her head drop into her hands.

"Ms. Stanhope? Are you there?"

"I'm sorry," she said, her voice sounding thick and foreign, "you said my daughter *urinated on the stage?*"

A pause. "You didn't know?"

"No," Alice replied, her voice rising. "Can you explain why didn't I know? Surely you would think to inform the parents when—"

"We called you immediately, Ms. Stanhope. I spoke with a woman named . . ." Alice heard the ruffle of papers. "Kate Littleton. She said you were unable to take the call. When she came to the school—"

"*Kate* came to the school?"

"Yes. I'm sorry, I thought you knew this." Mrs. Hunt sounded flustered. "I did call you, last week, to check up on Zoe, and I left a message on your voice mail."

Alice thought of all the messages stockpiled on her message service. She hadn't felt well enough to check them.

"Wait, did you say Zoe hasn't been at school? Before today, I mean?"

There was a long pause. "Well, after the debate she wasn't at school for, let's see . . . over a week. I assumed you'd allowed her to take some time off."

Alice heard the keys in the door.

"All right," she said to Mrs. Hunt. "Thank you for letting me know."

"Once again, Ms. Stanhope, I'm very—"

Alice hung up the phone as Zoe appeared in the living room.

"Uncle Paul?" she said, blinking as if her eyes were deceiving her. "What are you doing here?" Her eyes found Alice's. "Mom? Are you okay?"

"I'm fine. How about *you?*"

Paul instinctively retreated to the kitchen.

Zoe sat on the edge of the sofa, cagily. "I'm okay. Who was that on the phone?"

"Mrs. Hunt. She says you weren't in school this afternoon."

Somewhere in the back of her mind, it occurred to Alice that she'd dreamed about conversations like this. Having a daughter doing normal, irresponsible things like skipping school and lying about it. She had not, however, dreamed about the reason for the skipping and the lying—something about urinating on a stage.

"I was at Harry's," she said guiltily, clearly knowing the jig was up.

"And the last week, when you said you were going to school? Where were you then? At *Harry's?*"

Zoe turned crimson, looked at her hands.

"Zoe?"

"I . . . was at Kate's."

Somehow, even after what she'd learned about Kate's involvement, Alice hadn't expected this. It was a punch in the stomach. "*What?*"

Just like that, Zoe burst into tears. "I wanted to tell you but you've been so sick and I didn't want to give you anything else to worry about. It was so awful, Mom. The class had to do a debate. I was freaking out, but then I decided I should do it . . . I should challenge myself, you know . . . I actually got kind of excited about it." Zoe broke into another short burst of sobs. "Then when it was my turn, I froze. I was trying to talk myself out of a panic, trying to remember what I had to say, and suddenly I was peeing my pants. In front of the whole class."

Alice's anger was already gone. "Oh, no."

"I ran out of the school. Kate found me walking down the street. She already knew what had happened by the time she found me—she had your phone when the school called. I didn't want to worry you but I couldn't go back to school. I turned up at Kate's place the next day because I didn't know where to go."

The anger came back with a vengeance as she pictured Zoe at Kate's house.

"I know you are mad, but Mom, it wasn't her fault, it was mine. And she . . . she was great. She was the one who convinced me to go back to school."

"Well, good for her," Alice said sulkily. "I should have been the one to do that."

"I like her, Mom. I really like her."

"I don't care. This is nothing to do with her. This is our business. She shouldn't have had anything to do with it."

Zoe looked at her, head-on, in a way that Alice hadn't seen before. "But Mom," she said quietly, "what would we have done without her?"

51

Kate was used to dealing with upset people. Patients who'd
been given bad news. Families of patients who'd been given
bad news. Doctors who were overworked and on a short
fuse. But as Alice hurled abuse down the phone line, it felt different. Because this time, it wasn't Mother Nature that had betrayed
Alice, it was *Kate*.

"I understand why you're upset," she tried after five full minutes of uninterrupted shouting.

"Do you? Do you really? I've spent my whole life trying
to protect my daughter and I've done a pretty good job of it. And
during the one period I wasn't able to be there for her, you've
swooped in—a stranger—and started making decisions for my
daughter."

"You're right," Kate said. "I'm so sorry, Alice."

"You should be. You had no right."

Alice was right, of course. But it didn't change the fact that
some part of Kate was glad she'd been able to be there for Zoe.
And no matter how she tried, she couldn't regret it.

"How is Zoe?" Kate asked when there was a lull in yelling.

She heard Alice exhale. "She's all right."

"Good." Kate felt a small knot in her belly release. "You know,
Alice, she's a—"

"Don't you tell me anything about my daughter!" Alice interrupted, instantly incensed again. "Don't you dare do that! I'm her mother."

"I'm sorry," Kate said quietly. "I was just going to say she is an exceptional girl."

There was a short pause. Kate took a steadying breath, ready for a new torrent of abuse. But this time, when Alice spoke, her voice was calmer.

"Look, I appreciate everything you've done, Kate. I really do. You helped us out when we needed it, and I can't thank you enough. But from now on, if Zoe needs something she can come to me. Do you understand?"

All at once the knot in Kate's stomach was back. "Yes. I understand."

"Good. Well, I'll let you go then."

Kate let Alice hang up first; then she slowly lowered her own phone. She looked at Zoe, standing opposite her in the kitchen.

"What are you doing here this time of the morning, Zoe?"

She looked shy. "Um . . . I just wanted to see you. Actually I wanted to tell you about . . . this guy, Harry."

Kate fought the urge to smile, to tell her to join her in the sunroom so she could find out all about Harry.

"But . . ." Zoe's shy expression melted away. "Why was my mom calling you?"

"She's very upset with me, Zoe."

"Oh, no." Zoe closed her eyes. "This is all my fault."

"No it's not. I'm your mother's nurse, I should never have let you into my house without her knowledge. And I should have told her about what happened at school. She has every right to—"

"—to what?"

Kate sighed. "To be angry."

"She should be angry at *me*, not you. You're the one who . . . who . . ." Zoe blushed. Kate was starting to find it her most endearing trait.

"Zoe," Kate said. "I don't think it's a good idea that you're here, honey."

She was trying to do the right thing, trying to make it swift, but Zoe's eyes narrowed. "Did my mom say that?"

Kate couldn't speak. She knew she had to make Zoe leave, but she couldn't find the words.

"She did, didn't she?" Zoe said. "I can't believe this. I'll explain to her, I'll tell her—"

"Zoe."

"*What?*"

"I think it might be for the best."

Zoe blinked. The hurt and surprise in Zoe's eyes made Kate want to take the words and stuff them back into her mouth. But she couldn't. "You should go home to your mother. And honestly, I need some time too."

Zoe looked mortified. "Oh. You mean . . . you don't want me here?"

"That's not it," Kate said, but tears were already welling in Zoe's eyes. All Kate wanted to do was gather her in her arms and take it all back, but what would be the point? The result would be the same. So instead, she went against every instinct she'd ever had and remained silent and watched her walk out the door.

Kate couldn't stay in that empty house another second. So, she decided, she was going to work. At least there she could be of use to someone. She drove purposefully through the pretty suburban streets until, without deciding on it, she pulled up in front of her father's house.

She wasn't sure what she was doing here, rather than at work. Reaching out, perhaps, to the only blood relative she had? Maybe she was just desperate. In what she had thought was a full life, she was fast running out of people. She wasn't sure when her heart started to pound. Her palms were a little sweaty too, and she had that pain in her sternum—the one that felt like indigestion but was actually mild anxiety. All because of a visit to her father.

She rapped on the door. After about thirty seconds, it swung open.

"Kate." Her dad blinked a couple of times, then glanced at his watch. "Did we have an arrangement?"

"No, but I thought I'd pop in. If that's all right."

"Oh, well . . . I mean . . . yes. Of course."

It wasn't the reception that she'd been hoping for. But as he stood back, allowing the door to open further, Kate realized he was inviting her in.

Actions.

Inside, she sat on the same couch she'd sprawled on as a kid—after school watching TV or on a Saturday morning with a book. She didn't remember having any particular affection for it then, but now it filled her with emotion. Her dad sat beside her, stiffly. There were no hugs, no offers of a cup of tea. He looked as uncomfortable as she felt.

"I'm sorry to just show up like this," she said.

"It's all right," he said. "Is everything okay?"

"Not really," she admitted.

He watched her, not speaking but at least looking concerned. It was all it took for her to not burst into tears. "I don't really know what I'm doing here, Dad. I just . . . needed someone and—"

"Where's David?" he asked.

"In Mexico."

He considered that a moment. "Are you having marriage problems?"

"No!" she said. "Yes. I don't know."

"Why don't you tell me what's happened?"

It was amazing the difference a shift in attitude could make. Her dad's words alone had done nothing to make her feel like her visit was welcomed. But everything about his actions—inviting her in, asking her to confide in him—conveyed something else entirely. And it made her want to talk to him.

"David doesn't want to try for another baby," she sobbed. "He's done with miscarriages, he says. But all I've ever wanted was a child of my own. All we've done is fight about it. And now he's gone off to Mexico to have a think about things. I just . . . don't know what to do."

It occurred to Kate that she couldn't remember the last time she had come to her dad with a problem. She'd certainly never done it as an adult. She didn't think he would care. But as she watched him now, thinking really hard, she could see that wasn't the case. His forehead was pinched, and he chewed his lip, his gaze fixed on something in the distance. He cared very much.

"That does sound like quite a conundrum," he said finally.

He pushed a box of tissues toward her. It brought up a memory. Of the time when she was eleven, and had the flu. Her dad had taken the entire week off work to take care of her. She'd been so ill, all she could do was lie on the couch and cry. He'd slept on the floor of her room at night, and during the day he was always nearby, offering tissues.

Actions.

"I'm not great at these kinds of things, Kate," he said finally. "But if you want to talk . . . I'm not a bad listener."

This was true, she realized. Her father *had* always been a good listener. Now that she thought of it, he had lots of good qualities—it was just that his inability to communicate well hadn't allowed her to see them. It occurred to Kate how easy it must be for someone who was uncomfortable with social interaction to become isolated in the world. She also realized how easy it was to overlook the value that person could bring.

"You know what?" she said. "A good listener is exactly what I need."

52

Alice was lying on the couch, hoping a nap would come, when the door crashed open. By the time she opened her eyes, Zoe was standing over her, her finger pointed at her.

"Did you tell Kate she wasn't allowed to see me anymore?"

Alice sat up. "Zoe—"

"*Did* you?" she cried. Alice couldn't remember the last time she'd seen Zoe so angry.

"Yes, I did."

She saw it then, something she'd never seen on her daughter's face before—a flash of pure white rage. "How could you? After everything Kate has done for us?"

"Give you a place to hide, you mean, when you were playing hooky from school?"

"How about: let me stay at her house so I didn't have to go to foster care?" Zoe cried.

Alice felt a wave of indignation. But she forced herself to breathe. She was the adult here, she needed to remain rational and in control. "I was grateful to Kate for that, Zoe. But that doesn't excuse what she did."

"Help me, you mean? When I really needed it?"

"Why didn't you ask *me* for help?" Alice's voice broke unexpectedly. "I'm your *mother*."

With her mouth already open to respond, Zoe glanced at the cushion where Alice's head had just been. Alice followed her gaze to a chunk of hair left behind on the cushion—blond at one end and a lightish brown at the other.

"Oh," Alice said, her hand rising instinctively to her head. She knew now was the time to say something calming, to whisk the hair away with a smile so as to not traumatize Zoe. But she was momentarily frozen, unable to react. Her *hair.*

Zoe picked it up.

Years ago Alice had seen a stand-up comedian do a skit about hair. When attached to someone's head, he'd said, hair was lovely. People smelled it, brushed it, ran their fingers through it. But once it left your head, he said, hair became something to be feared. A hair in your soup could have a restaurant shut down. People had cleaning companies brought in to remove dog hair from furniture.

It had brought the house down. So true, Alice had thought. A hair off your head was not a good thing. It was gross. Disgusting. Yet here was Zoe, on the couch beside her, holding a chunk of her hair like it was the most precious gem. It undid Alice.

"You were sick, Mom. I didn't want to worry you with my problems."

Alice closed her eyes. "Honey. I shouldn't have got so upset with Kate. But when you confided in her, I . . . I was jealous."

"You were?"

"I can see how much you like her. And I . . . understand why you like her."

Zoe went quiet for a moment.

"I do like her," she said. "She's really nice and easy to talk to."

"All right, all right." Alice smiled.

"But I like you more," Zoe said. It was downright juvenile how silly that comment was. And it was even more juvenile how much Alice enjoyed hearing it. "Kate doesn't know the way I like to loop my Cheerios on a straw and suck them off."

Alice smiled. "That *is* quite weird."

"She doesn't know how I can only watch TV on the floor while folding laundry."

Alice saw the direction this was headed and she felt her eyes fill. "Yes, I never really understood that."

"I can't crawl into bed with Kate and sleep beside her because she'd probably think that was creepy."

"True," Alice agreed. That was definitely only something a fifteen-year-old girl could do with her mother. The tears began to slide, unchecked, down Alice's cheeks, and Zoe's. Zoe leaned over and laid her head against Alice's chest.

"I still need you, Mom," Zoe said.

"You have me, Mouse," Alice said, and at least for now, the words felt true.

THREE

The fear of death follows from the fear of life. A man who lives fully is prepared to die at any time.

—MARK TWAIN

53

made a comment in class this week," Zoe said. It felt childish, reporting back her success to Dr. Sanders, but Zoe couldn't deny it felt good. It almost made the horrors of putting up her hand worth it. She'd done it in English, of all classes. They'd been having a class discussion about *The Outsiders*. When she'd raised her hand, Mrs. Patterson had done a double take.

"Do you . . . have some thoughts on this, Zoe?"

"Uh, well . . . I think S. E. Hinton did a good job of looking at life as an outsider," she muttered. "Ponyboy felt like an outsider in his own town, he didn't feel safe walking the streets in his own neighborhood because he was a greaser. He felt angry about that, and that it wasn't fair. But he came to realize that, in a way, everyone is an outsider and he needed to change his outlook."

It had come out fast, in a long line without pause or inflection. By the time she finished, she was breathless and her heart was a drum in her ears. But the important thing was that she'd done it. There was something to be said for little wins. It almost made her want to do it again.

"I'm impressed," Dr. Sanders told Zoe. "How did it feel?"

"It felt uncomfortable," she said. "But . . . it could have been worse."

Dr. Sanders didn't smile exactly, but he seemed pleased. It made Zoe feel like punching the sky. Mrs. Hunt had made her promise she'd meet with Dr. Sanders at least three times, and she'd been dreading it, but now she realized it had some upsides. It was actually pretty nice, having someone to talk to.

The truth was, her week back at school had been brutal. For the first few days while Harry still had been suspended, Cameron had continued to spill water every time Zoe walked into the room. On top of Cameron's antics, there were the expected whispers and stares. Then there were those who felt bad for her, and Zoe suffered equally under their gaze. In fact, in a way, kindness was worse than cruelty because the pressure to respond graciously could be crippling, and she inevitably failed at it.

Still, things weren't all bad. She and Jessie Lee and Emily had taken to sitting with Harry and a few of his friends at lunchtime, which Emily, of course, loved. Most of the time Zoe sat in silence, worrying that everyone thought she was the weird mute chick, but she managed to follow along with the conversation, even laugh a little.

She hadn't seen Kate since that day at her house. She thought about her sometimes, hated the way they'd left things. But she couldn't do it to her mom.

"Well, I think we can consider that a successful first week, don't you?" Dr. Sanders said.

Zoe nodded.

"So," he said, glancing down at the folder in front of him. "I thought today we could talk a little about your parents." He looked up, expectant.

"Er . . . okay." It seemed like a strange thing to talk about; then again, maybe it wasn't. On TV everyone seemed to talk about their parents in therapy.

"Why don't you start by telling me about your childhood?"

He watched her carefully. Zoe felt uncomfortable under his gaze.

"Well . . . I guess, there's not much to tell. I've spent my whole life in Atherton. I lived with my mom and my great-great-grandma until I was two, when she died. Since then, it's just been Mom and me."

"And your dad?"

Zoe shook her head. "He's not in my life. I don't even know who he is."

Dr. Sanders was quiet for a moment. "It must have been strange, growing up without a father."

"It wasn't strange. You don't miss what you don't have. And my mom more than made up for him not being around."

"You didn't feel cheated, not having a father figure in your life?"

"No," Zoe said. "Although . . . I do think about him sometimes. You know, just wonder what he's like."

The truth was, Zoe *had* been thinking of her dad more lately. Maybe it was because of Kate's husband, David, the perfect, friendly nice-guy dad, or maybe it was because her mom was sick? In those moments—those horrible moments—when she entertained the idea that her mom might actually die, she couldn't help but think of him. Up until now, she'd been happy not to know anything about him. The thing about having social anxiety was that you weren't too interested in knowing someone who didn't want to know you. But things were . . . changing.

She'd started imagining seeing him on the street. The fantasy was almost always the same. He'd be at the gas station, or walking his dog, and she'd feel it—a zing of electricity in the air. He'd glance up and he would know, of course, that it was her. They'd run all the way home, together, to tell her mom. *Look*, she would say. *It's him!* They'd all squeal and have a revolting three-way hug.

It would be a turning point in their lives. The missing piece for both of them. They'd start spending time together—occasionally at first, and then more often. After a while she'd start texting him "Happy Father's Day" and then they'd become friends on Facebook, and he would write all those dorky comments on her posts that her friends were always mortified by. And she'd text him and say "Daaaaad!" And he would send back about ten emojis, because dads always overused those things.

But it was just a fantasy.

"I mean . . . it's stupid," she said. "If he was a good guy and he, you know, wanted me . . . he'd already be in my life. So I shouldn't even think about it."

Dr. Sanders's expression was doing something with his face, sucking at the inside of his mouth or something, that made him look really tense.

"I don't think it's stupid to think about it," he said. "The biological pull is strong. Studies show that children are nearly always better off with both biological parents in their lives. Even just knowing who your father is has the potential to bring you a lot of peace."

It was the first time Zoe had seen him be anything more forceful than neutral. But there was something in his tone that was stronger. It gave her a funny feeling.

The bell went.

"Zoe—"

"I need to get to class," she said, jumping up. But afterward, at her locker, she was still thinking about something Dr. Sanders had said. *Even just knowing who he is has the potential to bring you a lot of peace.* She wondered about this. And it occurred to her that maybe she should find him.

5 4

H ungover but still here," Paul announced, when Alice
opened the door. Indeed he did look worse for wear. His
eyes were bloodshot and his plaid shirt was buttoned so
badly Alice couldn't understand how he'd managed it. Also, she
caught the faint whiff of alcohol. The strangest thing was, instead
of feeling angry, she felt grateful that he'd shown up at all.

Paul had been more dependable than Alice expected. Apart
from twice, when he was drunk and uncontactable (Alice had had
to call Sonja for a last-minute ride), he'd managed to show up when
required, and even sometimes when he wasn't. Truth be told, Alice had started to enjoy having the company, and, she suspected,
so did Paul. After a while it occurred to Alice that she hadn't been
the only one alone all these years.

"You ready?" he asked.

"Do turkeys stampede at dawn?"

Paul's expression said he was too hungover to process humor.

"Forget it," Alice said. "Let's go."

Alice was more than ready. It had been a rough few weeks.
Not just the chemo, but the complications. She'd had infections.
Low white-cell count. A blood transfusion. She'd had to delay
chemo twice. Before she knew it, two months had passed.

As sick as it made her, Alice wanted to have chemo. There was power in the knowledge that she was fighting the disease. Sometimes, when she was stuck in that chair with the tube going into her arm, she'd visualize the poison flowing through her veins, attacking the cancer cells. Stopping it in its tracks. It was, if not a good feeling, the only thing that gave her hope.

Today, she was optimistic. She'd had a blood transfusion a few days before and her blood exam had shown that her white-cell count was up. Yesterday Dr. Brookes had given her the go-ahead for chemo. She was all set. Unlikely as it was, somewhere along the way she'd started to enjoy chemo. She'd trundle in there with Paul and watch a movie or have a cup of tea and chat. The nurses were so upbeat and happy. Last time the young girl and her mother had been there again, and they'd passed two whole hours talking and exchanging magazines.

Paul dropped her off out in front of the hospital, as was their routine, and she went on up while he parked the car. In the elevator she saw Iris, her favorite nurse, who asked about Zoe, and Alice asked her about Russell, the man Iris had met online and was planning to go on a date with. At her last chemo session Iris had shown Alice a photo of him and Alice had commented on his large muscles.

"His profile picture was quite deceiving." Iris chuckled. "Then again, so is mine."

By the time Alice got to the chemotherapy room, she was feeling quite chipper. It was nice, being surrounded by people. It was, she suspected, the kind of community most people would have if they worked in an office, or were members of a club. Alice found her community at chemo.

Alice went to her usual station. There were no rules about where to sit, but she always seemed to end up at the same spot. Remarkably, it was always free. "People are creatures of habit," Iris had said, when Alice had asked about it. "They sit somewhere once, it becomes *their spot*."

The spot beside her, typically, belonged to the young girl and her mother, but today it was taken by a woman who looked to be in her seventies, and a support person who must have been her son. They nodded hello, and Alice tried not to be disappointed. She didn't see any familiar faces. No patients she knew.

Suddenly Alice noticed Kate at the desk. Kate glanced up at the same moment, then quickly looked away again. It was the first time Alice had seen her since her verbal reprimanding a few weeks ago. Since then, as far as Alice knew, Zoe hadn't seen Kate again. These last few weeks, Alice felt like she had her daughter back. At night, Zoe slept by her side. In the morning, before she went to school, Zoe made her a breakfast that she wouldn't eat. Still, she felt thoroughly cared for. It was nice.

Paul came up, then promptly disappeared—presumably to the bar across the road for a little hair of the dog.

After a time, the woman next to her drifted off to sleep. Her son, Alice noticed, was about Alice's age, with a crop of thick, sandy hair and blue eyes made bluer by his thin, periwinkle V-neck sweater. All of this Alice happily registered from her seat, comfortably aware that as a bald, forty-year-old cancer patient, she was hardly going to attract his attention.

But then, he looked up and said, "Oh, hello." His smile was as earnest as it was lovely. "Sorry, I didn't notice you there."

"No, I'm sorry," Alice said. "I think I was staring. You start to lose social graces in here. Like being in an old folks' home. Or at a kindergarten."

He laughed.

"Is this your mom's first session?" she asked.

"My aunt," he corrected. "And yes. You?"

"Oh, I'm an old hand," she said with faux pride. "Anything you want to know, ask me."

"Is that right?"

"Uh-huh."

"So what do I need to know?"

Alice was in a good mood. It had been a while since she'd

chatted with anyone socially except Paul. She told the man—
Andrew was his name—about the good nurses and the bad
nurses, the secret parking spaces across the road (free!), the coffee carts to avoid. Andrew, as it turned out, was a doctor in the
hospital—a hand surgeon—so he didn't need her tips (he had
his own parking space) but he was very polite. Alice told him
not to mention that he was a doctor when her brother arrived
because he would probably try and get him to write out a pre-
scription for morphine for him. Andrew laughed. Alice told
him not to laugh, she was serious. He laughed more. He was one
of those people who laughed easily. A lovely trait, Alice had
always thought.

"If you think that's funny, get this! He drops me off here, then
goes to the pub on the corner and gets loaded. We usually share
a cab home!"

Now he looked like he wasn't sure if he was meant to laugh or
not. But Alice was laughing so much, he joined in. "Family," she
said. "Who'd have 'em."

"So what kind of cancer does your aunt have?" she asked when
the laughter died down.

"Breast," he said, after glancing at her quickly and finding her
still dozing. "But they caught it early. Her prognosis is good. Yourself?"

"Ovarian. Stage three."

A cloud passed over his face.

"No, it's not great," Alice admitted. "But it could be worse. I
could be . . . trampled by a herd of elephants. Or dragged through
a town square by my feet."

He chuckled.

"Hung, drawn and quartered," she continued. "Tarred and
feathered!"

By the time she was finished he was laughing helplessly and so
was Alice. It felt fantastic to laugh with another adult. A normal
non-drunk male adult.

She kept talking.

After what only seemed like minutes, Iris came over and unhooked her IV bag.

"You're good to go now, Alice," she said.

"Already?"

"Can you call Paul and tell him to come up?"

"Paul doesn't have a phone. But it's all right. I know where to find him."

"Well," Iris said, shaking her head. "I really don't know what to do. I need to release you to a person."

This was a first. Alice had never had to be released to a person before. Besides, Iris knew all about Paul. She had an uncle, she'd told Alice last time, who was the same way. At previous sessions she'd been happy for Alice to head on downstairs to find him.

"Perhaps if someone could take you to him?" Iris said, glancing around.

"Can I help at all?" Andrew said.

"Oh, Andrew, would you?" Iris exclaimed. "Alice just needs someone to deliver her to her brother."

She met Alice's eye. *Oh, Iris. You naughty, naughty thing.*

"I'd be happy to," Andrew said. Which was exactly what Iris was banking on.

Iris waved a little too brightly as they walked away. Alice made a mental note to thank her later. But in the elevator, alongside a couple of nurses and an old lady in a hospital-issue dressing gown, conversation suddenly dried up between Alice and Andrew. A few potential topics crossed Alice's mind but she couldn't seem to project any. She, as Zoe would have said, *literally choked.* (A stupid saying, Alice thought, because if she literally choked, she'd be dead. If they had to specify, why not say figuratively choked?) The elevator stopped on every floor—one person off, one on. Alice became very aware that soon this lovely little encounter would be over.

With one floor to go, they were alone. Alice knew she had to act fast. But to do what? All she knew was that she had enjoyed today. And she didn't want it to end.

"Andrew?" Alice said, and when he turned to her, she stood on tiptoe and kissed him, quickly, on the lips. She didn't know who was more startled—she or Andrew. Mercifully, in the very next moment, the doors opened.

"Thanks for escorting me down," Alice said, and burst through the doors.

"Wait!" Andrew called.

Reluctantly, Alice turned.

"I . . . promised Iris I'd hand you over to your brother," he said.

Alice scanned the foyer. Through the glass she saw the back of Paul's oval head as he slumped against the wall outside. Always a class act, her brother.

"There he is." Alice pointed vaguely. "Anyway, nice to meet you. You'd better get back to your aunt."

He nodded uncertainly. Alice had well and truly bewildered him.

"Sorry," she said. "About that. I needed to know that I still had it in me."

He smiled. "You do."

They looked at each other for a moment. Then finally, he turned and walked away.

Alice watched as he headed back to the elevator. When he turned to face her he was still smiling. And when Alice skipped out of the foyer toward her drunk brother, so was she.

55

Sonja's gaze had been fixed on the glass door of the diner for ten minutes when Agnes finally walked in. It had been years since she had seen her sister. Apart from a few more gray hairs, she looked the same. Sonja stood to greet her, but Agnes's gaze continued right past her.

"Agnes!"

"Sonja?" Agnes's jaw dropped. "I would never have recognized you."

Sonja had chosen a diner in the neighborhood where they'd grown up, thinking it would be a) convenient for Agnes, and b) a comfort to Sonja. The former might have been true but the latter was not. In fact, Sonja doubted she'd ever felt more out of place.

Agnes crossed the floor slowly and slid into the booth opposite her. There was no hug. No kiss. Not even a handshake. And although Sonja hadn't expected any of these things, she felt a little disappointed.

"What happened to your face?" Agnes asked, timidly, after a few silent moments.

It took Sonja a moment to realize what she meant. "Oh. Botox."

"Ah," Agnes said, pulling at her face as if she could smooth out the wrinkles with her fingers. "I could use some of that stuff."

"You look fine," Sonja said. "Great."

Agnes did look fine, but "great" was pushing it. She'd aged as one would expect—with the gray hair and deep lines. But she looked well. Healthy and happy in jeans and a white sweatshirt, with her hair pulled back in a scrunchie. It made Sonja feel ridiculous in her pantsuit and pumps. She'd spent an hour blowing out her hair that morning. Funny the things she did without even questioning it these days. It was as though she had turned into a robot—everything was on autopilot.

When the waitress came, Agnes ordered a diet Pepsi. Sonja had planned to order chamomile tea, but at the last minute she said, "Do you know what? Make it two diet Pepsis."

It felt rebellious, somehow. Sonja hadn't drunk diet Pepsi in years. People in her world didn't.

When the waitress left, Agnes looked at her. "You're not dying, are you?"

"No." Sonja surveyed her sister's face for any clue to whether this would be good or bad news. But Agnes wasn't giving anything away. "I just thought it might be nice to see my sister."

"Oh," Agnes said. But she seemed so surprised Sonja had to ask herself: Why *was* she here?

Ever since the night George had choked her, she'd been thinking about her conversation with Dagmar at the hospital. *Was* she a victim of abuse? The irony of a social worker being abused was not lost on her. She was trained in recognizing domestic violence— how could she not see it in her own relationship? Worse, how could she not automatically know what to do about it?

She thought of all the clients she'd counseled over the years who had turned around and gone right back into the abusive relationship. She'd never understood it. Hadn't she given the client the number of a women's shelter? Hadn't she explained the support programs that were available to her? And yet the client would always say the same thing. "But I love him."

Suddenly Sonja understood. These women weren't imbeciles who didn't care about their safety or the safety of their children.

They might have had feelings of fear for their abuser, but they also had feelings of love. Rarely was an abuser a monster. He could also be loving, charming, maybe even a good father. Staying with him might hurt . . . but then again, so would leaving.

Agnes was still waiting for Sonja to explain. Her frustration began to surface. "What is it, Sonja? It's not like you to just call up out of the blue. Shane thought you might have had a nervous breakdown or something!"

"I . . . I . . . ," Sonja stammered. She'd come here to reach out to Agnes, to ask for advice. But the woman opposite her seemed like a stranger. Of course she was! Sonja hadn't been in touch with her properly in years. It was stupid reaching out to her now. She was stupid to think she had anyone else to rely on, apart from herself. "It's just . . . I'm only working part-time these days and I thought it would be nice if we could catch up every so often. No big deal." She tried for a smile. "So, how are the kids?"

Agnes looked skeptical, but eventually she said, "Macy's got herself a new boyfriend."

"Really?" Sonja said. Macy was a great girl—bright and loud with a laugh that caught. "I hope he's good enough for her."

"He seems like a good guy. He's in I.T. I might even become a nana one of these days!" Agnes gave her first smile since she arrived and Sonja felt herself smile too.

"I'd love to see that."

The waitress came with their drinks and they sipped them, exchanging unimportant details about their jobs, Agnes's kids, the latest celebrity gossip. Nothing groundbreaking, but for today that was enough.

"Well," Agnes said, when her diet Pepsi was finished. "I've got to get home. It was nice to catch up."

"Yes," Sonja stood. "Very nice."

Despite the rocky start, Sonja felt sad watching Agnes slide out from the booth. "So," she said. "I'm off work Thursday, if you're free?"

Sonja blinked.

"You said you'd like to visit every now and again," Agnes said. "So . . . I'm off Thursday if you—"

Sonja threw her arms around Agnes and hugged her tight, nearly causing her to fall sideways. "I'll be here," she said into Agnes's ear.

That night, once George was snoring, Sonja crept into the bathroom. Naked, she stood in front of the mirror to survey her injuries. The bruises around her upper arms and wrists were already starting to form, from George's grip on her less than an hour before. That would do for now. She picked up her phone and snapped some pictures, then attached them to an e-mail. In the subject bar she wrote the date. She sent the pictures to herself. For her files.

Just in case.

56

Zoe's mom wasn't doing so well. Ever since her last chemo treatment, she'd gone downhill pretty fast. She hadn't eaten properly in weeks. She just lay in bed insisting that she was fine, just tired. Zoe didn't know what to believe. She was constantly cold, so she said, but Zoe slept with her every night and all she felt was sweat and heat.

Her uncle Paul took her to appointments and reported back to Zoe. She didn't really understand what he told her, and she could tell Paul didn't either. He'd just recite whatever the doctor or nurse had said. *No chemo today, blood test revealed low white-cell count. Antibiotics today for infection.* Zoe didn't know if this was normal for cancer patients, but she knew it wasn't normal for her mother.

Still, her mom kept up her verging-on-crazy positivity.

"I'm fine," she said constantly. "A few days of rest and I'll be back at chemo. This time next year everything will be back to normal."

She'd become weirdly obsessed with making plans, way in the future.

"You know where we should go next Christmas? Mexico! Or Hawaii? Or what about Australia! You can bring Harry!"

"Let's just get through this, Mom," Zoe would reply.

It wasn't that Zoe didn't like her being positive. She did. It was that it was so at odds with the way that she looked. Outwardly, she seemed to be getting worse. She'd lost weight and she always seemed sick. But maybe, if her mom said she was fine, she was. Wouldn't she know her own body better than anyone else?

Today, her mom was dozing on the couch when Zoe touched her hand to her forehead. An hour earlier, she'd been telling Zoe how, when chemo was over, she planned to grow her hair long and get highlights.

"Mom!" she said. "You're burning up."

Her mom moaned softly but didn't respond.

"Mom?" she tried again, shaking her.

Her eyes opened briefly then closed again. Zoe immediately thought to call Kate. Kate would know what all this meant, and she'd be able to explain it in a way that would make sense to Zoe. But Zoe hadn't spoken to Kate in weeks. It was the weirdest thing, but Zoe *missed* her. How was that even possible? A few overnight visits, a few conversations in the sunroom . . . it wasn't exactly a lifelong friendship. And yet now, when she was really worried, it was Kate that she wanted to talk to.

She dialed Kate's number. Kate picked up after a couple of rings. "Kate speaking."

Zoe's throat became thick and full of words that wouldn't come out. The relief that she felt, just hearing Kate's voice, was staggering.

"It's me."

"Zoe?"

"Mom's sick," she said. "She's burning up."

Kate paused just a second. "She's hot to the touch?"

"Yes."

"How long has she felt hot?"

"I . . . I don't know!"

"Okay, just listen to me. Do you have a thermometer there?"

"Yes," she said.

"Good. Can you take your mom's temperature for me? I'll wait."

Zoe put down the phone and ran to the bathroom. The thermometer was in the cabinet. She raced back to the sofa and popped it into her mom's mouth, resting against her cheek. She waited thirty seconds, then plucked it out again.

"It's . . . one oh four," she said into the phone. "Oh God. That's high, isn't it?"

Kate was silent for a moment. Long enough to make Zoe worried. "Zoe, is your uncle there? Or anyone else?"

"No," Zoe said. "It's just me."

Kate paused another beat. "Hang tight," she said finally. "I'm coming over."

57

D r. Brookes was wearing remarkably casual clothes, Alice thought idly as he appeared at her hospital bed. A polo shirt, a pair of trousers. If she hadn't been feeling so crappy, she'd have commented on it. She'd warmed to Dr. Brookes, these past months. Maybe he became more personable the better he knew his patients? Or maybe *she'd* become more personable.

Zoe had tried to reach Paul but he hadn't answered his phone for days. He was probably off on a bender.

Sonja was here, as usual. And at some point, despite their rocky start, Alice realized she'd started to appreciate her presence. In fact, over the past few weeks, Sonja had become one of the few people Alice could depend on.

Kate had become another one. She had driven Alice to the hospital. Alice was thinking of calling her Saint Kate. Always coming to the rescue when they needed it—taking care of Zoe, taking care of her. It made Alice feel a little sheepish, after the way she'd shouted at her the last time they spoke. Today, Kate had also managed to bypass triage and put Alice straight into a bed, and half an hour later, Dr. Brookes was here, seemingly on his day off. For an unassuming woman, she sure could make things happen.

Alice watched Kate now through the glass. She stood in the

corridor opposite Zoe. When Dr. Brookes came in, Alice thought she'd have to beg Zoe to leave. But all it took was a nod from Kate and she was gone. Now, the two of them chatted with an ease that Alice had never seen Zoe have before. Not even with Emily. Not with anyone except, well, Alice.

"How are you feeling?" Dr. Brookes said.

Alice made a face.

"Not great, huh? That was an impressive fever you came in here with. The antibiotics should start working soon. And I'll get the nurse to give you something to make you more comfortable."

"Make it a double," Alice said.

Dr. Brookes smiled but it didn't touch his eyes. There'd been a dip in his enthusiasm these last few weeks. Slight frowns when he looked at her chart. Words of encouragement were more strained; reassurances were vaguer.

"So?" Alice said. "Another infection?"

"Yes," Dr. Brookes said. "It's to be expected because of the way the chemo attacks your white cells."

Alice got the sense there was more. "But?"

"But it has me concerned."

"Why?"

Alice glanced at the window. Kate was giving Zoe a hug. Or was it the other way around? As if noticing her discomfort, Sonja moved in close beside Alice.

"We have your test results back," he continued. "As I explained, we knew your white-cell count was low, that's why you've had recurrent infections. Unfortunately these tests showed your levels are below five hundred cells per cubic millimeter, which makes you a grade-four neutropenic. The most severe kind."

Alice looked back at Dr. Brookes. "And that means?"

"That means you'll need to stay in the hospital until your neutrophil levels come up. We need to get you well and can't risk another infection while your white-cell count is so low. And no more chemo, for the time being."

"No more chemo?" Now he had her full attention. "But I *need* chemo. How am I supposed to beat the cancer?"

"Unfortunately your neutropenia makes it very difficult for us to treat your cancer at present," Dr. Brookes said.

Alice waited, but he didn't continue. "So what *do* we do?" she prompted.

"I'd suggest we take a break and when your blood improves we can revisit the chemotherapy, maybe with a different formula. Right now I'd be loath to do anything to deplete your neutrophils further. We'd be risking neutropenic sepsis, which can kill you a lot faster than cancer."

Alice felt the room swell around her. "But I . . . I need to be one of the twenty percent."

Sonja reached for Alice's hand and gave it a squeeze of solidarity. It was surprisingly comforting. Alice glanced at their intertwined hands—a universal sign of support—and in that second, felt grateful. Then she noticed Sonja's shirtsleeve had ridden up a few inches, revealing a purplish-black bruise. Immediately, Sonja tugged the sleeve down again.

Dr. Brookes laid a hand on Alice's shoulder. "Let's just take it one thing at a time, Alice. First, a few days in the hospital."

Alice nodded repeatedly, calming herself. She could do that, she told herself. She could take things a day at a time. Like Dr. Brookes said, when her blood improved they would revisit chemo with a different formula. A better formula, this time. The right formula.

"Do you need Sonja to make arrangements for your daughter?"

"Zoe has somewhere to go," Alice said, and she glanced back at the window, trying to ignore the fact that Kate and Zoe stood arm in arm, looking very much like mother and daughter.

58

"Mom?"

A week after her admission to the hospital, Alice was back home. At the sound of Zoe's voice, she sat upright in bed. It was crazy how her daughter—her voice, her smell, even her footfalls—could create such a yearning in her. She recalled the feeling from when Zoe was a little girl—standing outside her classroom at the end of the day, waiting to feel her sweet, soft body in her arms, to smell her sweet little head. Sometimes motherhood was a hunger, Alice thought. An addiction. Most people were gradually weaned from it as their child got older. Alice had got to indulge in it longer than most.

Zoe appeared in the doorway. "You're home!"

She crossed the bedroom floor in three giant steps. She looked as though she was going to launch herself at Alice, but she seemed to stop herself, and she gave her a gentle hug instead. Alice closed her eyes and tried to drink her in, the way she had when she was little. Zoe stayed there in her arms until Alice let go. After an eternity, she did.

"When did you get back?" Zoe asked, sitting up.

"An hour ago. Sonja drove me. How was Kate's?"

It was a silly question, since Alice knew how it had gone at Kate's. Zoe had visited her at the hospital every day and given her the lowdown. ("It's a bit weird," Zoe had said one day. "Especially when Jake and Scarlett are there. They all eat dinner together in the dining room and talk about their days!") But Alice could see that Zoe didn't hate it there. She smiled when she talked about them. As hard as it had been, imagining Zoe with another family, it had also been a relief, knowing that she was safe and happy. It allowed Alice to concentrate on getting well.

"It was okay," she said. "But I'm happy to be home."

"Have they rescheduled your next chemo session?" Zoe asked. She'd asked about this each time she'd visited—she'd obviously been Googling, and she'd come to the same conclusion that Alice had—if the chemo stopped, it wasn't good news.

"I have a meeting with the doctors next week to discuss next steps," Alice said carefully. And she smiled brightly. Dr. Brookes had told her she should remain optimistic and that's exactly what Alice planned to do.

Alice was having coffee with Sonja. And if that wasn't strange enough, the whole thing had been Alice's idea. This morning, when Sonja called around unannounced to check on her, Alice found herself suggesting it. There was only so much sitting around the house someone could do, and Alice didn't exactly have a huge selection of people offering to take her out and about.

"How are you feeling?" Sonja asked her.

"I feel good," Alice replied, sipping her coffee. It tasted bitter so she reached for a packet of sugar. "Much better since taking a break from the chemo."

Sonja's expression was hard to read. "Well I'm glad you're feeling good."

The truth was, Alice didn't feel all that great. She hadn't had any more infections, but she was constantly tired. A lot of days, she could barely get herself out of bed. Today was the first time she'd felt remotely like leaving the house. But no one liked a downer.

"I'll admit," Alice said, "I can't wait until it's all over."

Sonja looked surprised. "You . . . can't?"

"I just want things to go back to normal. Except," she said, when Sonja opened her mouth. "They won't go back to normal. They'll be better. I'm going to go outside more with my daughter. Go on vacation. Dance!" Alice ripped open the sugar sachet, spilling granules everywhere.

Sonja didn't say anything for a long time. "Did Dr. Brookes tell you things would go back to normal?" she asked, eventually.

"Well, he told me to be optimistic."

"Alice, while it's wonderful to be optimistic, it's also prudent to plan for all possibilities." Alice started shaking her head but Sonja held up a hand, silencing her.

"Just . . . think of it this way. Most people take out roadside assistance when they buy a new car. They don't expect anything to go wrong with it, of course, it's a new car. But it's insurance. It means they know they'll be taken care of. Just in case."

Alice didn't like the direction the conversation was taking. She'd been focusing her energy on remaining positive—for Zoe. She didn't see the point of "planning for other possibilities."

Sonja's hand was still in the air. Alice looked at her wrist. The bruise was yellow now, but still there. "What happened," Alice asked, "to your wrist?"

She hoped it sounded like a change of topic rather than an accusation—even though the truth was, Alice was suspicious. And her suspicions were confirmed when Sonja immediately shrugged it back under her shirtsleeve. "Oh, nothing," she said. Sonja looked for a moment like she was going to continue, but she just stopped as though she'd lost her train of thought. For the first time, Alice wondered what was going on behind her perfect, Botoxed exterior.

"Are you married?" Alice asked. Sonja wore a ring, but she never talked about her family—and Alice had never asked Sonja anything about herself.

"Yes," Sonja said.

"Kids?"

She shook her head. "Unfortunately not. I married too late for that."

"I'm sorry."

Sonja shrugged, sipping her coffee. "George and I have a full life."

"Lucky you."

"Well, it's not as though things are perfect. No marriage is." Sonja put down her cup.

"I wouldn't know," Alice admitted.

"You've never been married?" Sonja asked. "Not to Zoe's father?"

"Not to him or anyone else," Alice said. "I'm not sure if that makes me lucky or unlucky."

Sonja's eyes were downcast as she absently swept the loose sugar granules into a pile. "At the beginning, you think it's all going to be happiness, romance and charm. Then real life creeps in. You know, the ugly stuff." Sonja's mouth twisted on *ugly stuff*. She was speaking in a slightly detached way, as if she'd forgotten Alice was there.

"Ugly stuff . . . like your wrist?" Alice asked.

Sonja glanced up quickly. Consciously or unconsciously, she fiddled with her shirtsleeve again. "All sorts of ugly stuff," she said eventually.

Suddenly Sonja seemed to remember herself. "But . . . life has its ups and downs, doesn't it?" She pasted on a false, bright smile. "During the downs you just have to remind yourself that the next up is just around the corner."

"I agree," Alice said. "Although . . . while it's good to be optimistic, isn't it prudent to plan for all possibilities?"

They locked eyes. Alice cocked her head. For the first time, Alice felt like they were both actually seeing each other.

"That's familiar advice," Sonja said.

"It's good advice," Alice admitted. "And perhaps we should both take it?"

They both lifted their coffees in unison then, and after they put their cups down again conversation went in a different direction. But, despite herself, Alice had heard what Sonja was saying to her. Alice hoped Sonja had heard it too.

59

Zoe still walked to school these days. She was doing better with people, but she didn't know if she'd ever be comfortable on a bus. However, unlike before, when she was filled with dread on the way to school, now she looked forward to it. Because Harry met her halfway.

She could see him now, up on the corner, his hands shoved in his pockets. The sight of him, as always, started a flap of panic in her chest. By the time she reached him her heart was thundering and her hands were shaking, but if he noticed, he didn't seem bothered. He removed one of his hands from his pocket and put it around her, sneaking a kiss on her forehead. And then they walked to school, arm in arm—even as her cheeks flamed.

Inside, as they put their books in their lockers, Emily arrived. A few minutes later, Lucy Barker and Jessie Lee joined them. Everyone chatted, and Zoe listened as she rummaged in her locker for books before heading to class. It was nice being a part of the group—even if she was at the periphery.

English came and went. After class, as everyone funneled through the door, Mrs. Patterson called her name. "Zoe, can I see you for a moment?"

She paused, freaked out. "Uh . . . sure."

Harry glanced back, a question in his eyes. She shrugged.

"I'll wait for you outside," he said, then filed out of the room.

"Have a seat, Zoe," Mrs. Patterson said. "We need to talk about the oral component of your English grade."

Zoe tensed up. There had been no mention of this since the debate and she had hoped they would just give her an average grade and move on.

"I graded the written portion of the debate, and it was excellent. An A-plus. But you still need to deliver an oral component to pass English."

The tension in Zoe's stomach turned to horror.

"Now, given last time, I understand that you might not want to deliver it in front of the entire class. But I've spoken with Mrs. Hunt and also Dr. Sanders, and we all agreed that you are capable of doing something to fulfill this requirement. So we've decided to put you in charge."

"What do you mean . . . put me in charge?"

"Exactly what it sounds like. You will decide what material you want to deliver, and who you want to deliver it to. I, of course, need to be one of those people. But it can be as small or large as you like."

Zoe felt the terror release like a swarm of moths.

"You might like to arrange a small group of friends, people that you really trust. You don't even need to stand on a stage. You are in charge of this, Zoe. You let me know in the next couple of weeks what you're going to do and we can take it from there."

"I'm just . . . I'm not sure I can, Mrs. P."

Mrs. Patterson was silent for a moment; then Zoe heard her sigh. "You know, Zoe, many people are highly successful in spite of their fears. A lot of famous actors and actresses got into acting to address their fears of the public eye. They somehow learn to channel their fears and use them to make them better at what they do. Some of them have even won Oscars."

"I don't know how I could channel my fears into a good speech," Zoe said.

"Think about it. Maybe there is a way that you can do this presentation that is uniquely you." Zoe looked up, and Mrs. Patterson smiled. "For the record, I'm looking forward to it. You're intelligent. You're creative. Your speech-writing skills are the best in the class. Something tells me you have a lot to say that is worth listening to."

Mrs. Patterson pulled a document out of her folder and handed it to Zoe. "Here are the criteria you will be graded on. As long as your speech fits into these guidelines, you can be as imaginative as you like."

Zoe took the document, a feeling of dread brewing in her belly. But as she stood up and turned to walk out the door, she had an idea. *Something that is uniquely you.*

She had an idea.

60

uck!" Alice whispered as she heard the ringing in her ear. But whispering cusswords was horribly unsatisfying. From her bedroom she could hear the hum of the television out in the living room. Zoe would be curled up in front of it. So she needed to be quiet.

But all she could hear was Sonja's words swirling in her mind. *While it is wonderful to be optimistic, it's also prudent to plan for all possibilities . . . it's insurance.* Alice knew Sonja had a point. After all, healthy people did it all the time. They nominated someone to be a guardian for their child in the event of their death, jotted down their name in a will and never thought about it again. End of story. Alice decided it would be a good idea to do the same, but unfortunately it wasn't as simple as that. Even if there had been an abundance of possibilities (which there wasn't), it would have been hard to find the right person for Zoe. Zoe was a special kind of girl—she needed a special kind of parent. It took Alice a while, but she realized there was only one possibility. She just needed to pluck up the courage and ask.

"Kate speaking."

"Kate!" Alice's heart jumped. "It's Alice."

"Alice." Kate sounded wary, and Alice understood why. Even though Kate had come to the rescue when Alice was ill—and even after Zoe had stayed with her again—Alice still hadn't spoken to her properly since the day she'd told her on the phone to stay away from Zoe. "Hello. It's good to hear from you."

Alice marveled at how a person could be so nice. Part of her hated it. Part of her was counting on it.

"I must apologize again," Kate started.

"Please don't," Alice said. "After all you've done for Zoe, I think we can call it quits."

"Okay. Good." Kate was quiet a moment. "Dr. Brookes told me your white-cell count was still low. Try not to be discouraged. Hopefully your levels will come up in a few weeks and we can try more chemo."

It was genuine, Alice realized. The way Kate cared.

"Yes, I'm sure they will," Alice said.

"Is there anything I can do for you?" Kate asked.

Alice choked back a small sob that leapt out of nowhere. "Actually yes . . . I wanted to ask you a favor."

"Anything."

Alice swallowed. What on earth was wrong with her? "Could I . . . could I come over tomorrow?"

Kate didn't hesitate, not even for a second. "What time?"

Alice got Kate's address and made a plan to go over there the next day. After she hung up, she pulled herself together. It was just insurance, after all. Nothing more. Yet for some reason she cried until the world became as blurred as she felt inside.

61

The next afternoon Kate squinted at the figure standing in front of her house. She was bundled in a navy blue coat with a red scarf flapping in the breeze. Her hands were ungloved and clasped together, wringing. Kate raced down the stairs. The house was empty again, for now. David was back from Mexico, but their issues, unfortunately, had returned with him. They'd had a few talks, made a few inroads, but the baby dilemma hovered between them, threatening to ruin every pleasant dinner, every nice conversation. Now, it felt like he was gone more than he was home. And the kids were at Hilary's this week, which made the house eerily quiet. There was only so much aloneness one person could take.

She opened the front door. "Alice?"

"Hello," she said, but remained where she was. She looked thin, small. Her face was gaunt, and her head was covered in a red knitted hat.

"Would you like to come in?"

"Yes. Thank you."

"Have a seat," Kate said, once they were inside. Alice seemed strangely stiff and formal. Kate wondered what was going on. "Shall I make coffee? Or tea?"

"I'm fine." Alice sat in the armchair.

Kate sat opposite. "How are you feeling?"

"Better for not having the chemo," Alice said. "And worse, for not having chemo."

"And how is Zoe?"

"She's involved in her own life. She has a boyfriend, some friends. She's probably doing better than she ever has."

"That's fantastic," Kate said.

"But I've been thinking," Alice continued. "About what would happen to Zoe . . . I mean, I have no intention of dying. But it seems the . . . prudent thing to plan."

"I see," Kate said slowly. "Well, yes, that makes sense."

"Problem is, I don't have a lot of options."

"Zoe's father definitely isn't a possibility?" Kate asked.

"No." Alice's voice was firmer than Kate had ever heard it. At first Kate thought she was going to leave it at that, but then she sighed. "The truth is . . . how can I put this? . . . Zoe wasn't conceived consensually."

"Oh, Alice, wow."

"It was the best thing to ever happen to me," Alice continued quickly. "It gave me Zoe. But, no, Zoe's father is definitely not an option."

"Of course not," Kate said.

They descended into silence again. And Kate had a sudden feeling that she and Alice had become a team. A team responsible for looking out for Zoe. Surprisingly, it was a team she very much wanted to be on.

"Well, how about your brother?" Kate said.

"Paul's been pretty good these last few weeks. He's come nearly every time I've needed him. But he's not a potential parent for Zoe." Alice dropped her gaze. "Kate . . . Zoe really likes you."

Kate edged forward, trying to catch Alice's eye. "I really like her too. She's a wonderful girl."

Alice's face suddenly seemed to spasm. It took Kate a moment to realize she was trying not to cry. "Well, then I hope you'll humor me when I ask if you'd consider . . . becoming her guardian. If something happens to me."

For a moment, silence engulfed them. Kate felt something shift in the room.

"It's just insurance," Alice continued, lifting her head now. "I have no plans to die. But . . . Zoe feels comfortable with you. You understand her. Maybe even better than I do."

"That's not true," Kate said.

"Maybe it is, maybe it isn't. The fact remains, I think . . ." Alice swallowed. "I think she'd be happy with you."

Kate hadn't seen this coming. And still, somehow, the idea wasn't shocking. But it wasn't as simple as that. She imagined bringing this up with David. *You know how you don't want a baby, how about the teenager of one of my dying patients?* Just what every troubled marriage needed.

"Oh, Alice, I . . . I am so touched that you asked me. And you know I adore Zoe. It would be a privilege but . . . honestly, I don't know. I have to talk to David and—"

"I understand," Alice said too quickly.

"I want to be clear," Kate said. "I care about Zoe. I want Zoe to be all right more than anyone."

"Not more than anyone," Alice corrected. "But you're a close second, and that's why I hope you'll take her."

62

"David," Kate said. "I have to talk to you about something."

Kate had been watching David silently for several moments. She'd promised Alice she'd think about her request, talk about it with David, and get back to her. She wanted to wait, to choose her moment, but Kate knew Alice didn't have much time. Which meant, neither did Kate.

David was pouring himself an after-work Scotch. Without looking up, he said, "Sounds serious."

"It is. I had a visitor this afternoon. Alice Stanhope. Zoe's mom."

David brought his glass over and sat down on the other end of the couch. "How's she doing?"

"Not so great. There's a real possibility she won't make it."

"Wow," David said.

"Alice asked if we would take Zoe after she dies." Kate knew she shouldn't blurt it out like that, but there was no right way to have this kind of conversation. Tentatively, she looked at David.

"Us?"

"Yes. I said I'd talk to you about it."

David blinked slowly, taking it all in. Kate steadied herself.

The fact that this was the longest conversation they'd had all week didn't bode well for a positive response. It also, likely, didn't make them a perfect choice for welcoming a troubled child into their home. Even so, Kate found herself holding her breath. She wanted this, she realized. Not just for Zoe. For herself.

"Well," he said finally, "what do *you* think?"

She felt vaguely optimistic that he was, at least, willing to discuss it.

"Well," she said, tucking her legs up under her on the couch, "on one hand, it's probably not the best idea bringing a new person into the family when things are not . . . completely harmonious with us. On the other hand, she exists. A fifteen-year-old girl with severe anxiety is about to lose her mother and have no one left in the world. She can either come to live with us, or she can bounce around in foster care until she is spat out at the age of eighteen. And David . . . I care about her. I mean . . . I care about all my patients and their families but . . . I *really* care about Zoe."

David put his glass on the coffee table.

"I'm not trying to emotionally blackmail you," Kate said.

"I know. It's just a lot to take in." He leaned back in his chair and rubbed his eyes. "And it's very out of left field. But I guess . . . my initial response is . . . maybe we *should* help her."

Kate suddenly realized she'd been holding her breath.

"We'll have to speak to the kids about it. But . . . you're right. She exists. She has no one. Her mother has come to us. We have to consider it."

Kate allowed herself to wonder how it might look if Zoe *did* join their strange blended family. With stepchildren, ex-wives and their new husbands, they all had a story of how they'd come together. Perhaps Zoe would find a place amongst them all?

"Why don't we talk to the kids tonight?" he continued. "See what they think. Then we can take it from there."

"Yes," Kate said. She scooted across the couch and sat beside him. "Yes, okay."

David reached out and took her hand. That's when Kate realized. The way you got past an obstacle in your marriage was through trying. David was trying. And so would she.

63

lice sat on the couch with Kenny in her lap. Across town, Kate would be speaking to her husband, making a decision about whether or not she'd be Zoe's guardian. It was agony, waiting for someone to make the most important decision of *your* life.

It got Alice thinking about people. Pre-motherhood, if she had pictured this inconceivable situation, she'd have thought there would be a dozen people willing to take her child. Her child's father, of course. Her parents. Her friends. And yet, she found herself in the kind of situation that most people swore could never happen to them. With no one. The irony was, since the cancer diagnosis, her life had more people in it than it had had in years. Kate. Sonja. Paul. Andrew. And still, she didn't have enough people.

She needed someone to talk to, or she'd go crazy waiting to hear from Kate. But it was late, nearly 10 P.M. It was too late to call Sonja and besides, Alice wasn't sure it would be appropriate. It was another reason people needed multiple friends, she realized. The night owls, the early risers. A friend for every season. She'd missed having friends. She missed having a door that swung continually with neighbors and friends coming and going.

Alice stood suddenly. She strode across the apartment and out into the corridor and knocked hard on Dulcie's door.

Dulcie answered dressed in a peach candlewick robe, and clasping a steaming mug. "Oh," she said. "It's you."

"Hi, Dulcie. I was just about to put the kettle on. I see you already have a drink, but I wondered if you'd like to join me."

Dulcie frowned at Alice. "But . . . it's ten o'clock at night."

"Suit yourself," Alice said. "I'll be across the hall if you change your mind."

Alice turned and walked back to her apartment, leaving the door ajar. A few moments later she heard Dulcie's door close and the sound of her slippers scuffling across the hallway toward her apartment.

"It's nice to have someone to have a cup of tea with sometimes," Dulcie said, getting comfortable at one end of Alice's couch.

Alice nodded. "I know what you mean."

64

When George appeared in the kitchen, Sonja had his coffee ready.

"Here you go," she said, handing him a coffee.

"Thank you," George said.

It was almost as if they were a normal couple.

Ever since speaking with Alice, Sonja had thought a lot about leaving George. She'd even packed a bag of clothes and money and put it in the trunk of her car.

But George had been in a good mood these last few weeks. Only last night, he'd come home talking about Christmas. "Are we going to get a real tree this year?" he'd asked. "Stockings by the fire, that sort of thing?" Sonja didn't know what to say. Usually she put up a few decorations—a wreath on the door, a small artificial tree in the front window—but it hardly seemed worth going all-out on decorations for just the two of them.

"Sure," she'd said eventually.

It made Sonja wonder. Maybe retirement was starting to agree with him? Maybe he was finally starting to relax? She'd heard about it happening. Men who were harsh, cutthroat business people all their lives, suddenly becoming old softies in their golden years. Maybe that was happening to George? If so, after all the hard yards she'd put in, there was no point leaving just as things were looking up.

"Got much on today?" George asked her.

"I'm going to see Alice Stanhope," Sonja said. "She's out of the hospital but doesn't have much support. I'm going to see if I can convince her to take Meals on Wheels."

George was looking at her with an expression that was hard to read. "Alice Stanhope?"

"My client," she said. "Ovarian cancer. She's not doing well."

George put down his coffee. He blinked, as though he'd received startling news, instead of a status report on her client. "Alice Stanhope?" he repeated.

"Yes," Sonja said, confused. "Alice Stanhope. Why? Do you know her?"

George ignored the question. "You said Alice . . . isn't doing well?"

"Not well at all. She's dying."

He stared off, his brow puckered. Sonja looked at him, wondering what on earth was going on in his mind.

George took another sip of his coffee, then put it down. He inhaled, steepling his fingers against his lips. "Sonja," he said. "I have to tell you something."

65

Kate wondered if it was ominous that she'd never shown anyone the box she kept in the top of her closet. It was, she thought, the aspirational area of her wardrobe. The clothes for holidays and vacations. Her wedding dress, wrapped in tissue. Some of her mother's jewelry. And the box.

As she got it down, she thought about yesterday evening. When David had brought up the idea of Zoe coming to live with them with Scarlett and Jake, Kate had been floored by their responses. Jake had listened carefully when they'd explained the situation, and then said, "Wow, she has no one? Well, yeah. Of course we should help her." Scarlett had been more inquisitive. "Where's her dad?" she asked. "What about her grandparents? Her friends? Her neighbors?" She'd wanted specifics—how it would work, would they adopt her, would they be sisters? Many of the questions Kate and David didn't have answers for, but they'd worked through them, one at a time. Finally she'd said, "Well, I'm cool with it, if you are."

After the kids went to bed, Kate and David stayed up talking until 3 A.M. when they finally decided that they would keep Zoe. They also decided to find a relationship counselor to help them deal with their unresolved emotions around their fertility issues. It wouldn't be resolved overnight, but they were both committed to fixing it.

She opened the box, and reached for the tiny white sleep suit—the one item she'd allowed herself to buy when she'd found out she was pregnant for the first time. Also in the box were her first positive pregnancy test and the letter she'd written to her baby that day. She'd planned to show the letter to her child, maybe when he or she was five, maybe on his or her eighteenth birthday or wedding day. When it felt right.

Now, she opened it out.

Dear You,

All my life I have dreamed about being your mother and today, we found out that you are coming into our lives. I want you to know that I grew up without a mother, so I understand the significance of the role. I want you to know that I may not always be perfect, but I will always try my best. Most of all, I want you to know . . . you will be loved. You are going to have a protective big brother, an adoring sister, and a doting father. Most of all, you will have a mother who will move Heaven and Earth for you. I promise. You will always be safe. You are the final piece of our puzzle.

All my love.
Mom

Kate read it twice, noticing but not bothering to wipe away the tears on her cheek. Then she stuffed everything back into the box and took it downstairs. And, because she had the house to herself and because she was feeling indulgent, she lit a fire. She planned to toss in the whole thing and watch it burn until nothing was left, but at the last minute, she tucked the letter into her pocket. It occurred to Kate that she might have someone to give it to after all.

66

t was a week after George had told Sonja the truth and she still didn't believe it. At least she wouldn't, if it didn't make so much sense. But George had explained it all. It was the reason for the sudden move to Atherton. The reason he'd been so adamant to volunteer at local high schools. The reason he'd been so highly strung these few months. It had all been because of Zoe. And, inadvertently, because of Alice.

It was a one-night stand, he told her. Alice had been his receptionist. She was young and wild, but he thought he could tame her. After all, young people were his specialty. She wasn't a bad receptionist, he said, but her behavior was very erratic. She was overly chatty with the clients, and not as careful as she should have been with private files. Then one night she arrived unannounced at his home, ostensibly to drop off some documents. George had been on an important call, so he waved her inside. By the time he got off the phone she'd made herself at home and helped herself to his wine. She *threw* herself at him. Father issues, George said.

He tried to fend her off, but she was determined. And in a moment of weakness, George couldn't resist. He'd had a few glasses of wine himself and she was an attractive young woman. And she wouldn't take no for an answer.

Afterward, George felt terrible. He offered to drive her home, to talk about it, but she just walked out into the night. A wild child, he said. Couldn't be tamed.

The next day, she didn't come back to work. She didn't answer her phone. He kept trying to find her but she might as well have disappeared off the face of the earth! After a while, he assumed she'd died or left the country.

Fifteen years later, he saw her face in a news article.

When Helping Others Becomes a Career

Sonja looked at it now, for the hundredth time. It was worn and yellowed and curved at the edges. Alice's face smiled back at her.

No one had been more surprised than George to learn that Alice had a child. She didn't seem the mothering type, he said. Then he noticed the dates and he did the math.

He needed to see for himself that Zoe was his child before he told Sonja. It was why he'd started volunteering at local high schools. Then, he found her . . . Zoe. There was never any doubt that she was his. She had the same black hair and nearly black eyes. It had been like looking in the mirror, he'd said. The strangest part was he'd actually been *counseling* her!

"She's beautiful," he'd said. "She has problems, though. With anxiety."

Which meant, of course, he would be the perfect person to help her.

"Don't you see?" he'd said. "It's not just about us getting Zoe in our life—this is about *her* life. She needs *us*!"

George had taken Sonja's two hands in his own. The tears that shone in his eyes were impossible to fake. It had made Sonja pause. What if this was their second chance? She could finally be a mother!

They would be good parents, Sonja thought. They were financially stable. George was only working part-time at the school, and

Sonja could retire, if need be. They'd be able to give her opportunities, money, love. Maybe they'd travel more—take Zoe to Europe. They'd put up Christmas decorations, start traditions. The house could fill up with Zoe's friends, and maybe, down the track (if George allowed it), her boyfriends. It might be just what they needed. It might change everything.

67

Alice never knew whether Paul was late or not coming, because he didn't have a cell phone. Who didn't have a cell phone? She would have bought him one if she wasn't sure he would just lose it or forget to turn it on. Today she was giving him the benefit of the doubt, because it was too late to get the bus and she didn't want to call Sonja again. She was having her full blood work done today to see if her white-cell count had risen enough to try more chemo. Or perhaps she could do another blood transfusion? Whatever it was, she was going to remain positive. If only Paul would get here.

Zoe was at her boyfriend's house. It felt good to say it. Zoe's *boyfriend*. There was a time not so long ago when Alice couldn't imagine saying those words.

It was a relief that Zoe wasn't here, though. Alice was fairly good at pretending she wasn't in pain, but keeping a straight face could be torture when she had to do it for hours on end. These days Alice found herself looking forward to Zoe heading out, so she could flop on the couch and moan. It was in her belly, mostly. Constipation. A feeling of heaviness. Bloatedness. Waves of nausea and pain. She had drugs for pain—lovely drugs—but they didn't help with the feeling of heaviness. It was like a really bad period that never ended.

After an eternity there was a knock at the door. "Finally!"

She stood, slowly. When she eased the door open, Sonja was standing there. "Sonja! Oh, didn't I tell you? My brother is taking me to the hospital today."

"Oh, you're going to the hospital, of course. Sorry, I forgot."

Sonja seemed even more flustered than usual. Sometimes Alice wondered what on earth was going on with her.

"If you forgot . . . why are you here?" Alice asked her.

"Actually, I need to talk to you."

"What is it, Sonja?" Exhausted, Alice leaned against the door-frame.

"It's about George," Sonja said, but Alice's face was blank. "George . . . Sanders?"

Alice pulled herself upright. "What did you say?"

Alice must have been hallucinating, because she could have sworn she saw him then, standing right behind Sonja.

Dr. Sanders.

She was going to faint.

Sonja turned, just as startled as Alice. "George?" she said. "What are you doing here?"

Sonja's face became pure white. Alice registered it only for an instant before she grabbed the door, and shoved it closed with all her might. But it jammed, a few inches short of shut. Alice looked down and saw Dr. Sanders's foot wedged in the opening.

68

Zoe was making out with Harry on his sofa, which looked like Barbie had barfed on it. Bits of tiny pink clothing kept appearing between their bodies and the cushions, and were scattered across every surface, along with tiaras, tutus, and fairy wands.

"What is this?" Zoe said, holding up what looked like a tiny, sequined bikini top.

"It's Maggie's," he said, rolling his eyes.

"Seriously? This stuff's not yours?"

"You're pretty funny, you know that?" Harry said, mock-annoyed, but it descended into more making out. It was playful at first, but it quickly became more intense. Harry cupped her face in his hands and then gently slid his hands down her body. Finally he rolled over so he was hovering over her. "You're not laughing anymore," he commented, kissing her neck.

"No," she agreed. She felt hot, but not in the usual way. In a good way. She found herself wanting to take things further. But every time her thoughts got carried away she suddenly snapped out of it.

"I'm sorry," she said, breaking off.

"What's up?" he said, pushing a piece of hair behind her ear.

She sat up. "Don't take this the wrong way, but I was thinking about my mom."

Harry gave her an abashed smile. "I'll try not to take that personally."

"She's sick, Harry. Really sick."

His smile fell away.

"But she's pretending she's not. Pretending or, I don't know . . . maybe she is delusional."

"She probably is," he said. "Who wouldn't be delusional? She has cancer. She's choosing to believe that she's going to live. The only alternative is to accept that she's going to die."

"I guess," Zoe said. "It's just . . . weird. She's making plans for next year, and the year after that. She never even used to make plans for next week!"

Harry shifted on the couch, so they faced each other. "When I got sick, I told myself that I was fine. That it was a virus, that it would pass, that I'd be back playing football in a week or two. Even after months of it, I was convinced it would be resolved. Even after I was diagnosed with Crohn's I didn't believe it. Check my browser history to see how many times I Googled 'people misdiagnosed with Crohn's disease'! I was in denial. And with good reason. I wanted a normal life. Your mom has even more reason to be in denial. Cancer can kill her."

"So what made you accept it?"

"My body." He smiled sadly. "Eventually I realized that wishing for things to be different wouldn't change anything."

Zoe felt a stab of pain right around her heart. "So . . . what should I do?"

"Just be there for her. Either she'll accept it . . . or she won't. And whatever is going to happen will happen anyway."

Zoe had heard people talk about how grief came in waves, ebbing and flowing. It had been that way for her. Some moments she felt almost normal—at least as normal as she could feel. Other moments it lapped around her. But now it hit her like a tidal wave.

"When will the moment come for me to accept it?" she asked brokenly, and she buried her face in Harry's chest and began to cry.

69

Alice. Please hear me out."

Dr. Sanders was in Alice's doorway. He was trying to get inside. When this happened in her nightmares, Alice was ready. She had a weapon and superhuman strength. She had all the lines ready to demoralize and humiliate him, the way he had done to her. But today she had none of those things. She only had one thing in her favor and it was the most important.

Zoe wasn't home.

"Get your foot out of my door." Alice's voice sounded much more impressive than it felt. It boomed. She could feel her face, taut and mean—her *don't fuck with me* face. But she had nothing to back it up. She was weak, and already losing the battle on the door. With a single shove, he could throw the door open, and send her flying across the room.

"I'm not going to hurt you, Alice," he said. "I just want to talk."

"About *what?*"

Dr. Sanders, she noticed, was ignoring Sonja. Though, from the way he'd greeted her he clearly knew her. But how? For now, Alice was too panicked to try to figure out the connection.

"I want to talk about Zoe," Dr. Sanders said.

A chill ran the length of Alice's spine. "What did you—?"

"My daughter. Zoe. I know all about her," he said. "You and I have a lot to talk about, don't we?"

"I don't know what you're talking about," Alice said weakly.

"I saw the article in the newspaper, Alice, about your home-helper business. It referred to your daughter. I had to see with my own eyes if she was mine."

Alice gripped the doorframe. This couldn't be happening, Alice told herself. Not now, of all times.

"I moved to Atherton earlier this year," he continued. "And I've been offering my services to local high schools to see if I'd run into Zoe."

"You stay away from Zoe!" Alice screamed. "Do you understand? If you go anywhere *near her*—"

"I've already seen Zoe," he said calmly. "Several times."

The room began to spin.

"I've been counseling her, helping with her social anxiety." When he smiled a little, Alice felt vomit rise in her throat. "She has my eyes."

Dr. Sanders—why the hell did she still call him that, even in her mind?—looked at Sonja. "And, as it turned out, my wife is your social worker—"

Alice looked at Sonja. "*What?*"

"I didn't know Zoe was his daughter," she said. She seemed apologetic. "Not until last week."

Alice knew she needed to get it together, but it was all too much. Dr. Sanders was here. He'd seen Zoe. Sonja was his wife.

"You can't just show up like this," Alice said finally. "How did you even know where to come?"

"I followed Sonja," he said. "But you're right. I haven't gone about this the right way. But neither did you. You should have told me I had a daughter, Alice. You owed me that much."

"I *owed* you—"

"Yes," he said. "What's more, you owed it to Zoe."

Alice stared at him. She thought about how awed she'd once been by his confidence, the authority he commanded. But now she saw him for exactly what he was. Delusional.

She drew herself up to her full height. "Let's get one thing clear. You have no rights here, *George*. Rapists aren't owed anything."

Dr. Sanders flinched a little, and Alice realized it was because she'd called him George. After all these years, after everything that had happened, he still thought he was owed respect. She was ready to continue, but before she could she felt a great twist in her belly that stole her breath.

"Where is Zoe now?" he demanded.

"It's none of your business," Alice panted.

"I'm her father."

"Like hell you are!" Alice opened the door a little and slammed it again, hard, against his foot. He barely flinched.

"Alice, can we just talk for a minute? Like adults?"

"No." Her stomach was full of knives. "We can't."

"I know you're ill," he said. His voice was quiet, but somehow it carried strength.

"It's none of your business," she repeated. "Get your foot out of my door."

"I want to know what you've put in your will. For guardianship of Zoe!"

Alice shoved again on the door, but it was useless. "Hey! What's going on here?"

Paul stood behind George in the hallway. He looked at George, then at Alice, in confusion. But it only took a moment before understanding came to his face. "This is the guy?"

Alice had barely nodded before Paul grabbed him by the back of the shirt. He spun him around and punched him, clean, in the jaw. Sonja cried out. Despite herself, Alice felt a tingle of satisfaction. She yanked Paul by the wrist into the apartment, locking the door. "What was that?" she cried.

Paul shrugged. "I told you I was going to step up and be a good brother."

In other circumstances, Alice might have been touched. Unfortunately these weren't other circumstances. And Alice couldn't hold it any longer, she doubled over and vomited.

70

He can't do this," Paul said, pacing. Alice lay on the sofa. She felt hot in the face, and her stomach radiated pain. She'd vomited another two times, mostly bile—a strange greenish color.

"He might be able to," Alice said. "I'll have to get a lawyer."

"But he's a rapist!" Paul said.

"I never filed a report. As far as the law is concerned, he's an upstanding citizen."

Alice felt weak. The pain in her abdomen was getting worse—little twisting blades in her gut.

"He won't get her, Alice."

Alice thought about Sonja. Alice couldn't believe she'd found herself becoming fond of the woman who had been plotting to take her daughter away. All this time she'd thought Sonja was concerned about her when actually she'd been George's wife! But it wasn't just the betrayal that worried Alice. Frustrating as it was, Sonja lent a certain legitimacy to George. A judge might not give a child to her biological father if he was an alleged rapist. But if he was happily married to a social worker who could vouch for the fact that he was a good man? What happened then?

"Where's my phone?" she asked Paul.

Paul had no idea. Eventually Alice located it, charging, by her bedside. She called Kate.

"Hello?"

"It's Alice."

There was just something about her voice that undid Alice.

She opened her mouth, but all that came out was a giant sob.

"Alice?" Kate said. "What's the matter?"

In that moment the pain in Alice's belly was so sharp that it stole her breath.

"Kate," she said, when she recovered. "Can you come over here?"

"Are you all right, Alice? Tell me."

"Just . . . come over," she said, and then felt her stomach seize.

"All right," Kate said. "I'm on my way."

It was a good thing, because after that Alice couldn't talk any more.

71

As soon as Kate got off the phone with Alice, she grabbed her keys and drove to Alice's. A familiar-looking man answered the door.

"You're Kate?" he said.

"Yes. Who are you?"

"Paul," he reminded her. "Alice's brother. Come in, quick."

Kate strode into the apartment. Alice was bent over the couch.

"What happened?" she asked Paul.

"Zoe's father turned up."

"Zoe's *father*? But . . . I thought he wasn't involved."

"He's not. At least he shouldn't be. But now he's saying he wants Zoe."

"He's saying . . ." Kate's fingers found her temples. "No!"

"We won't let him," Paul said. "We'll fight it. But—"

But Kate wasn't listening; she was looking at Alice, half kneeling, half lying on the couch. Her face had a faint sheen to it. She kept moving around, agitated. "Alice? Are you all right?"

Alice muttered something about stomach pain, then turned her head and vomited onto a towel.

"I'll get another towel," Paul said, but Kate was staring at this one. Her vomit was green.

Kate yanked up Alice's top. Her belly was distended and

stretched taut. Kate launched to her feet, snatched up the phone, and dialed 911.

"What is it?" Paul said, returning with a fresh towel.

"Yes, I'm a nurse," she said into the phone. "I have a woman in her home with acute abdominal pain and vomiting. I need an ambulance right away." She looked at Paul. "Where's Zoe?"

"I . . . I think Alice said she's at her boyfriend's place."

"Do you know the address?" Kate said.

"It's written down in the kitchen."

"Fine. Do you want to get Zoe or should—"

Alice responded to the sound of Zoe's name. It was, perhaps, the first time she'd even noticed that Kate was there. But as she caught Kate's gaze she looked surprisingly cognizant.

"You get Zoe," she said, and she didn't break her gaze until Kate promised she would.

72

George! George, wait!"

He was striding into the house. Sonja had to run to keep up with him. They'd returned from Alice's in separate cars, so she had no idea what was going on his head. Certainly he'd seemed calm when he was speaking to Alice, reasonable even, but that was because he wanted something. It was no indication of how he would behave in the privacy of his own home.

Sonja closed the front door but she had barely turned around when she was suddenly slammed against it. The air rushed from her lungs. His face was right up close, so close she could feel his breath on her face.

"What *the hell* were you doing there, Sonja?"

"What do you mean?" she choked out. "Alice is my client."

His hands teetered just below her throat, around her collarbones, like a threat. He pressed harder. "You said you wanted to talk about me. Why?"

Sonja struggled to catch her breath. Why *had* she gone there? Ostensibly it had been to find out what had happened between George and Alice the night Zoe was conceived. But she needn't have bothered. Even before she'd heard Alice say it, she'd known the truth.

"You raped her," she said to George.

George released his grip on her. All of a sudden he seemed almost . . . bored.

"Tell me I'm wrong," she said.

George rolled his eyes and turned away. As if he were admitting to a speeding ticket that he'd tucked away, hoping she wouldn't find it, rather than a heinous crime. "It was . . . just a moment," he said. "I lost it."

Sonja felt a rumbling start from somewhere down deep. Although she had suspected this since the moment George had told her about his relationship with Alice, it still was a shock to hear him say it. Her husband was a rapist.

"You can't do this," she said, because in that moment it was clear. All this time she'd made excuses for him. She'd thought his sexual aggression was *her* fault! But it had nothing to do with her. "You can't try to get custody of Zoe."

"Sonja, she's my flesh and blood," George said. "This could be good for all of us. This would be good for you."

His demeanor had changed now. The threatening man who had just pinned her to the wall had vanished. He was appealing to her sense of reason. Five minutes earlier she might have fallen for it.

"No," she said.

"Sonja—"

"No," she repeated, slowly and clearly. "You're not fit to look after a child. And I won't allow it."

A muscle flickered in his jaw. "You won't *allow* it? Why would I need you to—"

"Because no one is going to give a child to an abuser."

George became frighteningly still. Sonja waited for him to quip back, tell her she couldn't do anything. But he didn't say anything. She had his attention.

"I've documented everything you've done to me. The bruises, the bumps, the injuries. I'm keeping an official log of it all." She was fudging a little, but what did it matter? "Call it what you want, but it's abuse. And the courts won't just have to take my word for it. From what you've told me, Alice will be pretty keen to tell the story of how Zoe was conceived."

George still didn't move. Sonja had never seen him so uncertain. She remembered the first time George had assaulted her, the way she'd justified her staying. *If you are this weak-willed and skittish with George, what on earth will you be like without him?*

Now, as she stood before him, she repeated the thought in her mind. And suddenly, she could picture *exactly* what she could be.

"You're not getting Zoe," she said evenly. "I'm going to make sure of it."

This time Sonja didn't deliberate. She simply turned and walked out the door.

73

W hat is it?" Zoe hurriedly put on her seat belt. She'd arrived home to the sound of an ambulance siren and Kate standing in front of her building. "Another infection?"

"No," Kate said. "Not an infection."

"Then . . . what?"

Kate remained quiet as she pulled out onto the road. Too quiet. She was blinking a lot, and chewing on a thumbnail.

"Is it serious?" Zoe asked.

Kate's gaze flickered to her for second before she answered. "Yes it is, Zoe."

Usually Kate had an extraordinary way of—a gift for—reassuring her when it came to her mother. Not today.

"Is . . . is she going to die?" Zoe asked. "Today?"

Kate put her hand over Zoe's and squeezed it. "Let's just get you there, sweetheart."

74

When Zoe walked into the hospital room, her mom was asleep. She had a tube in her nose and an intravenous line in her arm. Zoe went to the side without the tube, lowered the rail on her bed and lay down beside her.

"Mouse?"

Zoe lifted her head. "Mom!"

"Are you all right?" she mumbled. She was pretty out of it, on all sorts of painkillers. And still she was asking how Zoe was. Only a mother could do that.

"I'm good," Zoe said.

Her mom said something else then, which didn't make any sense. Then she winced as a flash of pain overtook her.

"I love you, too, Mom," she said, taking a stab in the dark, and her mom drifted back to sleep. But Zoe stayed there for hours, holding her mom's hand. Neither of them was ready to let go.

75

W hat's your pain between one and ten, Alice?" Dr. Brookes asked.

Alice knew it was Dr. Brookes without having to open her eyes. During the past days his voice had become as familiar as her own. So had the voices of other members of the hospital staff—the nurses, the orderlies. All of these people that surrounded her, caring for her. As sick as she had felt, there was something lovely about being so cared for.

"A four?"

"Good," Dr. Brookes said. "Much better."

"Can I go home now?" Alice asked.

A pause. "Not yet."

Alice opened her eyes. Kate stood in the corner of the room. Her expression was somber. "What is it?" Alice asked.

"I've just had a look at your CT scan," Dr. Brookes started.

"And?" Alice prompted.

"And it shows you have a number of secondary metastases in your peritoneal cavity."

Alice was about to ask him to speak English when Kate came to her side and took her hand, obscuring him from her view. "The cancer has spread, Alice. Most worryingly, it's in your bowel, and a tumor has partially blocked your small intestine. That is what has been causing you such pain. It's not allowing you to digest food."

"So how do we . . . fix it?"

"Well . . . we'll continue to hydrate and rest the bowel until the return of bowel sounds, and you're feeling more comfortable. But the likelihood is that when you start eating again the problem will return."

There was a long pause.

"So," Alice said. "What's the plan? Surgery to remove the tumors?"

Kate glanced at Dr. Brookes, who had come to stand on the other side of Alice. "Unfortunately, due to the multiple sites of obstruction, it's not a possibility."

"So what *is* a possibility?" Alice asked, frustrated. "Will we just continue with the chemo when I'm feeling better?"

Another pause. Another exchange of glances.

"Alice, the cancer has spread too much. Your illness is now terminal and we are recommending a palliative approach . . . treating the symptoms. We wouldn't recommend any more chemo."

It was Dr. Brookes talking, but Alice looked at Kate.

"A . . . *palliative* approach?"

Kate squeezed her hand. "I'm so sorry."

At first the news hovered around Alice. She had the urge to say "What?," "What do you mean?," "Explain this to me again," but she understood what they were saying. It was just that it felt like they were talking about someone else. Telling someone else that the end of her life was near.

"If we can get your obstructive symptoms under control," Dr. Brookes continued, with something resembling positivity, "you'll only have to stay in the hospital for a few days, maybe a week."

"And then?" Alice said.

"And then a hospice staff member will come in to evaluate you."

A hospice. Alice felt the news start to penetrate.

"How long?" she asked. Her voice sounded calm and stoic—
the very opposite of how she felt.

"A few weeks," Kate said. "Maybe a month."

A few weeks. The words bowled her over. A *month*. Alice's eyes
roamed the room, looking for something . . . what? A cure? A
candid camera? Suddenly she saw Sonja hovering in the doorway. Alice felt a swell of rage but almost instantly it gave way to
something else. Something more important than rage.

"Sonja, Kate—we need to talk," Alice said.

She'd realized, as all mothers did at one point or another, that
nothing was about her anymore. Not her cancer. Not even her
death. It was all about Zoe. And Kate and Sonja might be the
only two women on earth who could help her.

76

Sonja never expected to be invited in to Alice's room. She expected Alice to scream and cry and threaten her, the way she had when she'd had Zoe put in foster care. To this end, she had brought in a letter which she'd planned to give to Alice. It explained that she'd had no idea that George was Zoe's father until last week. That since the altercation at Alice's door, Sonja had resigned from her job, left George, and moved in with her sister, Agnes. Most importantly, the letter explained that she had no intention of letting George anywhere near Zoe. But before Sonja could open her mouth to say any of this, Alice was speaking.

"I've asked Kate if she will be Zoe's guardian," Alice said. Her voice was calm and matter-of-fact. "I think this is the best home for her, and that Zoe will be happy there."

"I'd heard you'd asked Kate," Sonja replied. "And that's why—"

"I'm assuming," Alice interrupted, "that if George is your husband, you know what kind of man he is. You know that he wouldn't make a good father, to Zoe or anyone else."

"No," Sonja agreed. "He wouldn't."

Alice stopped. "You mean . . . you agree? That Zoe should go and live with Kate?"

"I do," Sonja said. "In fact, I've spent this morning getting the legal paperwork together so you can make this official as soon as possible. I figured it was the least I could do . . . after everything."

Alice appeared to be lost for words.

"I've left George, Alice. You may not believe this, but I had no idea that he was Zoe's father. And I'm going to do everything I can to prevent him gaining custody of her."

Alice was suddenly teary. "Really? But George . . . he can be pretty convincing."

"Yes, but so can I. And I'm pretty experienced in this area."

"What are you going to do?" Alice asked.

"I'm going to start by filing a restraining order against him. I have documented proof of his abuse, which I want on the record. Then I'm going to do a little digging. My guess is that you and I aren't the only ones that George has abused. If I can get any other women to come forward, this is just the beginning. I can try to get him deregistered as a therapist. And we may be able to have charges brought against him. No judge in their right mind will give a child to a man like that."

"Do you really think you can do this?"

For a person who'd been so uncertain of everything these past few years, Sonja had never been surer or more determined. "I do."

Alice looked from Sonja to Kate. After a long time, she reached out and took Sonja's hand. "Thank you, Sonja."

Sonja nodded.

"I'm glad you're getting away from him," Alice added.

"Me, too."

And then, there was nothing left to say. Sonja took a deep breath. This was it. It had been over a decade since she'd been alone. She said good-bye to Alice and Kate, slung her purse over her shoulder, and put one foot in front of the other. She'd be doing that for a while, she suspected. Taking things one step at a time. But Agnes was waiting for her. And she had a lot to do these next few months, making sure George wouldn't get Zoe.

She made it to the elevator and then out into the foyer. Outside on the street, an ambulance pulled up and people leapt out. A woman walked past pushing a stroller. Sonja moved around them and kept on walking. She wasn't all alone at all, she realized. There were people everywhere.

77

A few days later Zoe's mom was doing better. Sitting up in bed. She wasn't eating or drinking and she still had the strange tube in her nose, but she was alert and oriented. And she wanted to talk.

"You seem better," Zoe said to her. She was painting her mom's nails. "Kate says you can leave the hospital tomorrow."

"Yes, I'm feeling better. These look nice." She lifted her hands to admire them, then dropped them carefully onto her knees. She was quiet for a long time. "Honey, there's something I need to tell you."

"What is it?"

"I am leaving the hospital in a few days. But . . . the doctors said I won't be able to come home."

"What do you mean?"

"My scans showed that the cancer has spread. There are new tumors on my bowels and that is why I was in such terrible pain."

"But you're better now." It was meant to be a statement, but the sentence rose at its end, seemingly of its own volition.

"Yes," her mom said. "Because I haven't been eating or drinking. Everything has been going in and out of this tube. If I start eating and drinking again, this would just happen again." Her mom took her hand. "When I leave here, hon, I'll have to go to a hospice."

"A . . . hospice?" Zoe reared back. "Isn't that where people go to—"

"Yes, Mouse."

Zoe's hands tented over her mouth. "No!"

"I'm so sorry, honey. I have to tell you the truth."

Zoe shook her head, a sob building at the base of her throat. "I don't want to hear this truth."

"I know. But you can handle it."

Now the sob burst from her. "I can't."

"Yes, you can."

Zoe took a deep breath. The rest of what her mom was saying slowly caught up. She wasn't going home.

"But . . . what will happen to me?"

"They . . . they told me that you can come and stay with me at the hospice. After that, I've asked Kate if she and her husband would consider becoming your legal guardians."

"*What?*" Zoe's hands fell from her mouth. "But . . . you hate Kate."

"I don't hate Kate. But what's more important is how much *you* like her. And how much she cares about you. I believe you would be loved and taken care of with Kate. Nothing is more important to me than that."

Her mom's voice was calm and soothing, but she had tears in her eyes. They hovered on her bottom lid, defying gravity.

"I don't want to live with Kate," Zoe blurted out, more of a cry than a shout.

"You don't?" Her mom's tears started to fall.

"No!"

"Oh." Her mom wiped furiously against the tears that refused to stop. "Well . . . who do you want to live with?"

"I want to live with *you!*" Zoe cried, and she lay down next to her mother. There, in the hospital bed, they sobbed, until their tears mingled together and it was impossible to tell whose were whose.

78

Kate stood in the doorway of Alice's hospital room. Zoe was curled up on her mother's bed, asleep. She hadn't left Alice's side in nearly a week. Alice had stabilized now and discharge planning had commenced. That afternoon, she would be transferred to a hospice.

"Hello," Alice said, noticing her there.

Kate walked into the room and they both looked down at Zoe, sleeping peacefully. Kate had an overpowering urge to stroke her hair back off her face, but she held back. For now, her mother could do that.

"So," Kate started at the same time as Alice grabbed her hand.

"Zoe loops Cheerios on a straw and then sucks them off," she said. "It's weird, but she likes it."

Kate stared at her, confused.

"She's a little OCD. She never watches TV without doing something else to occupy her hands. A puzzle. Folding laundry. Stuff like that."

"Alice—"

"She's surprisingly cuddly. You wouldn't think that, would you? She loves things that are cozy—cushions and throw rugs and blankets. As you can see, she still likes to sleep with me. When she was younger, it was for her—because she was scared or just wanted a cuddle. Lately, it's been for me."

Alice's chin quivered, but she kept it together, always stronger than she looked. "She loves her cat, Kenny. I don't care for him much—he leaves fur all over my couch—but she loves him."

Alice's eyes filled with tears and suddenly Kate understood. She was handing Zoe over.

"Alice, you don't have to—"

"Please, let me. I don't have time to tell you everything, but at least I can tell you this."

A ball of emotion lodged itself in Kate's throat, so enormous it was nearly unbearable. No mother should have to say good-bye to her child like this. Not when their time together was already too short. Finally she nodded. "All right."

"Knock, knock."

They both glanced at the door, where Dr. Brookes stood.

"I've sent a discharge summary to the hospice," he said to Alice.

Alice lips were taut, controlling the emotion. "Great. Thank you."

Dr. Brookes came to her side and took her hand. "I wish you all the best."

"Thank you," she repeated. She looked so small, Kate noticed, in that bed. So vulnerable. For the first time, she reminded Kate of . . . Zoe.

"Kate, will you tell Sonja to inform the hospice that Alice is coming," Dr. Brookes said. He got as far as the doorway before Kate found her voice.

"No."

He paused, turned. "I'm sorry?"

"Alice isn't going to the hospice. She's coming home with me." She looked at Alice. "I have the room. I can care for you myself. And you'll have Zoe right there, in the very same room if you like."

The emotion in Alice's face nearly brought Kate to her knees. "Really?"

Kate managed to nod. "Hold on to your memories for now. We have time. I plan on hearing every last one."

Dr. Brookes nodded and excused himself from the room. Zoe continued to sleep. And for several minutes, Kate and Alice stayed right where they were, looking down at the sleeping girl who would bind them together forever.

79

T his," Zoe said into the microphone. The room was quiet, ready. "This is the scariest thing I've ever done. Most people would say skydiving, and I'm terrified of skydiving too, but probably not for the same reasons as you. Heights don't scare me at all. I'd be terrified about how I'd look with a parachute strapped to my back."

There was a slight hum of laughter, and Zoe realized that, until now, they'd all been holding their breath, just like she had. She'd decided to do her presentation with her back to the audience. She was still terrified, but it was bearable.

"And not just that. I'd be worried that someone might have to talk to me on the way up, you know, give me instructions. Then, when we jumped, I'd be terrified that I'd fall the wrong way—not because it would kill me, but because I might be embarrassed in front of my instructor."

The laughter was louder now. It was, she supposed, kind of funny.

"It *is* pretty funny," she said. "Even though it's not a joke, how bad I feel sometimes."

The laughter died down, which was good. It was textbook, in fact. Start with an anecdote, make them laugh, then get serious.

"The reason I'm messed up is, I have social anxiety disorder."

She paused for a few beats to let that sink in. "What does that mean? Honestly, I don't know. There are enough of us with it that the condition has a name, but all of us experience it differently. I have panic attacks, not everyone does. My panic attacks are not trigger-based, or at least, I don't know what the trigger is. Anything can start them, but usually it's a fear of being judged."

The silence behind her was terrifying. It also meant that, hopefully, she was making her point.

"The last time I tried to talk in front of you all, I peed my pants. I have no guarantee that this won't happen again today. I never have any idea what is coming. Whether it will be a good day or a bad day. That's why this is the scariest thing I've ever done.

"I didn't sleep last night," she said. "People say that a lot, when what they really mean is that they didn't sleep much. Their sleep was interrupted. They tossed and turned. But I *literally* didn't sleep. I spent the night in battle, batting negative thoughts away as fast as they could come at me. I did a pretty good job of it, clearly, because I'm here. But I'm tired. And doing something scary when you're tired, I'll tell you, really sucks."

Zoe's mouth was devoid of moisture. There was a bottle of water on the table in front of her and she picked it up, tried to unscrew the lid. But her hands were useless, weak and sweaty. She took the hem of her T-shirt, tried to open the lid with it, but it was no good.

"This, for example, is particularly mortifying," she said, and there was another burst of laughter. Harry appeared on the stage beside her and opened it with annoying ease. She took a sip. "I'm going to be honest. I'm not doing this because I'm trying to face my fear, or even because I want others to know that they are not alone. I wish my reasons were so noble. I'm doing this because my English grade depends on it. More importantly, I'm doing it because I want my mom to know that I can."

Zoe glanced over her shoulder now and looked directly at her mom, in a wheelchair in the first of six rows of people. She looked so thin, so unbearably ill, but she'd insisted on coming. Kate sat beside her. Zoe held it together pretty well, until she noticed they were holding hands, squeezing so tight that the bones of their knuckles protruded like tiny mountains.

"I spent some time looking at the grading criteria before I wrote this speech," Zoe continued, turning back. "There were five points to be graded on, and five marks for each. The first criterion was . . . originality. As far as I know I'm the first person to do her presentation with her back to the audience, so I'd say I have those points in the bag. The second was participation." Zoe looked theatrically around. "Unless my speechwriter pops out, I'm thinking I got those points covered too. The third was eye contact, which I guess I've failed . . . Then again, if you consider criterion one, originality, I suspect you might find some points for me too. The fourth was content, which I'll admit, there isn't much of. But a good speech shouldn't be measured in terms of content, but more in terms of *reaction to* content. And I'm going to go out on a limb and say that, judging by your silence, punctuated by interspersed laughter, I have your attention."

Another round of laughs.

"The fifth criterion was conclusion or opinion, which you are probably wondering about. Why on earth is Zoe committing this public social suicide? She could have done this speech in front of a group of five, why oh why would she choose to do it in front of the entire class? Which brings me to my powerful, five-point-worthy conclusion. We're all scared. Maybe we're scared of stuff that is truly, legitimately scary like skydiving, or maybe we're scared of what other people think of us. Maybe we're scared for someone else. Maybe we're scared of something that might never happen, or something that is going to happen next week. It's scary being scared. But what's scarier than being scared is being alone."

Zoe paused to let that sink in.

"Cheesy, maybe, but it's true. I used to think that, when I was scared, I needed to be alone. But that was the opposite of what I needed. The answer to fear is *people*. Which is why you're all here.

The truth is, I'll never be normal. I'll never be able to stand in front of a group and ad-lib a speech. I'll probably never walk down the street without worrying if people are looking at me, I probably won't be able to talk to a boy without sweating and shaking. But I'll try to do these things anyway. So I won't be by myself anymore. So I'll be out in the world . . . with you."

Zoe turned around. Two dozen pairs of eyes looked in her direction, which made her weak to her knees. But she looked back anyway. At her mom. At Kate. And finally, to the right of the faces, to where Mrs. Patterson stood.

"If that isn't worth five points, Mrs. P., I don't know what is."

80

t was late. Zoe lay on her side, looking at her mom. Kenny the cat lay on the other side of her mom, pressed against her, almost as if he knew it was time. In spite of her mom's relentless positivity, Zoe knew it was time too. Her mom had been mostly asleep these last few days.

Kate had taken a leave of absence from work and was caring for her around the clock. There were lots of visitors. Paul came by regularly. Even Dulcie had visited. Zoe had transitioned pretty well to life at Kate's. On the nights that Jake and Scarlett were there, she didn't say much, but she usually managed to at least eat something. It was easier when Harry was there. He made enough conversation for both of them. A few times, Kate's dad came over for dinner. He was a kind of awkward old guy, which Zoe found oddly comforting. It made her feel like she wasn't the only one who wasn't socially gifted.

But despite the number of people who'd been around, Zoe and Kate were the main team. When Zoe wasn't at school, they'd developed something of a routine. Kate would administer the medicine while Zoe took her temperature or readjusted her pillows. Until a few days ago, her mom had been making inappropriate jokes ("When I was diagnosed with a tumor I was horrified, but then it really started to grow on me"), but today she'd barely spoken. She was on a lot of morphine—more every day. Soon, Kate said, she wouldn't talk at all.

"Hey Mom?"

Alice's eyes fluttered, then opened a little. Zoe shuffled closer. "Do you want to go to Comfytown?" she asked. She started pulling the blankets up and arranging the cushions, but her mom shook her head.

"We don't need Comfytown anymore, Mouse."

Zoe left the blankets where they were. Slowly she looked around. Her mom was right. They lived in a big house, surrounded by wonderful people. They didn't need blankets and pillows to feel safe.

"You'll be happy with Kate." Her voice rose at the end, making it a question.

"I will," Zoe said. "I promise I will."

Her mom nodded. Her eyes were closed, but somehow, a tear slid out. "I need to sleep now, baby."

Zoe slid up farther until her body was pressed alongside her mother. Several hours later, when her breathing became labored, Zoe held her tighter and whispered, "I'm here." More than anything, she wanted her mom to know that she wasn't alone. She had the feeling her mom wanted her to know the exact same thing.

In the morning, Zoe didn't think she'd ever manage to untangle herself from her mother's arms, but somehow, she did. It might have been the fact that she was stronger now, because of the past few months. It might have been because she knew it was what her mother wanted. But Zoe suspected it was mostly the fact that there was another set of arms waiting for her, right down the hall.